What's Michael?

Show Time

Story and Art:
Makoto Kobayashi

Translation:
**Dana Lewis, Lea Hernandez,
& Toren Smith**

Dark Horse Manga™

Lettering and Retouch:
Digital Chameleon

publisher
Mike Richardson

series editor
Tim Ervin-Gore

series executive editor
Toren Smith for **Studio Proteus**

collection editor
Chris Warner

designer and art director
Mark Cox

English-language version produced by
Studio Proteus and
Dark Horse Comics, Inc.

What's Michael? Vol. VIII: Show Time

This volume collects What's Michael? issues
twenty-three through twenty-seven and twenty-
nine through thirty-one of the Dark Horse comic-
book series Super Manga Blast!

The artwork of this volume has been produced
as a mirror-image of the original Japanese
edition to conform to English-language standards.

Published by
Dark Horse Manga
A division of Dark Horse Comics, Inc.
10956 SE Main Street
Milwaukie, OR 97222

www.darkhorse.com

To find a comics shop in your area, call the
Comic Shop Locator Service toll-free at
1-888-266-4226

First edition: September 2003
ISBN: 1-56971-972-1

10 9 8 7 6 5 4 3 2 1

Printed in Canada

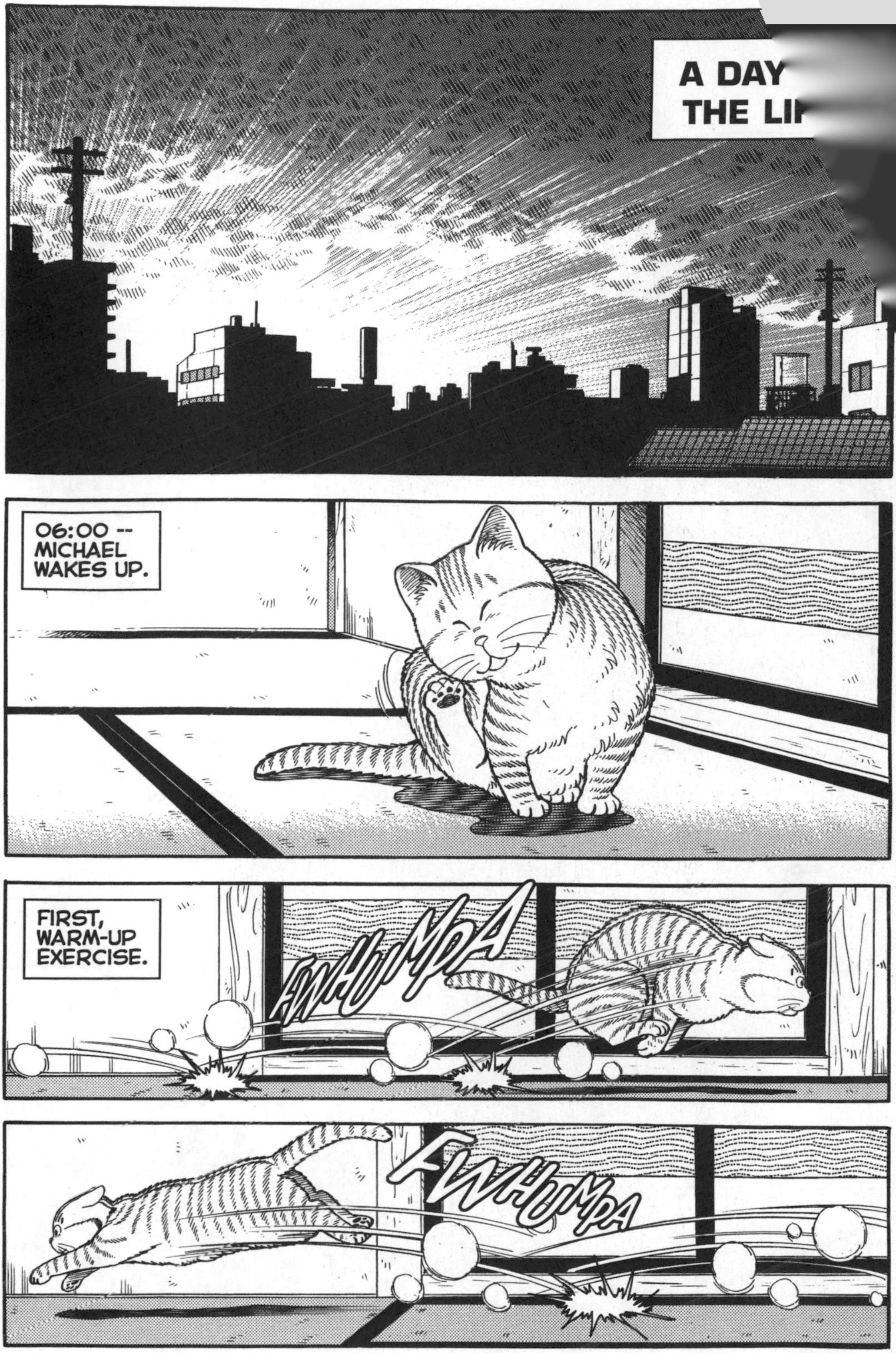
A DAY
THE LI
06:00 -- MICHAEL WAKES UP.
FIRST, WARM-UP EXERCISE.
FWHUMPA
FWHUMPA

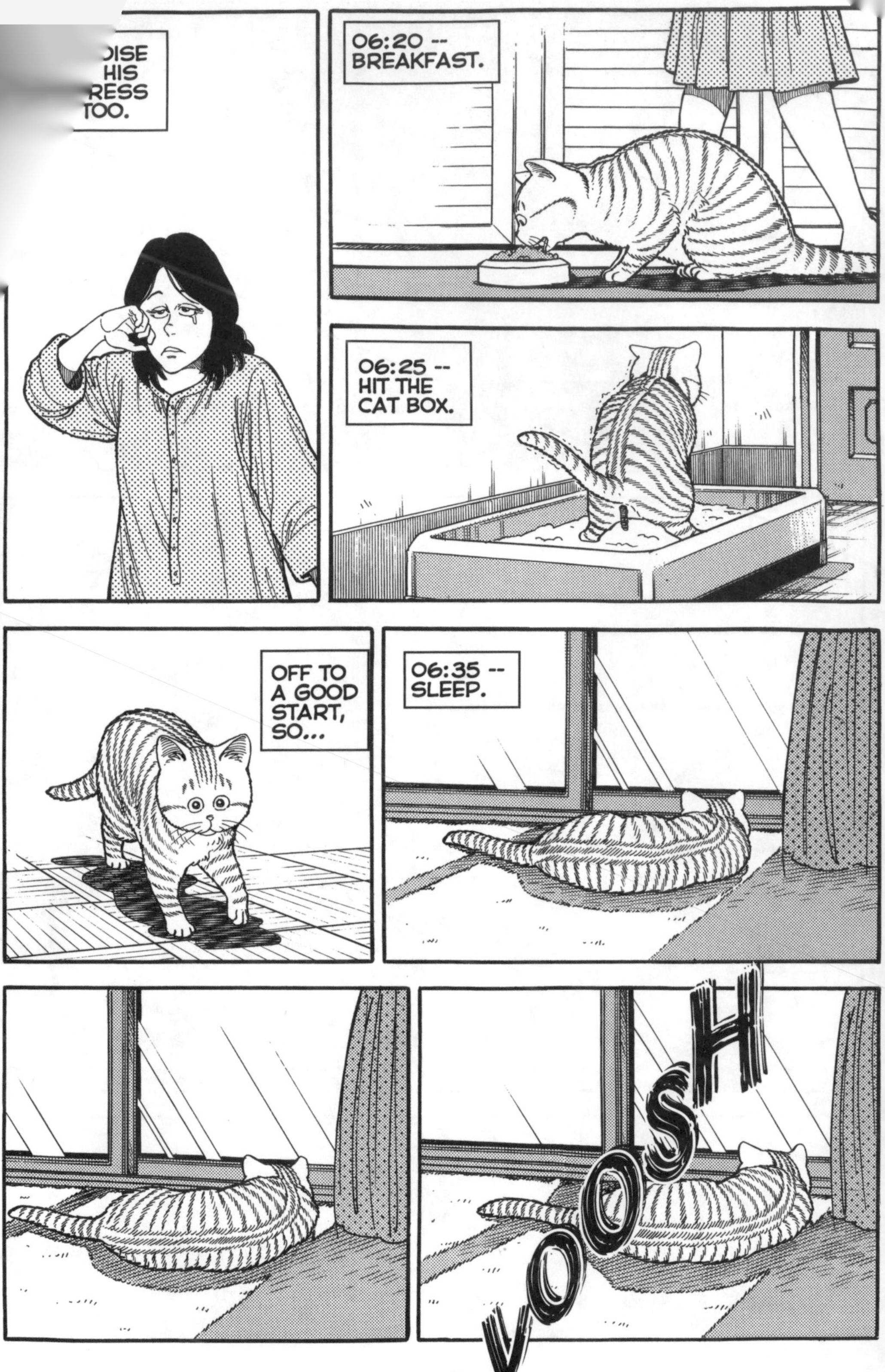
OISE HIS RESS TOO.
06:20 -- BREAKFAST.
06:25 -- HIT THE CAT BOX.
OFF TO A GOOD START, SO...
06:35 -- SLEEP.
VOOOSH

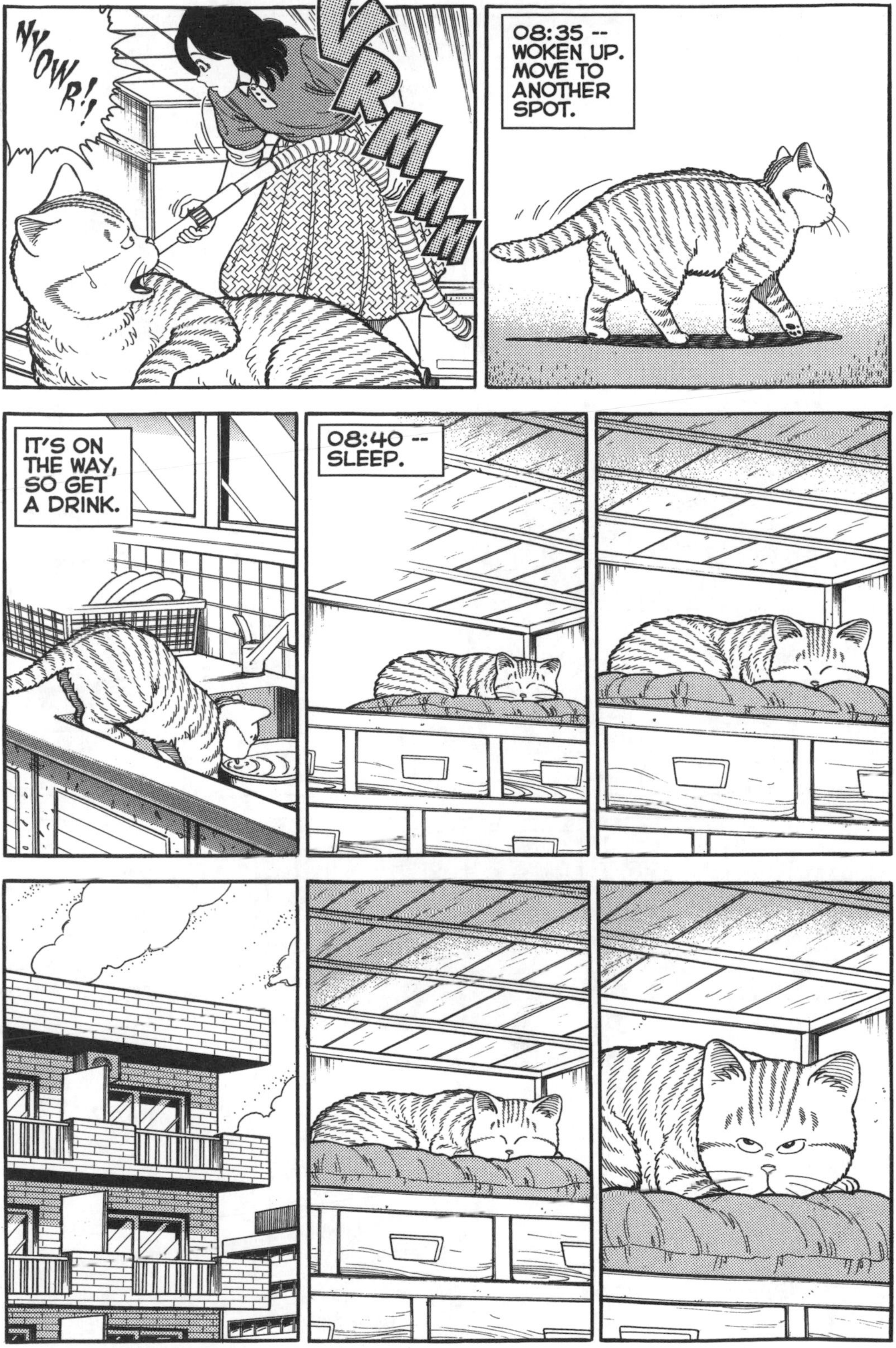
NYOWR!!
VRMMMM
08:35 -- WOKEN UP. MOVE TO ANOTHER SPOT.
IT'S ON THE WAY, SO GET A DRINK.
08:40 -- SLEEP.

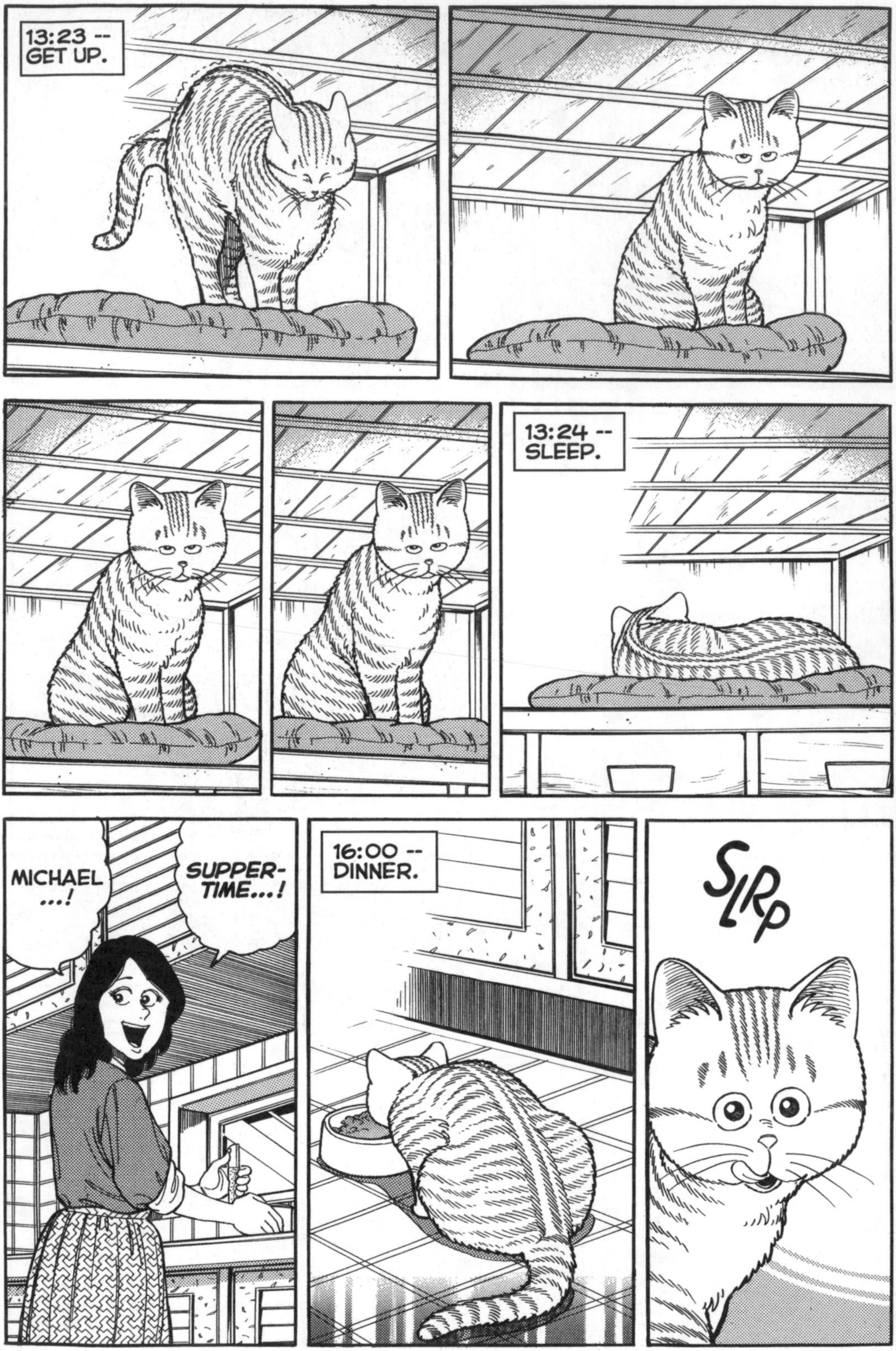
13:23 -- GET UP.
13:24 -- SLEEP.
MICHAEL ...!
SUPPER-TIME...!
16:00 -- DINNER.
SLRP

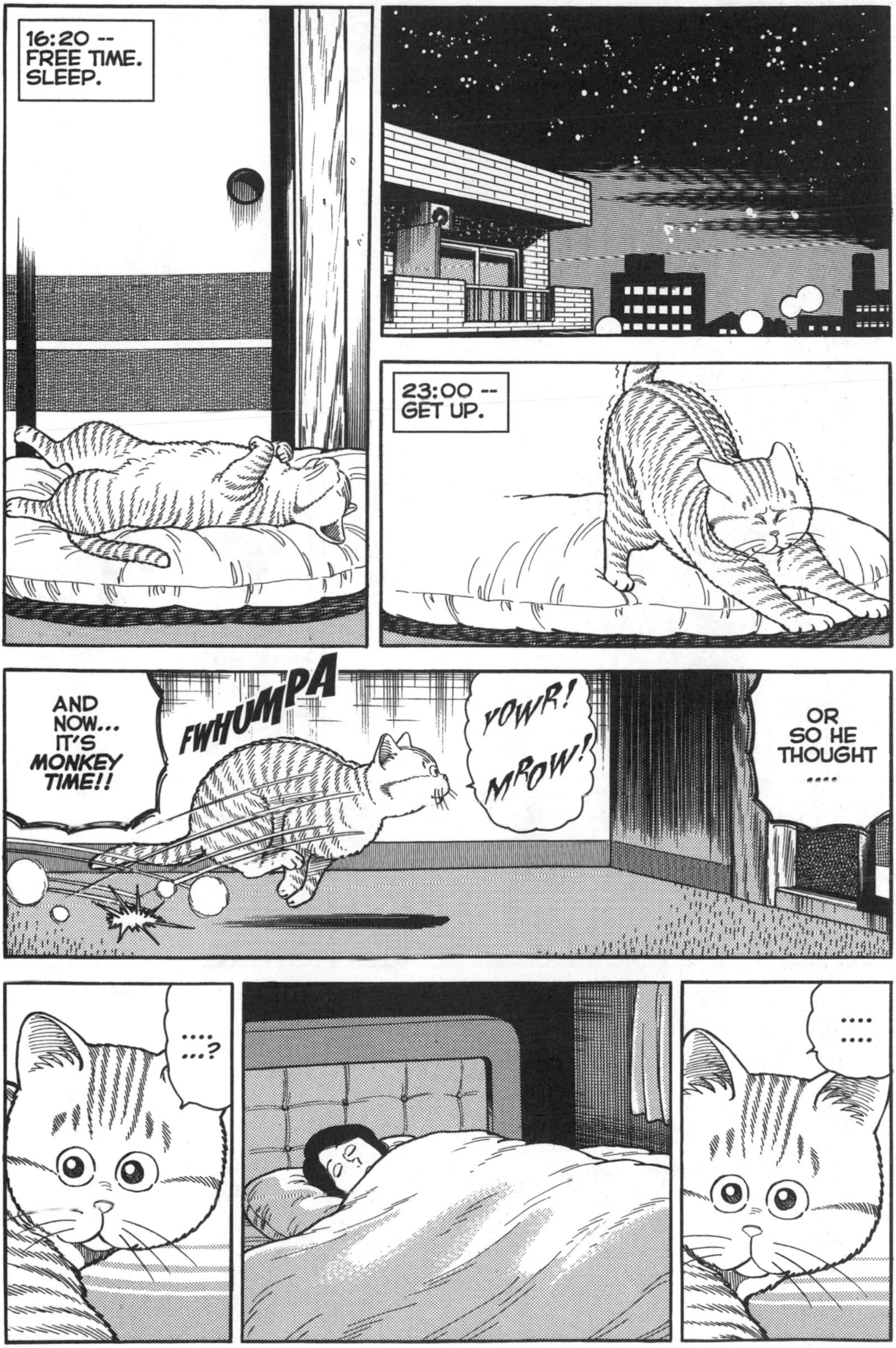
16:20 -- FREE TIME. SLEEP.
23:00 -- GET UP.
AND NOW... IT'S MONKEY TIME!!
FWHUMPA
YOWR! MROW!
OR SO HE THOUGHT ....
....?
....
....

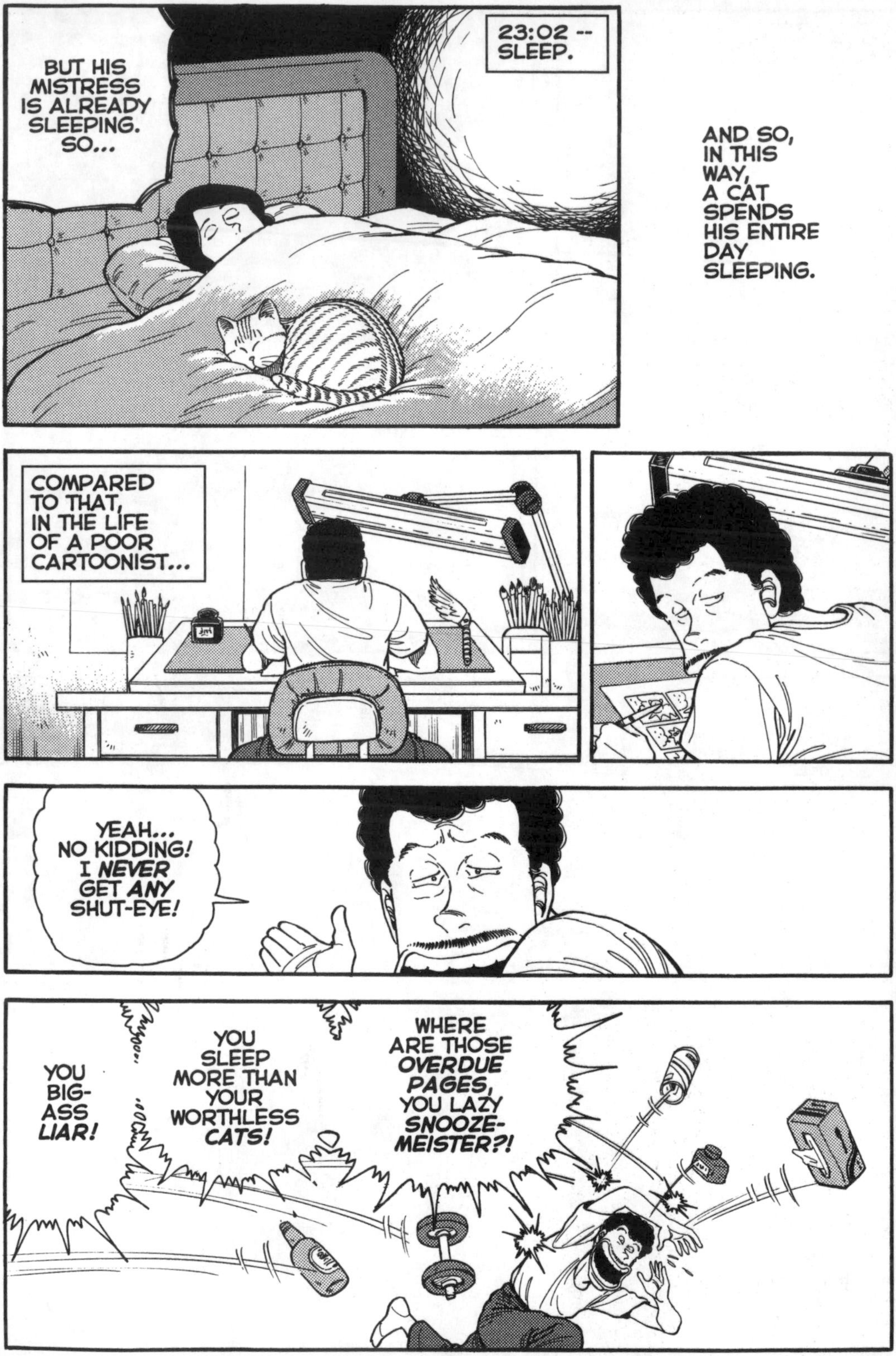
BUT HIS MISTRESS IS ALREADY SLEEPING. SO...
23:02 -- SLEEP.
AND SO, IN THIS WAY, A CAT SPENDS HIS ENTIRE DAY SLEEPING.
COMPARED TO THAT, IN THE LIFE OF A POOR CARTOONIST...
YEAH... NO KIDDING! I *NEVER* GET *ANY* SHUT-EYE!
YOU BIG-ASS *LIAR!*
YOU SLEEP MORE THAN YOUR WORTHLESS *CATS!*
WHERE ARE THOSE *OVERDUE PAGES,* YOU LAZY *SNOOZE-MEISTER?!*

THE END

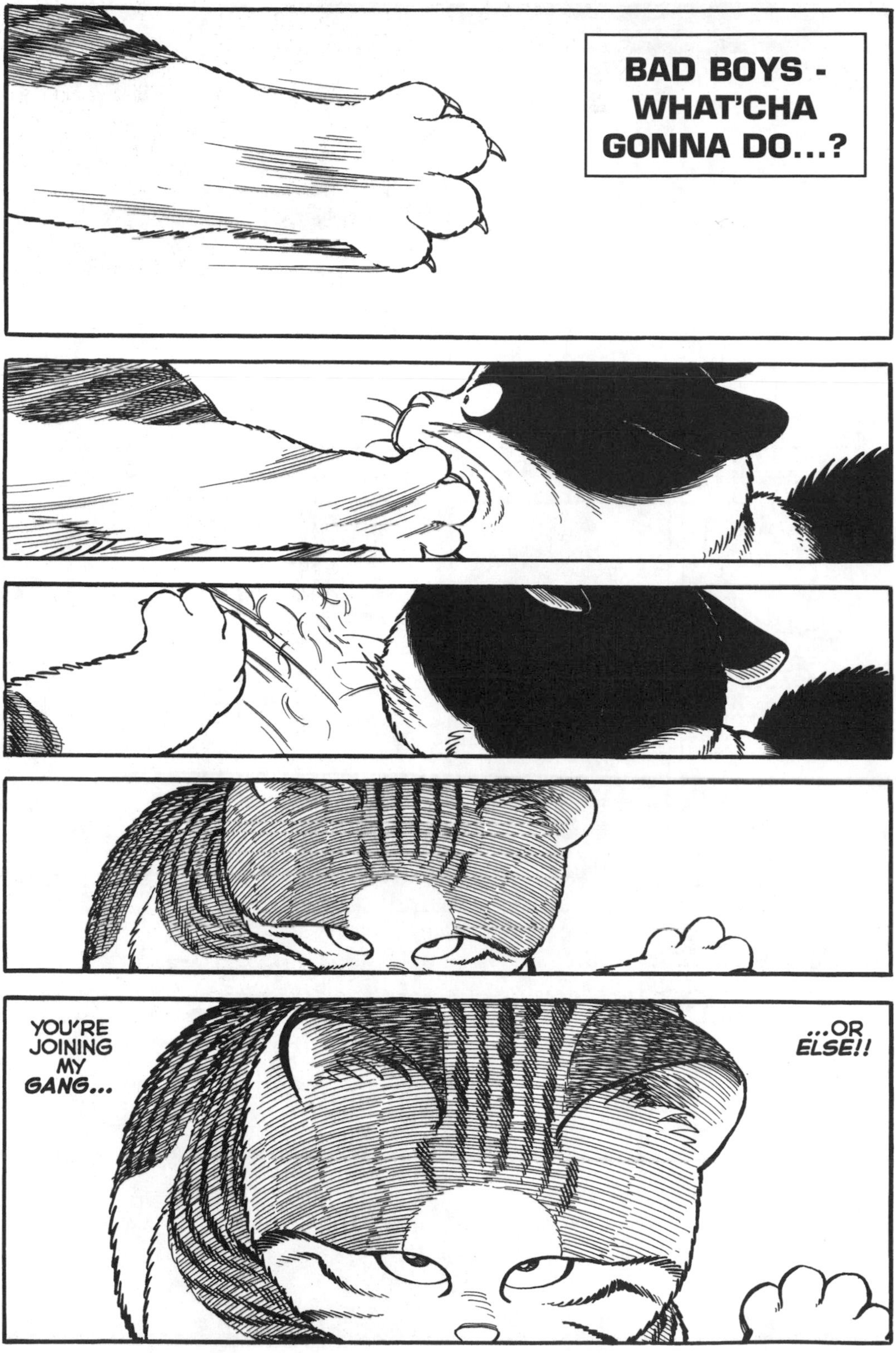
BAD BOYS - WHAT'CHA GONNA DO...?
YOU'RE JOINING MY GANG...
...OR ELSE!!

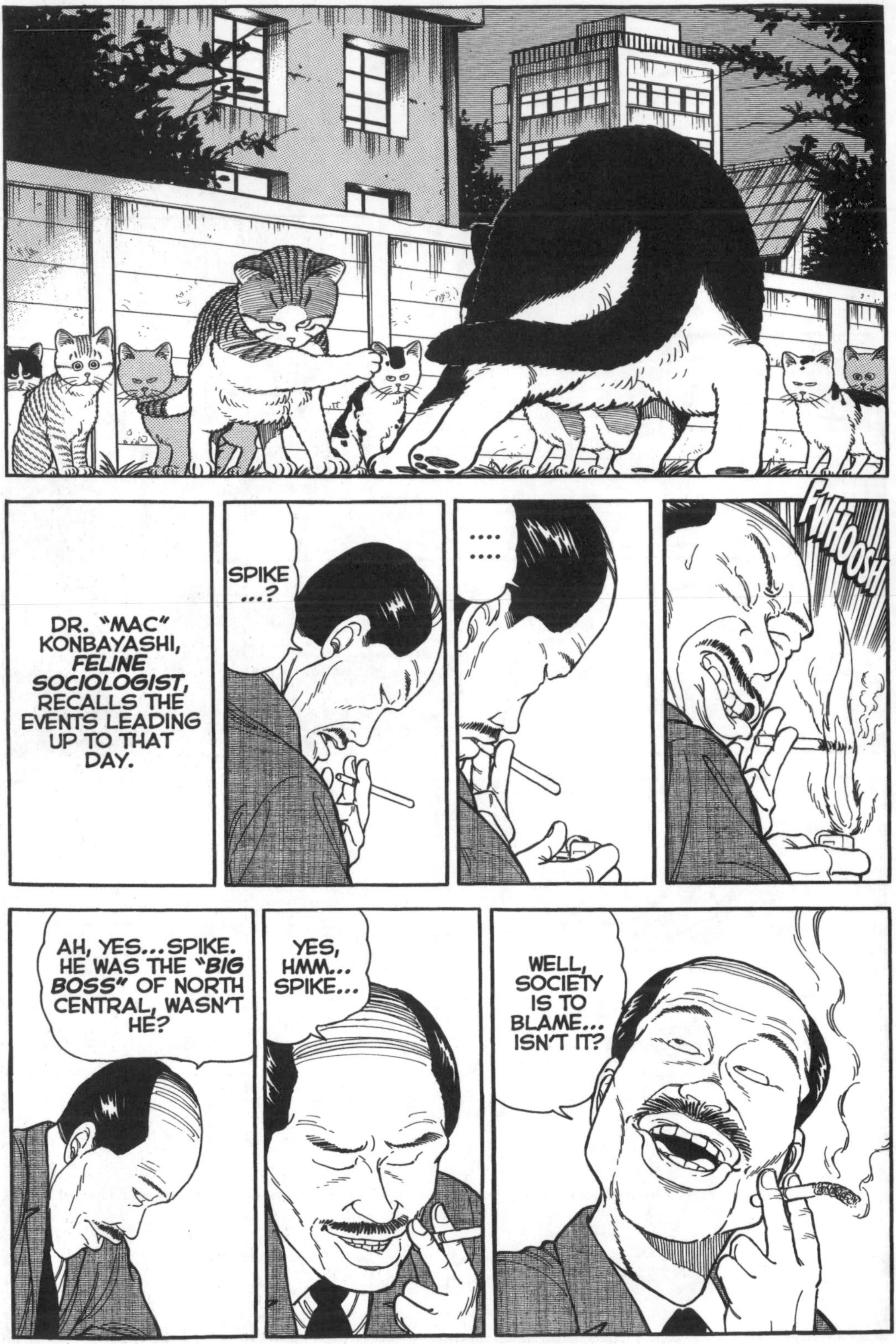
DR. "MAC" KONBAYASHI, FELINE SOCIOLOGIST, RECALLS THE EVENTS LEADING UP TO THAT DAY.
SPIKE ...?
....
....
FWHOOSH
AH, YES...SPIKE. HE WAS THE "BIG BOSS" OF NORTH CENTRAL, WASN'T HE?
YES, HMM... SPIKE...
WELL, SOCIETY IS TO BLAME... ISN'T IT?

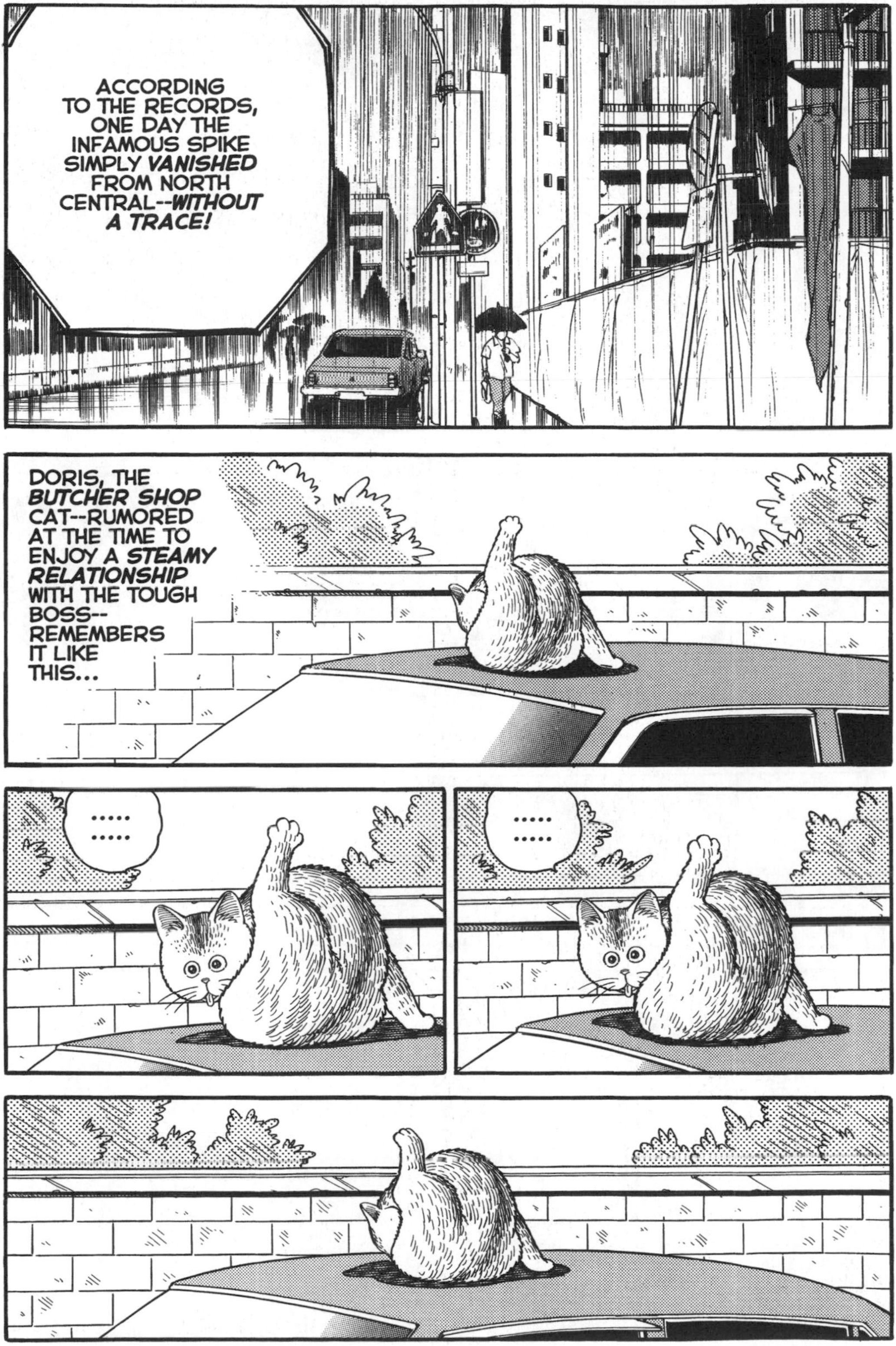
ACCORDING TO THE RECORDS, ONE DAY THE INFAMOUS SPIKE SIMPLY *VANISHED* FROM NORTH CENTRAL--*WITHOUT A TRACE!*
DORIS, THE *BUTCHER SHOP* CAT--RUMORED AT THE TIME TO ENJOY A *STEAMY RELATIONSHIP* WITH THE TOUGH BOSS--REMEMBERS IT LIKE THIS...
.....
.....
.....
.....

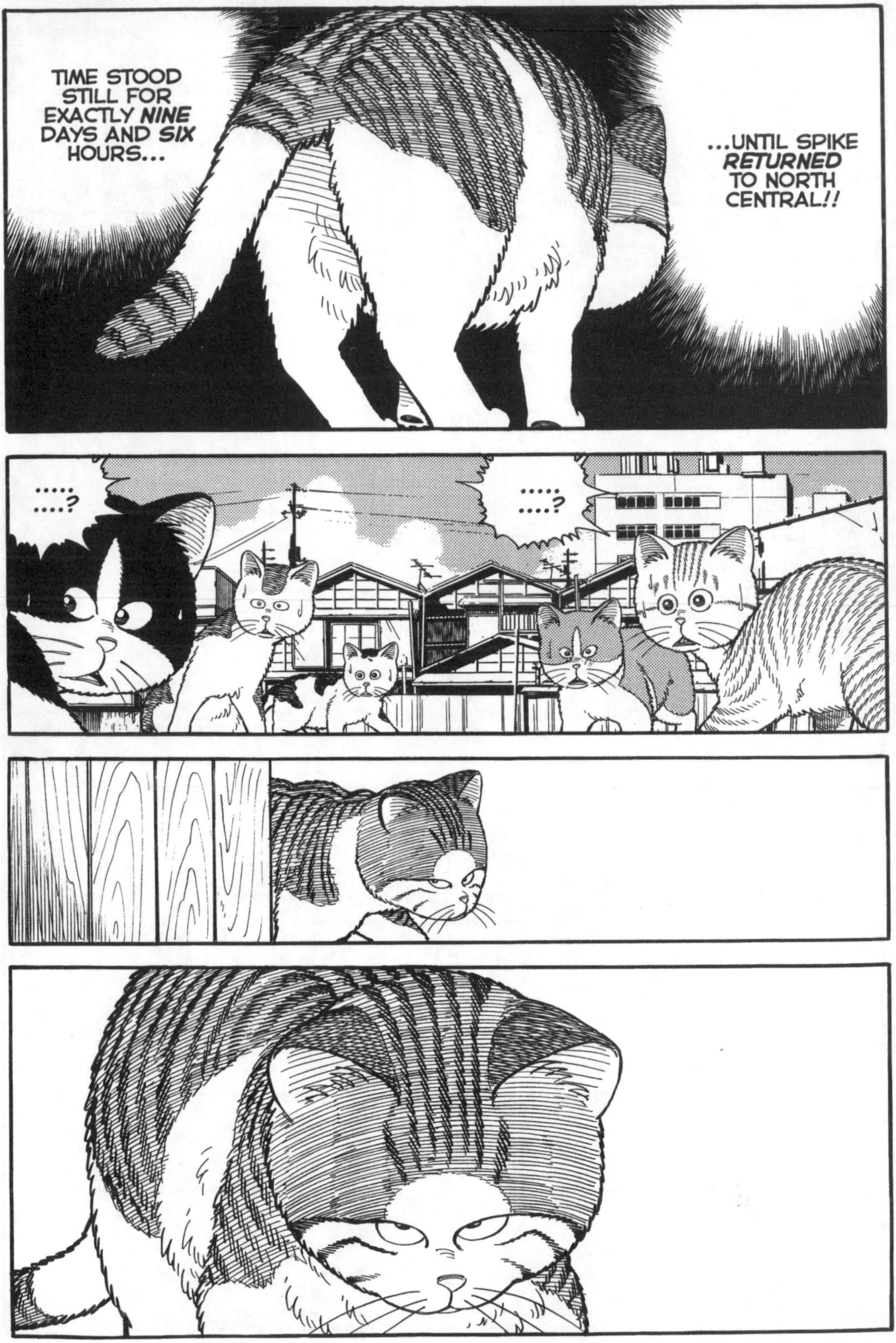
TIME STOOD STILL FOR EXACTLY *NINE* DAYS AND *SIX* HOURS...
...UNTIL SPIKE *RETURNED* TO NORTH CENTRAL!!
....?
....?
....?
....?

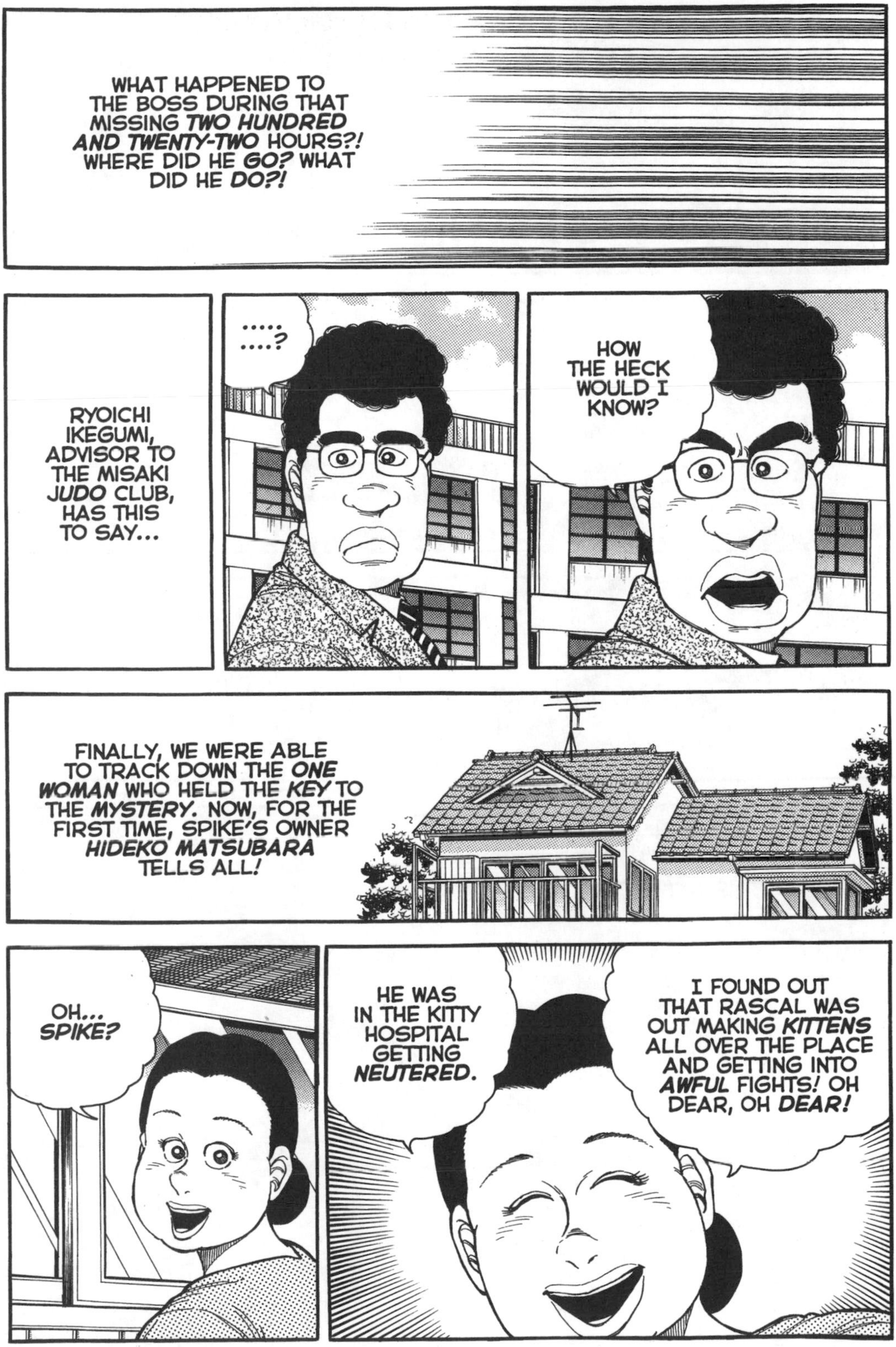

WHAT HAPPENED TO THE BOSS DURING THAT MISSING TWO HUNDRED AND TWENTY-TWO HOURS?! WHERE DID HE GO? WHAT DID HE DO?!
RYOICHI IKEGUMI, ADVISOR TO THE MISAKI JUDO CLUB, HAS THIS TO SAY...
.....
....?
HOW THE HECK WOULD I KNOW?
FINALLY, WE WERE ABLE TO TRACK DOWN THE ONE WOMAN WHO HELD THE KEY TO THE MYSTERY. NOW, FOR THE FIRST TIME, SPIKE'S OWNER HIDEKO MATSUBARA TELLS ALL!
OH... SPIKE?
HE WAS IN THE KITTY HOSPITAL GETTING NEUTERED.
I FOUND OUT THAT RASCAL WAS OUT MAKING KITTENS ALL OVER THE PLACE AND GETTING INTO AWFUL FIGHTS! OH DEAR, OH DEAR!

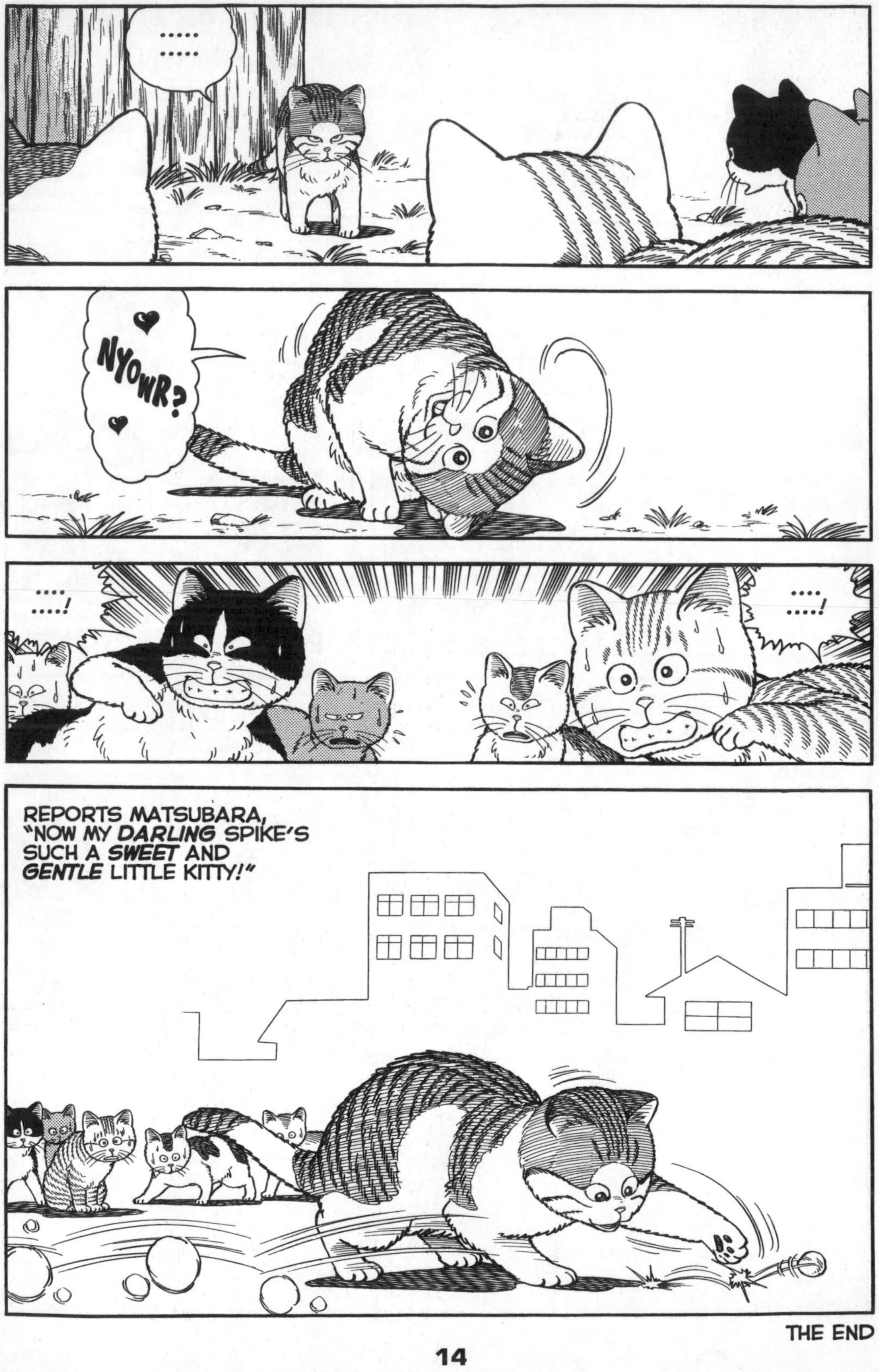
.....
.....
NYOWR?
....
....!
....
....!
REPORTS MATSUBARA, "NOW MY DARLING SPIKE'S SUCH A SWEET AND GENTLE LITTLE KITTY!"

THE END

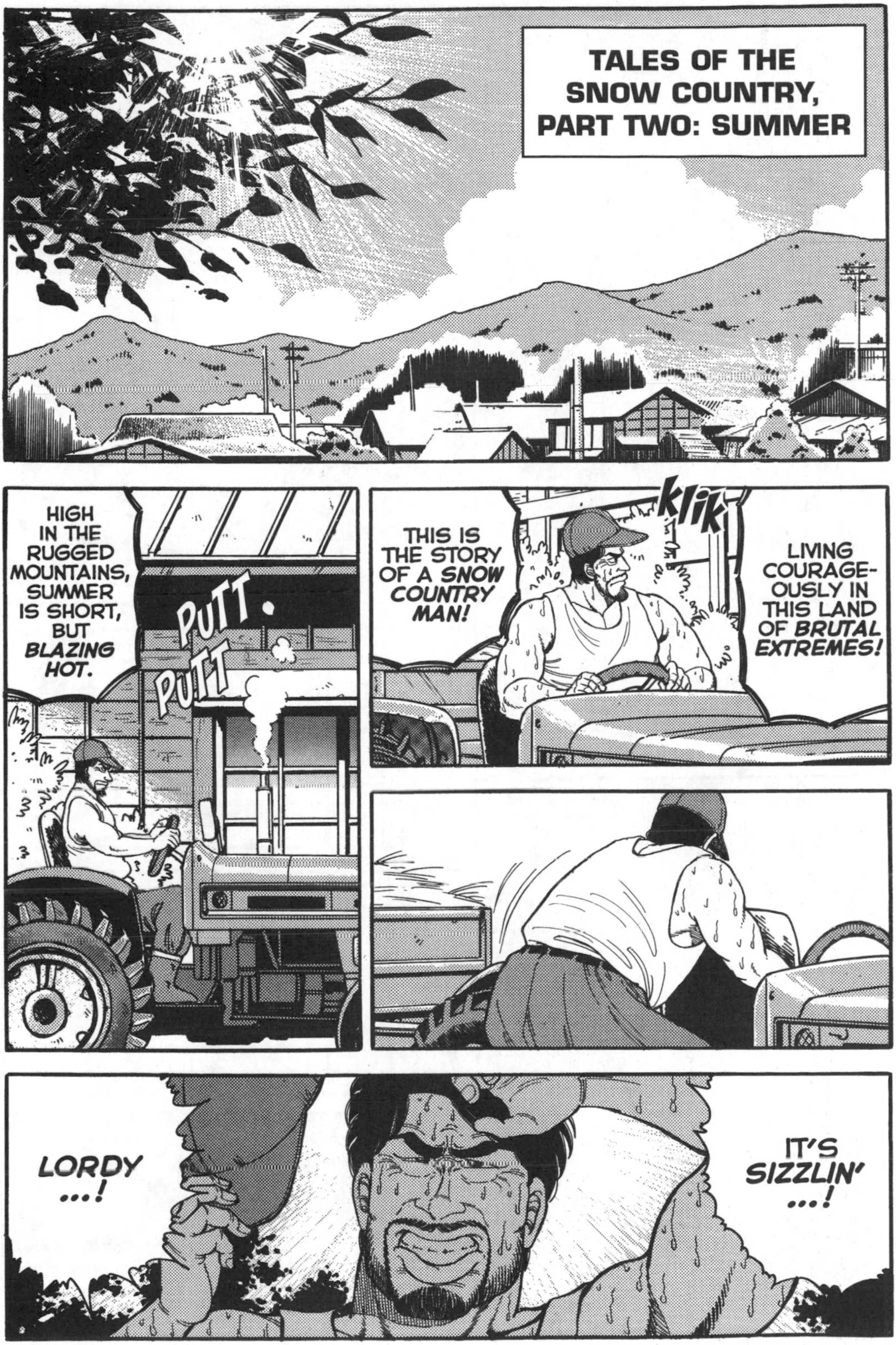
TALES OF THE SNOW COUNTRY, PART TWO: SUMMER
HIGH IN THE RUGGED MOUNTAINS, SUMMER IS SHORT, BUT BLAZING HOT.
PUTT PUTT
THIS IS THE STORY OF A SNOW COUNTRY MAN!
KLIK
LIVING COURAGE-OUSLY IN THIS LAND OF BRUTAL EXTREMES!
LORDY ...!
IT'S SIZZLIN' ...!

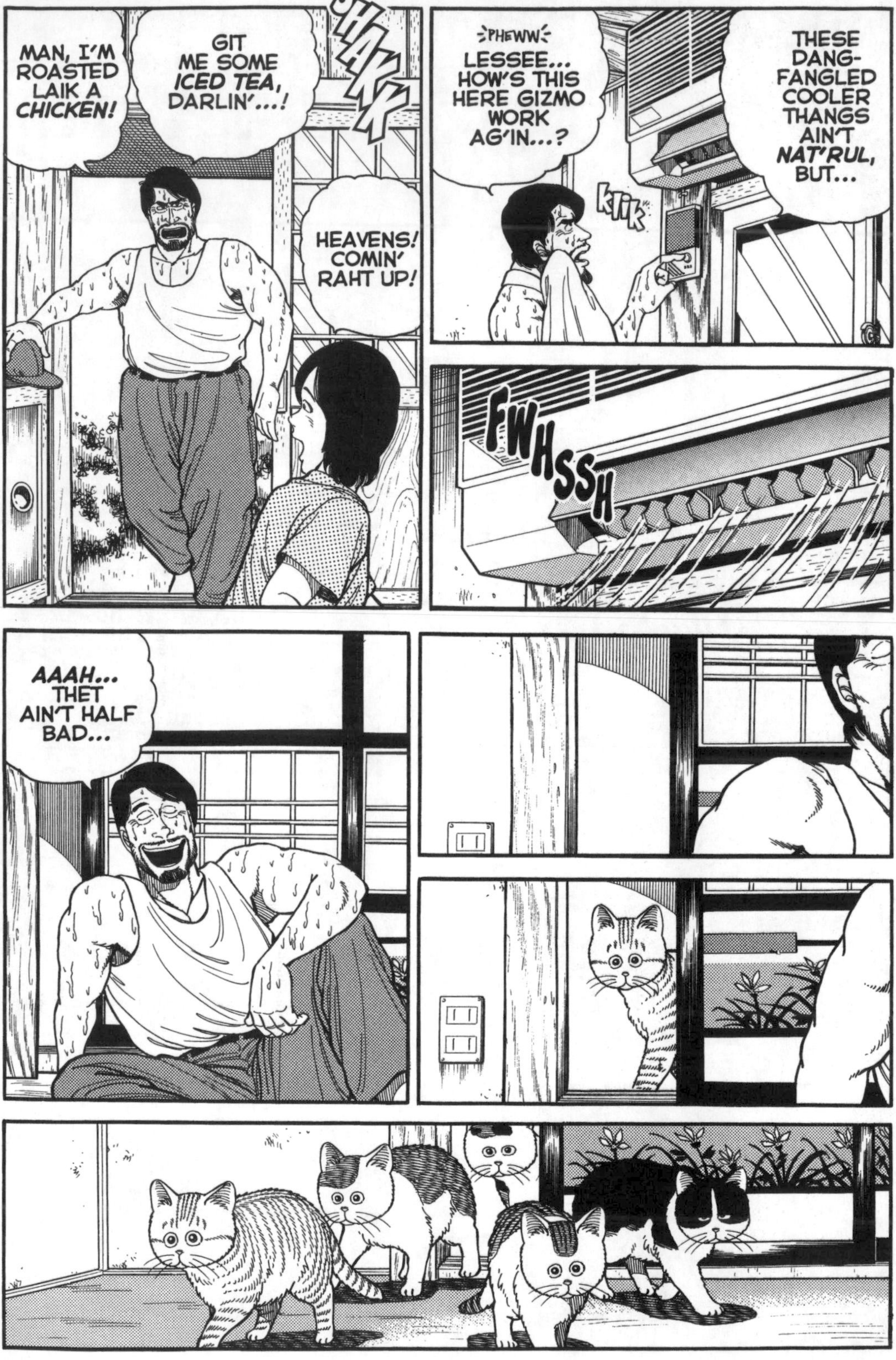
MAN, I'M ROASTED LAIK A CHICKEN!
GIT ME SOME ICED TEA, DARLIN'...!
SHAKK
HEAVENS! COMIN' RAHT UP!
PHEWW
LESSEE... HOW'S THIS HERE GIZMO WORK AG'IN...?
THESE DANG-FANGLED COOLER THANGS AIN'T NAT'RUL, BUT...
KLIK
FWHSSH
AAAH... THET AIN'T HALF BAD...

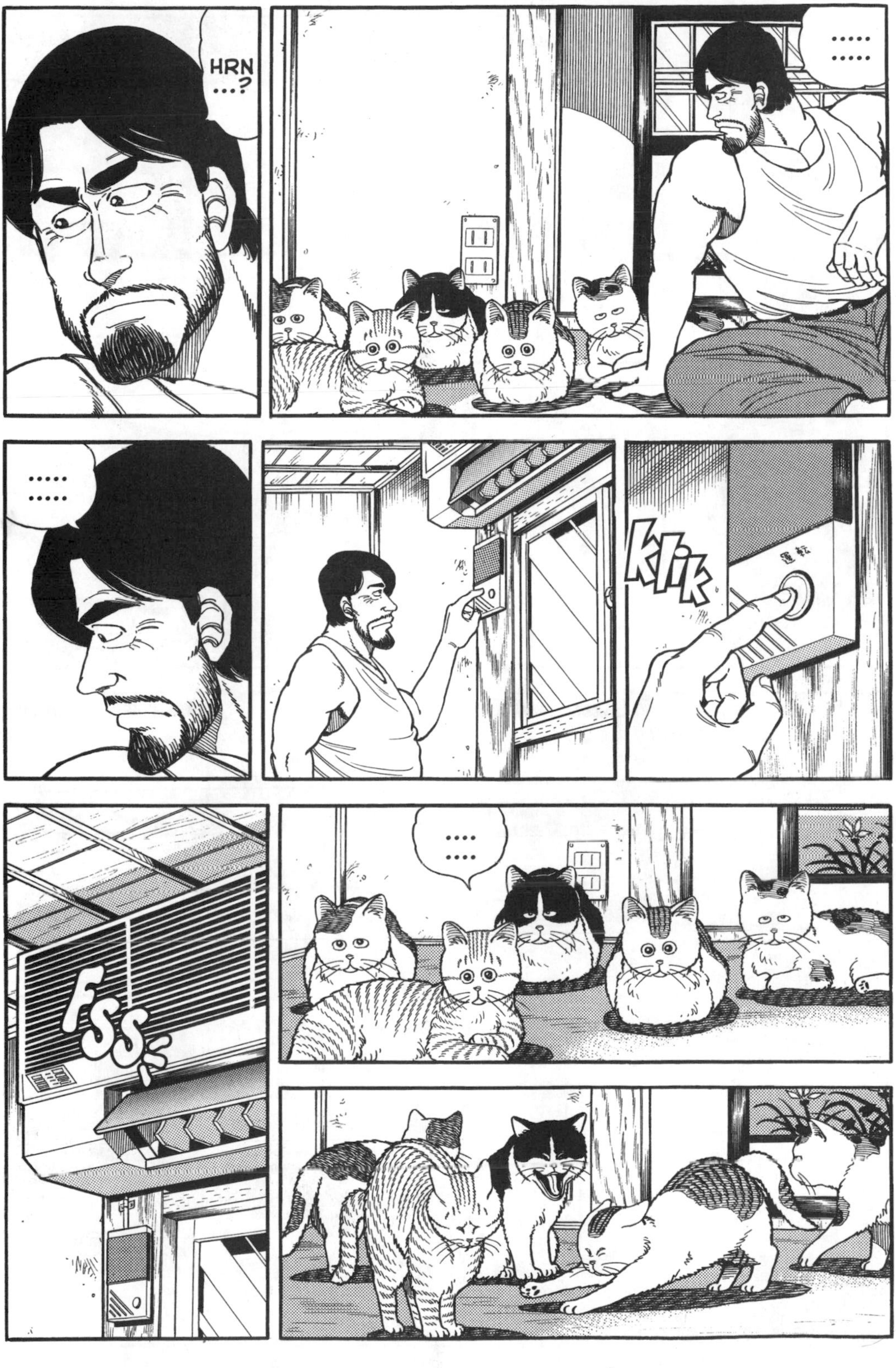
HRN ...?
.....
.....
.....
.....
KLIK
運転
FSS
....
....

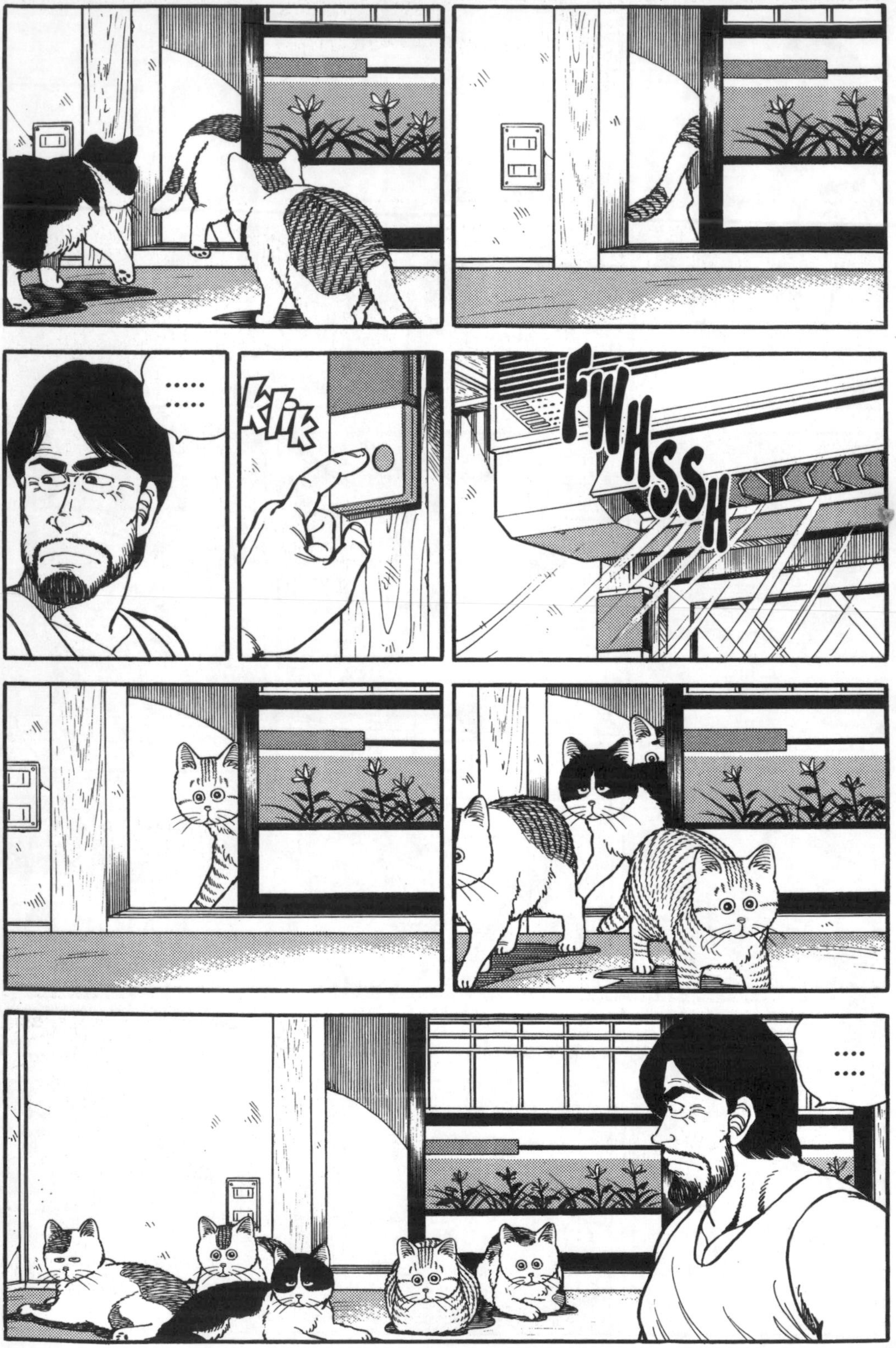
......
......
KLIK
FWHSSH
....
....

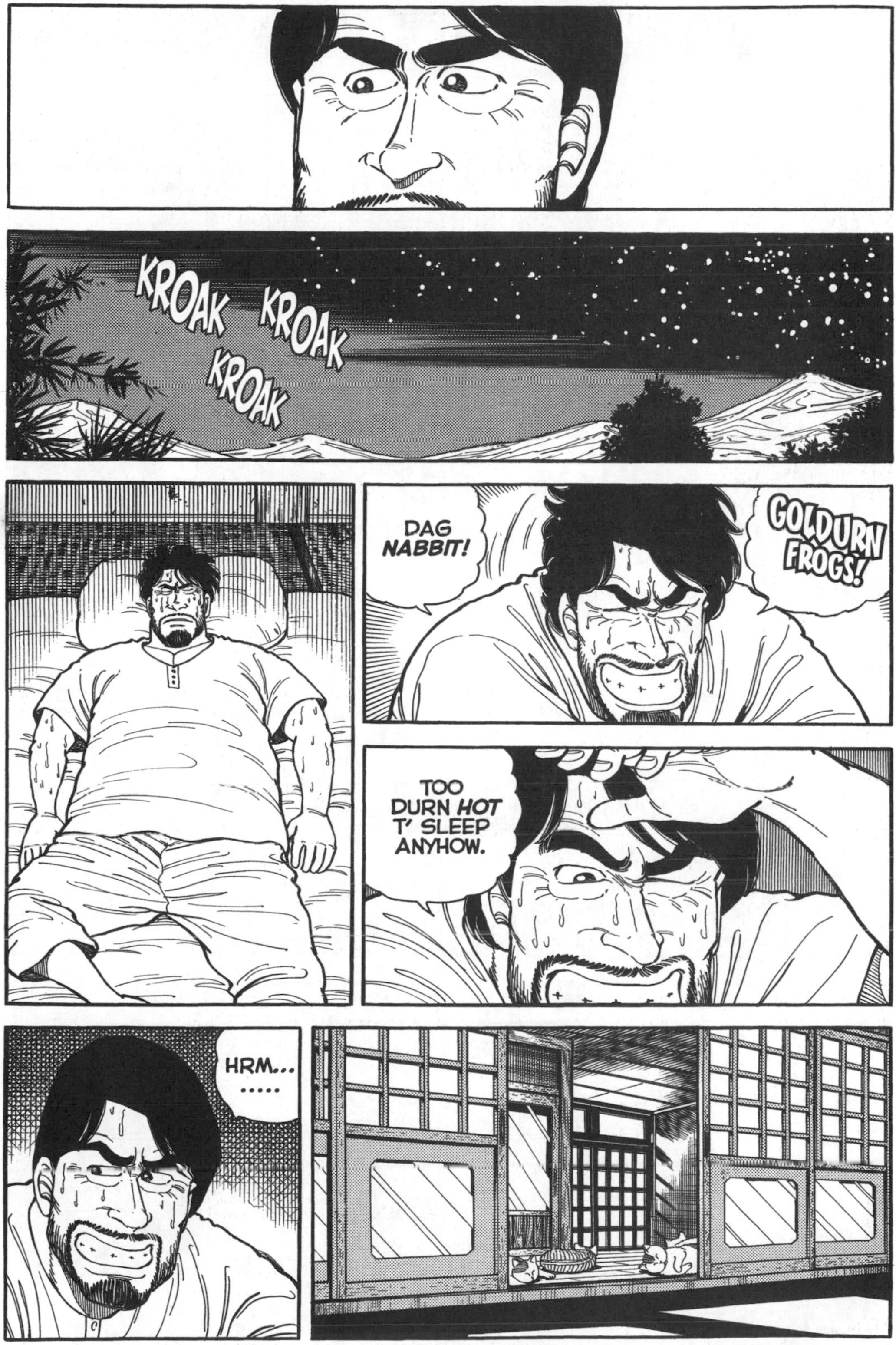
KROAK KROAK
KROAK
DAG NABBIT!
GOLDURN FROGS!
TOO DURN HOT T' SLEEP ANYHOW.
HRM... ......

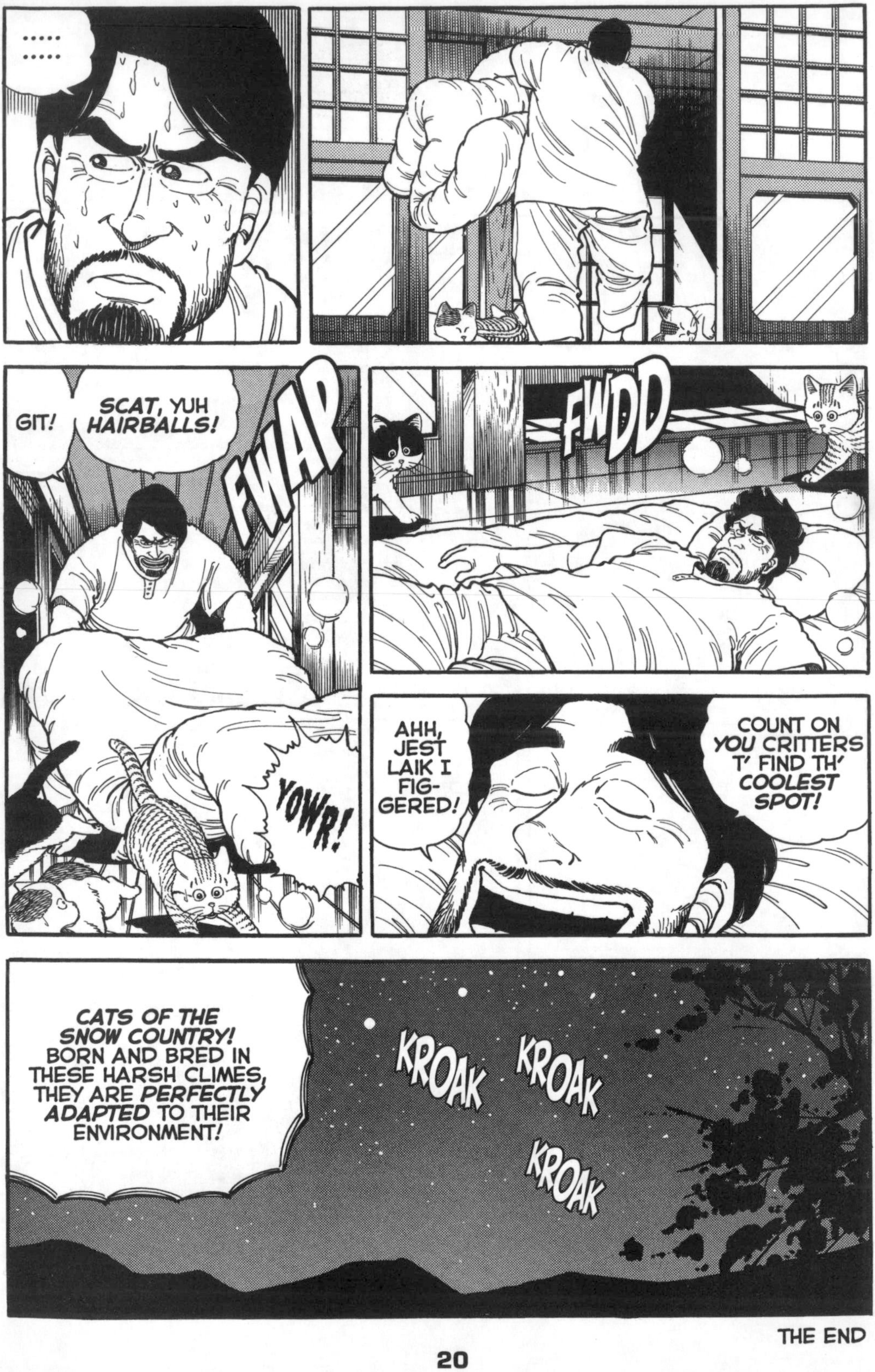
......
......
GIT!
SCAT, YUH HAIRBALLS!
FWAP
YOWR!
FWDD
AHH, JEST LAIK I FIG-GERED!
COUNT ON YOU CRITTERS T' FIND TH' COOLEST SPOT!
CATS OF THE SNOW COUNTRY! BORN AND BRED IN THESE HARSH CLIMES, THEY ARE PERFECTLY ADAPTED TO THEIR ENVIRONMENT!
KROAK
KROAK
KROAK

THE END

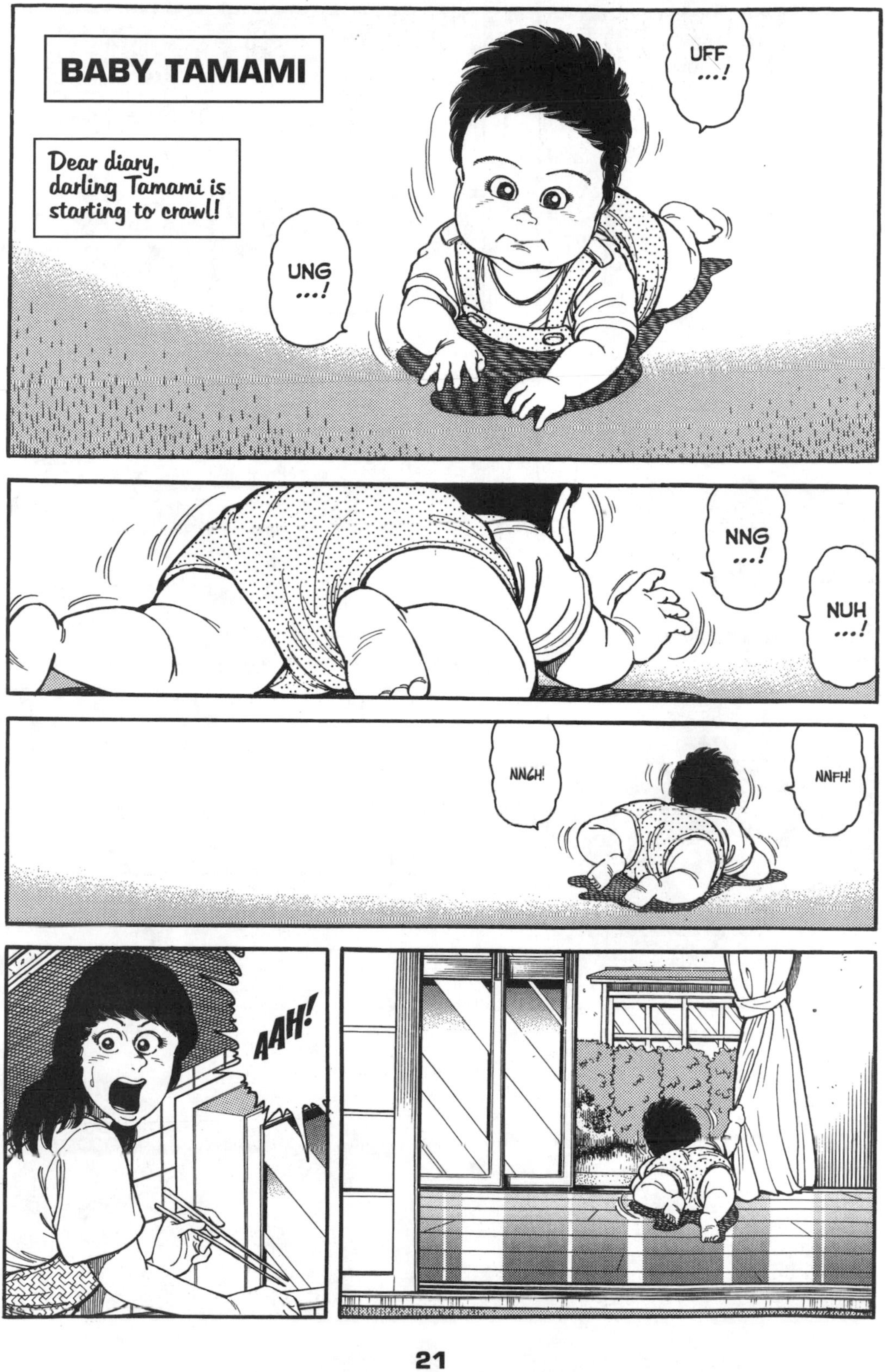
BABY TAMAMI
Dear diary, darling Tamami is starting to crawl!
UFF ...!
UNG ...!
NNG ...!
NUH ...!
NNGH!
NNFH!
AAH!

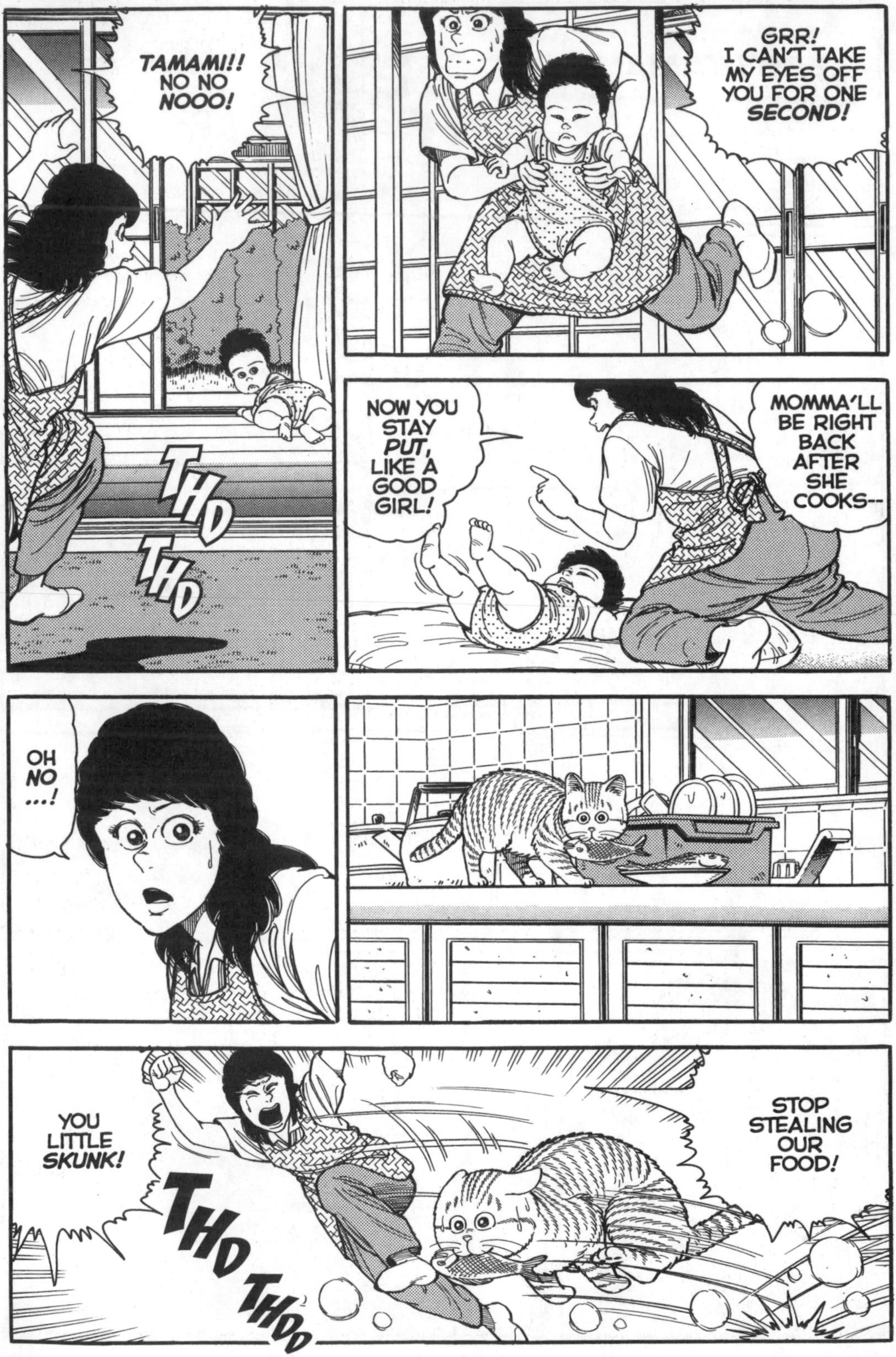
TAMAMI!! NO NO NOOO!
THD THD
GRR! I CAN'T TAKE MY EYES OFF YOU FOR ONE SECOND!
NOW YOU STAY PUT, LIKE A GOOD GIRL!
MOMMA'LL BE RIGHT BACK AFTER SHE COOKS--
OH NO ...!
YOU LITTLE SKUNK!
STOP STEALING OUR FOOD!
THD THDD

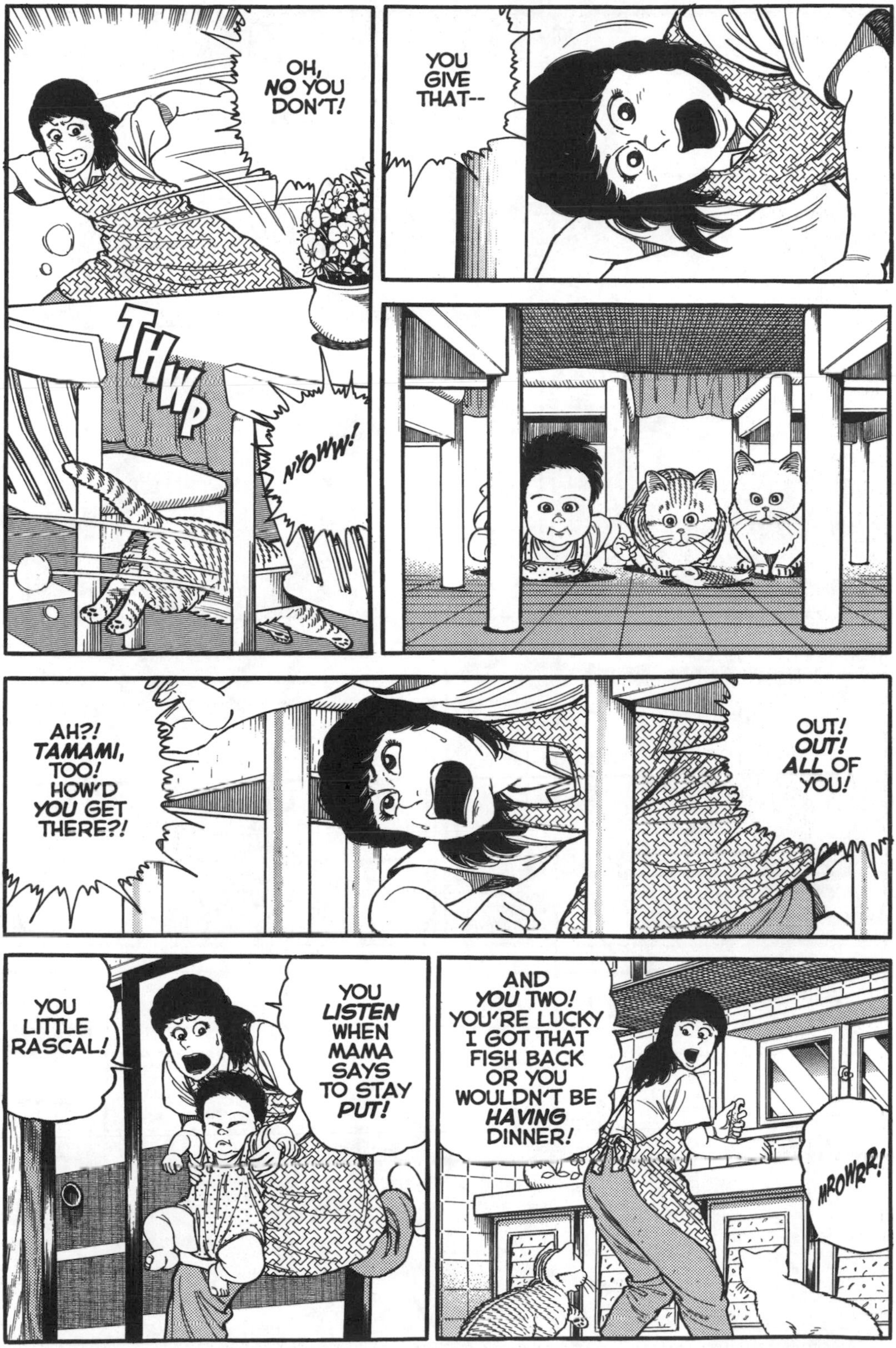
OH, NO YOU DON'T!
YOU GIVE THAT--
THWP
NYOWW!
AH?! TAMAMI, TOO! HOW'D YOU GET THERE?!
OUT! OUT! ALL OF YOU!
YOU LITTLE RASCAL!
YOU LISTEN WHEN MAMA SAYS TO STAY PUT!
AND YOU TWO! YOU'RE LUCKY I GOT THAT FISH BACK OR YOU WOULDN'T BE HAVING DINNER!
MROWRR!

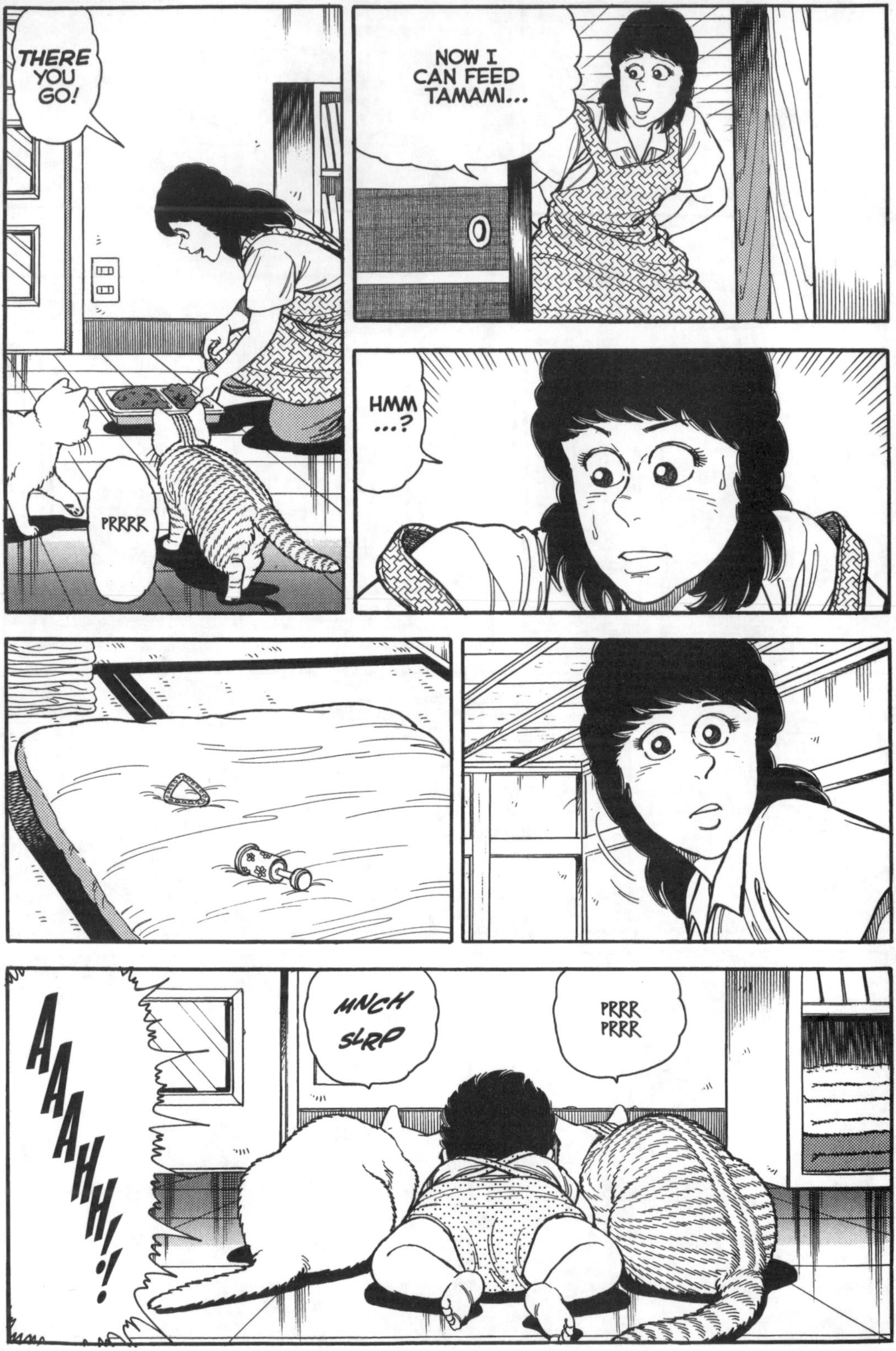
THERE YOU GO!
PRRRR
NOW I CAN FEED TAMAMI...
HMM ...?
MNCH SLRP
PRRR PRRR
AAAAHH!!

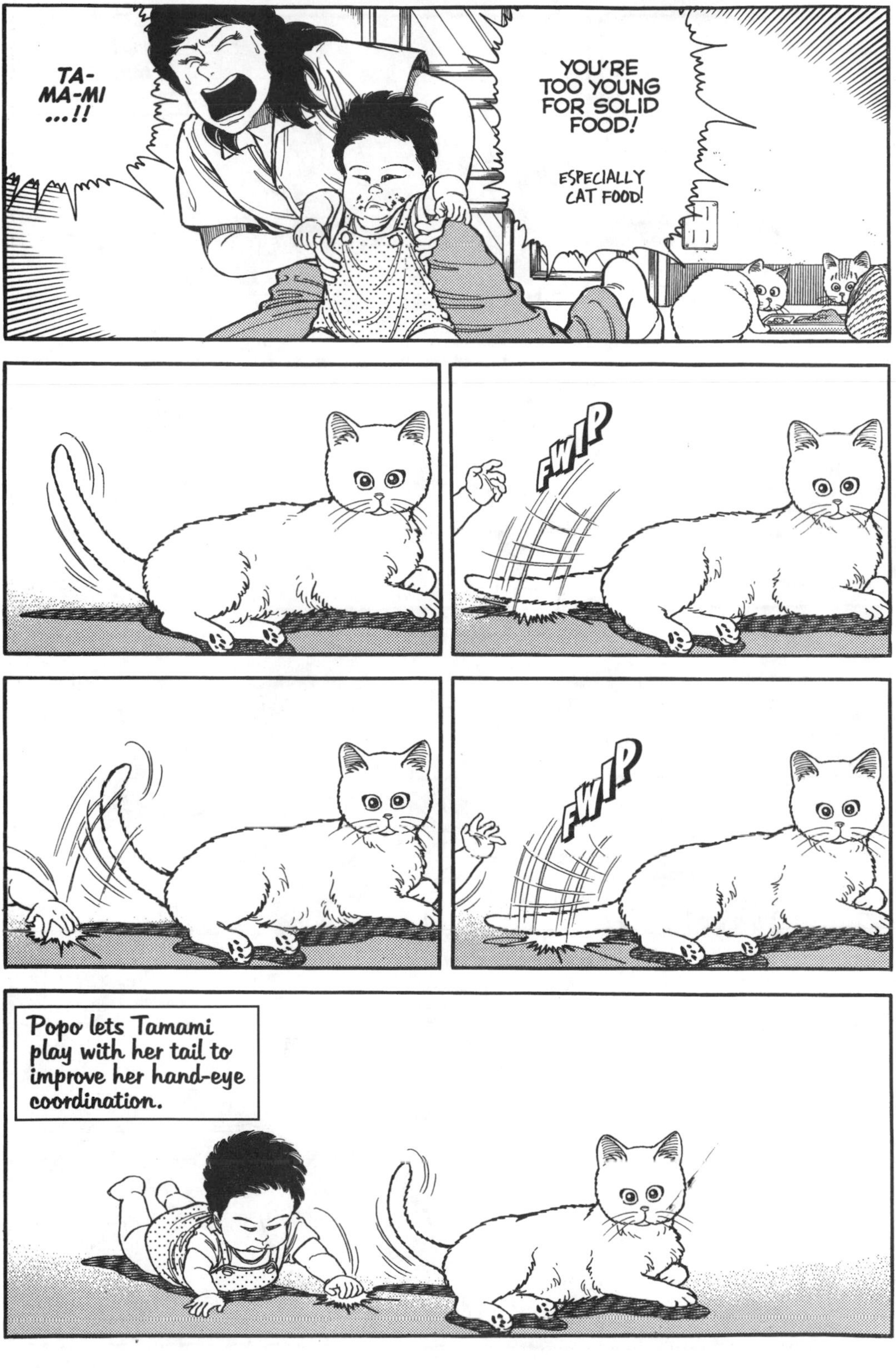
TA-MA-MI ...!!
YOU'RE TOO YOUNG FOR SOLID FOOD!
ESPECIALLY CAT FOOD!
FWIP
FWIP
Popo lets Tamami play with her tail to improve her hand-eye coordination.

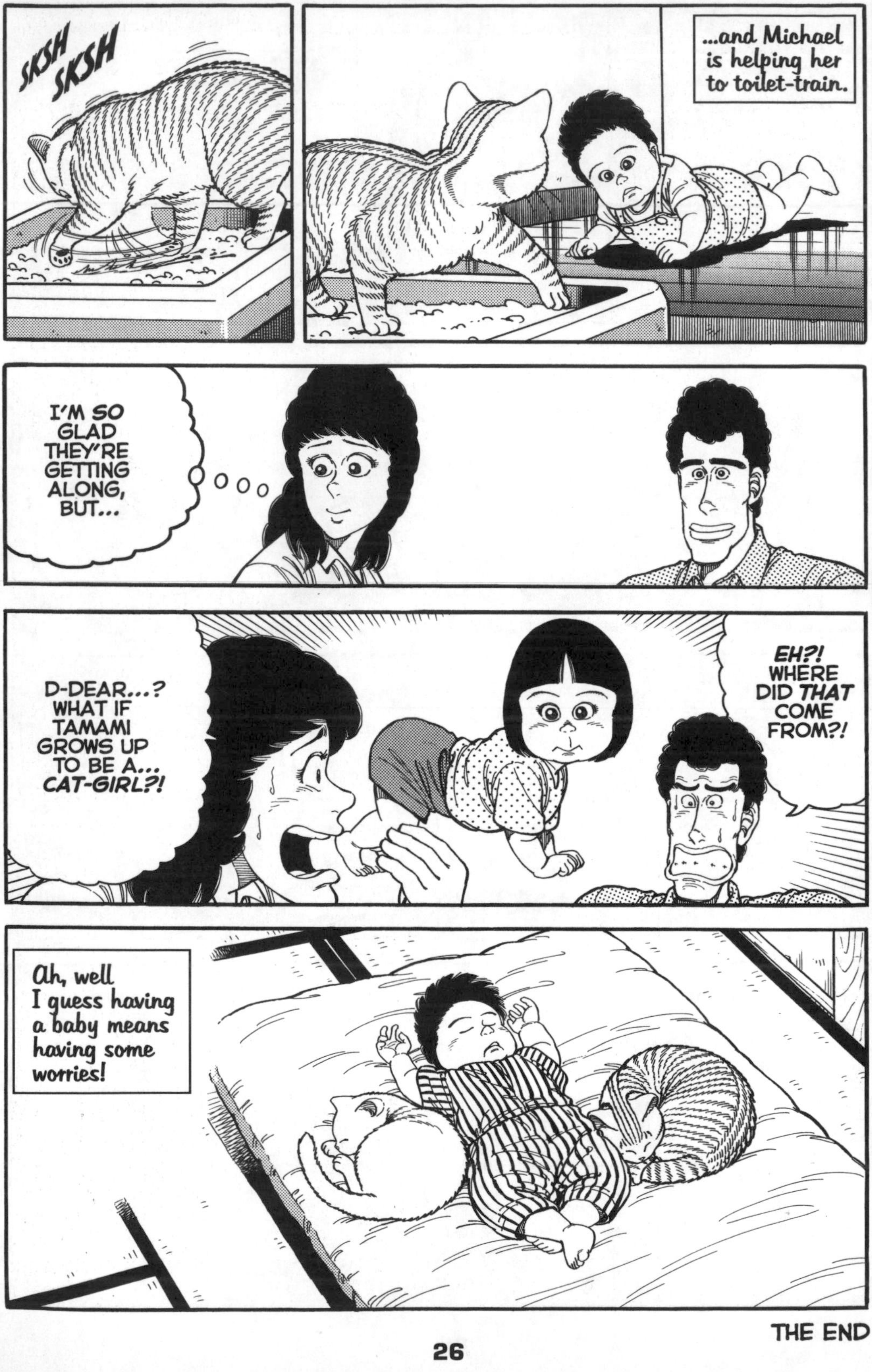
SKSH SKSH
...and Michael is helping her to toilet-train.
I'M SO GLAD THEY'RE GETTING ALONG, BUT...
D-DEAR...? WHAT IF TAMAMI GROWS UP TO BE A... CAT-GIRL?!
EH?! WHERE DID THAT COME FROM?!
Ah, well I guess having a baby means having some worries!

THE END

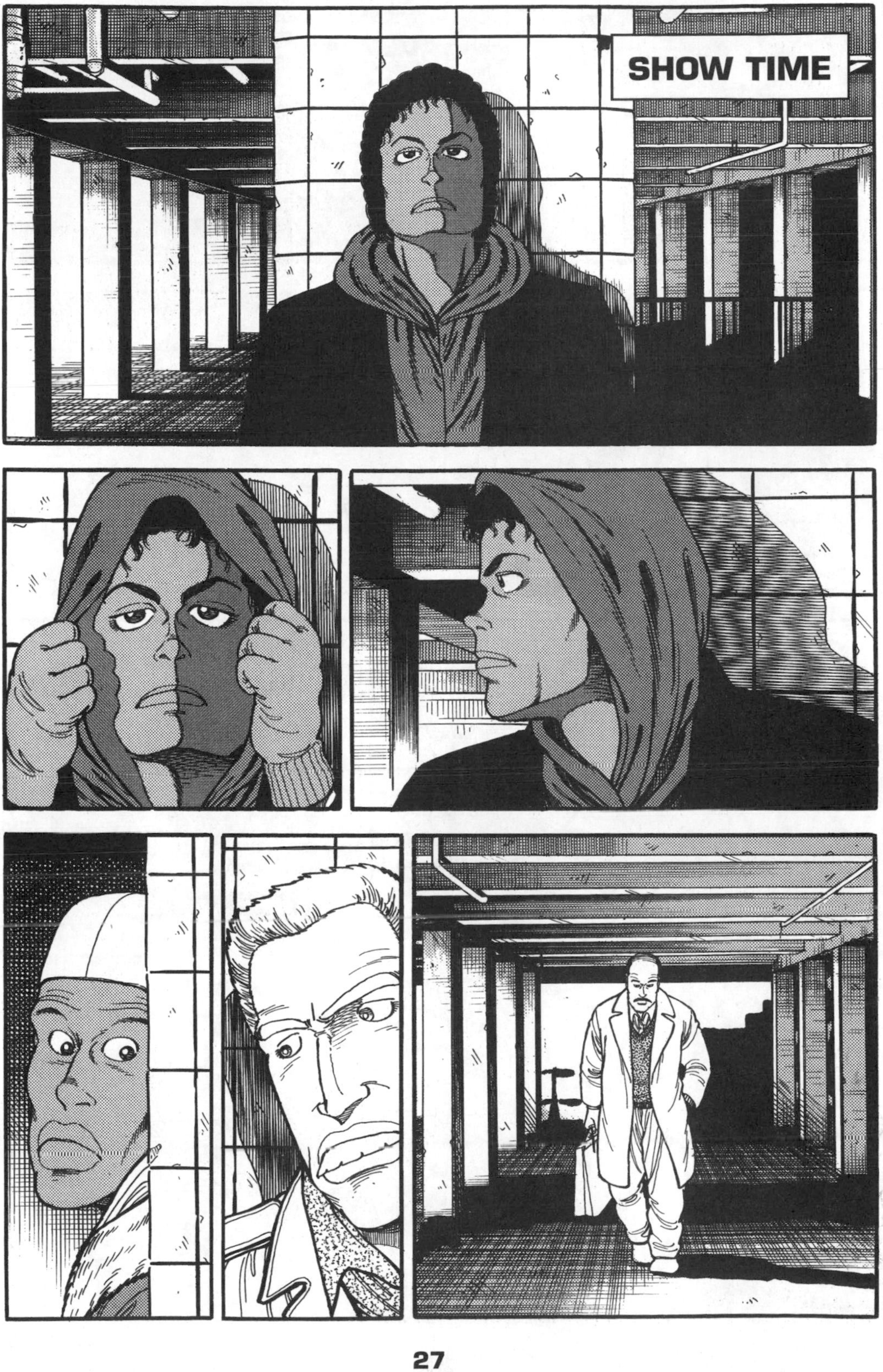
SHOW TIME

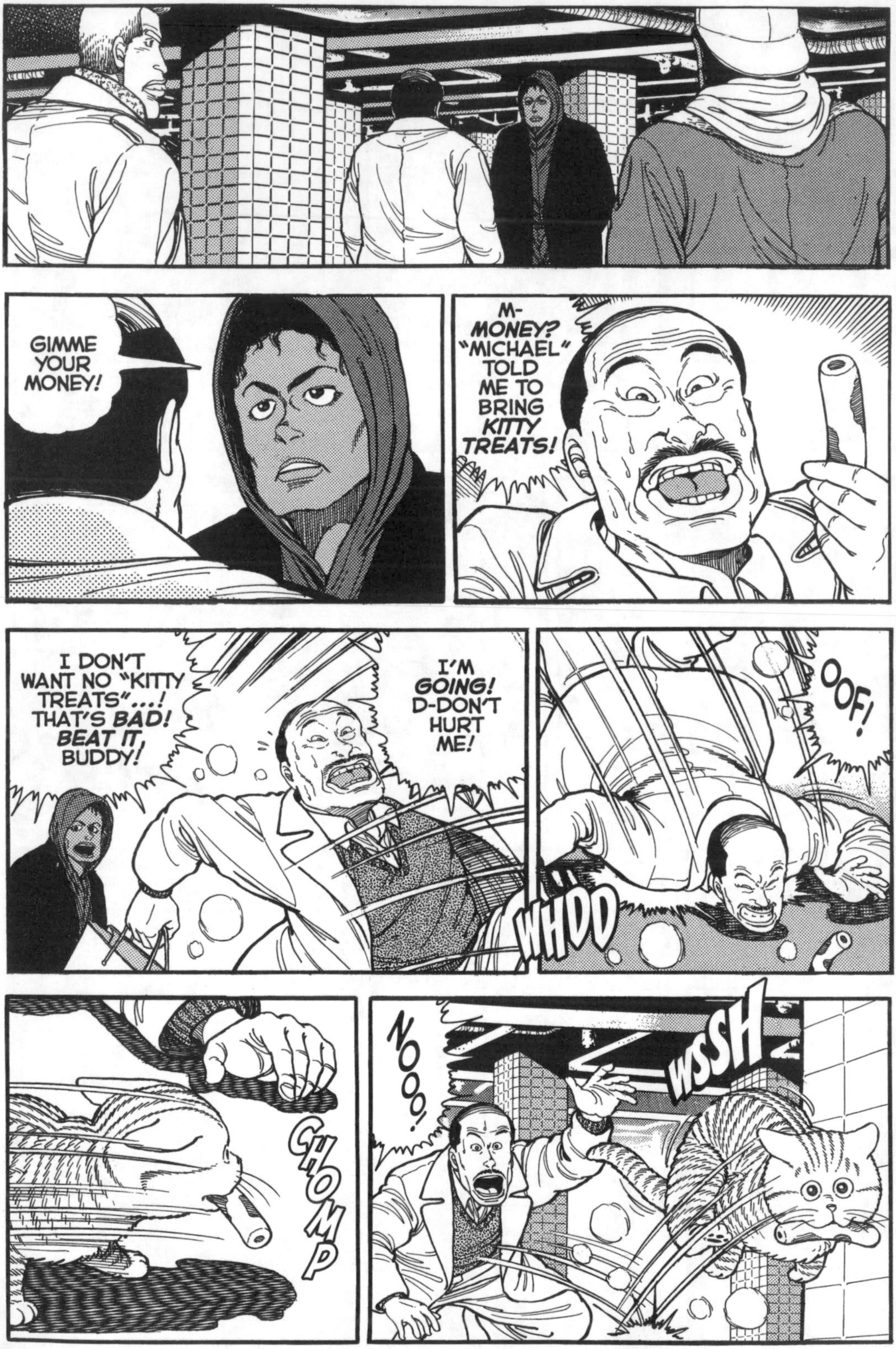
GIMME YOUR MONEY!
M-MONEY? "MICHAEL" TOLD ME TO BRING KITTY TREATS!
I DON'T WANT NO "KITTY TREATS"...! THAT'S BAD! BEAT IT, BUDDY!
I'M GOING! D-DON'T HURT ME!
OOF!
WHDD
CHOMP
NOOO!
WSSH

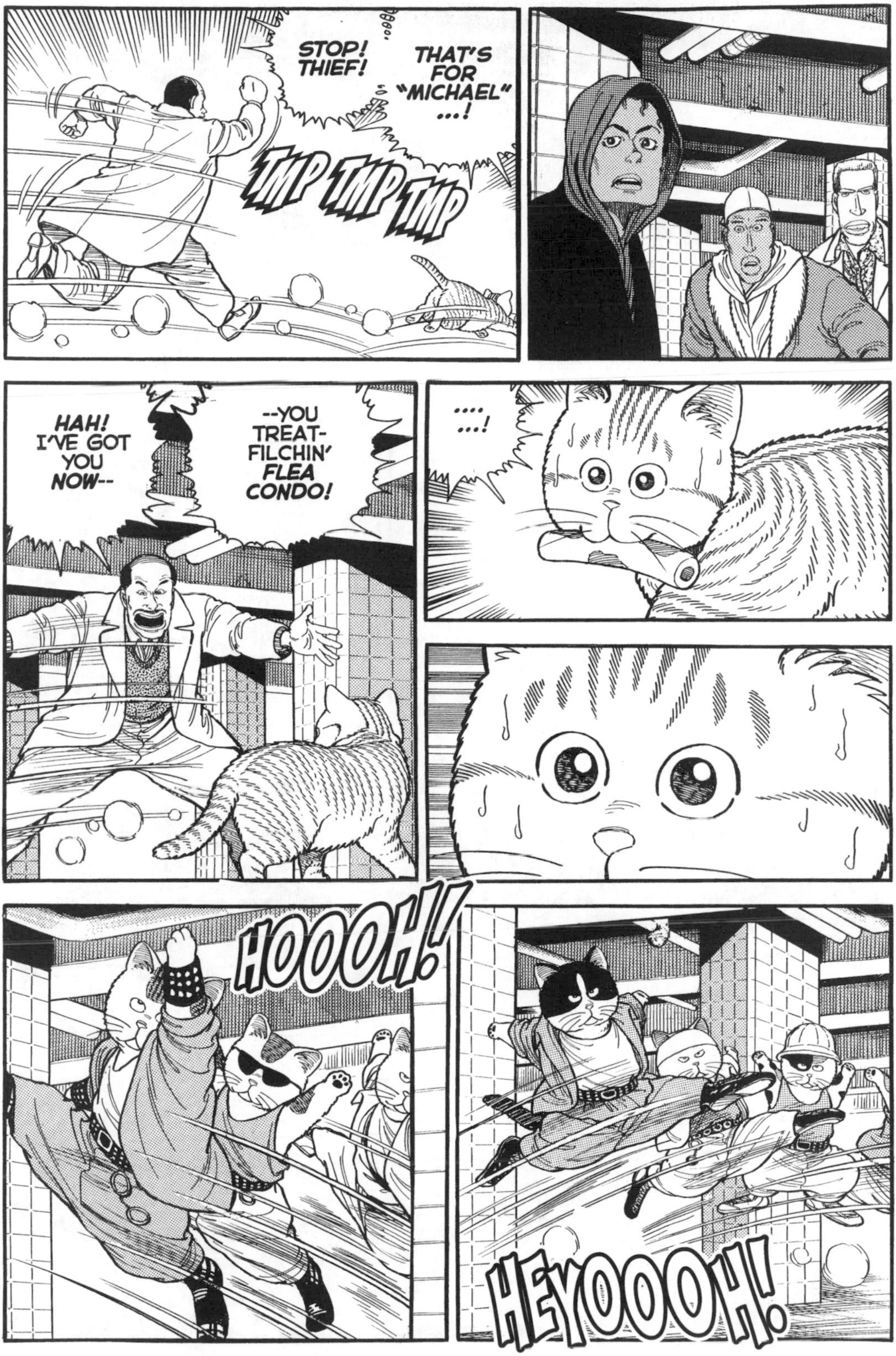
STOP! THIEF!
THAT'S FOR "MICHAEL" ...!
TMP TMP TMP
HAH! I'VE GOT YOU NOW--
--YOU TREAT-FILCHIN' FLEA CONDO!
....!
HOOOH!!
HEYOOOH!

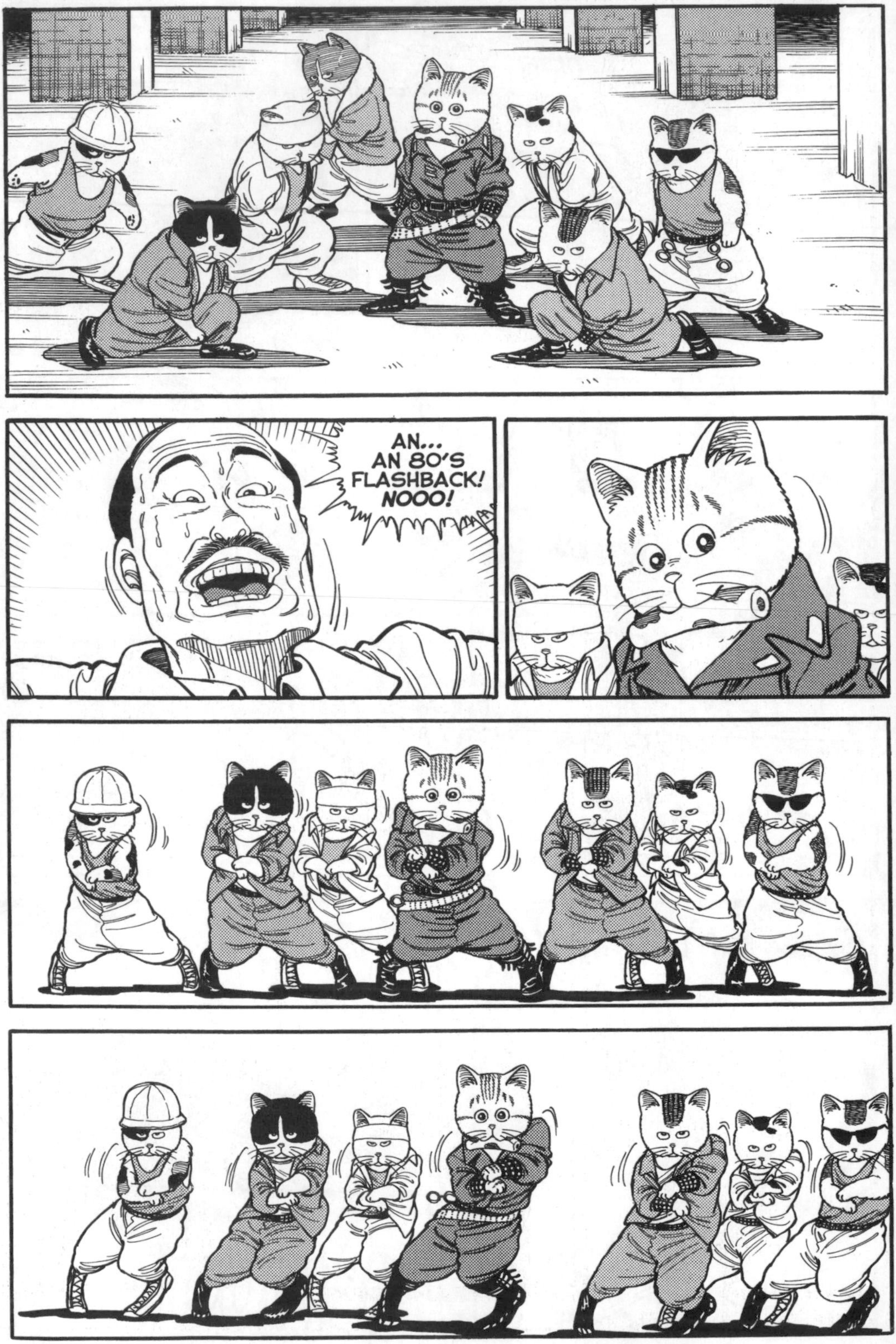
AN... AN 80'S FLASHBACK! NOOO!

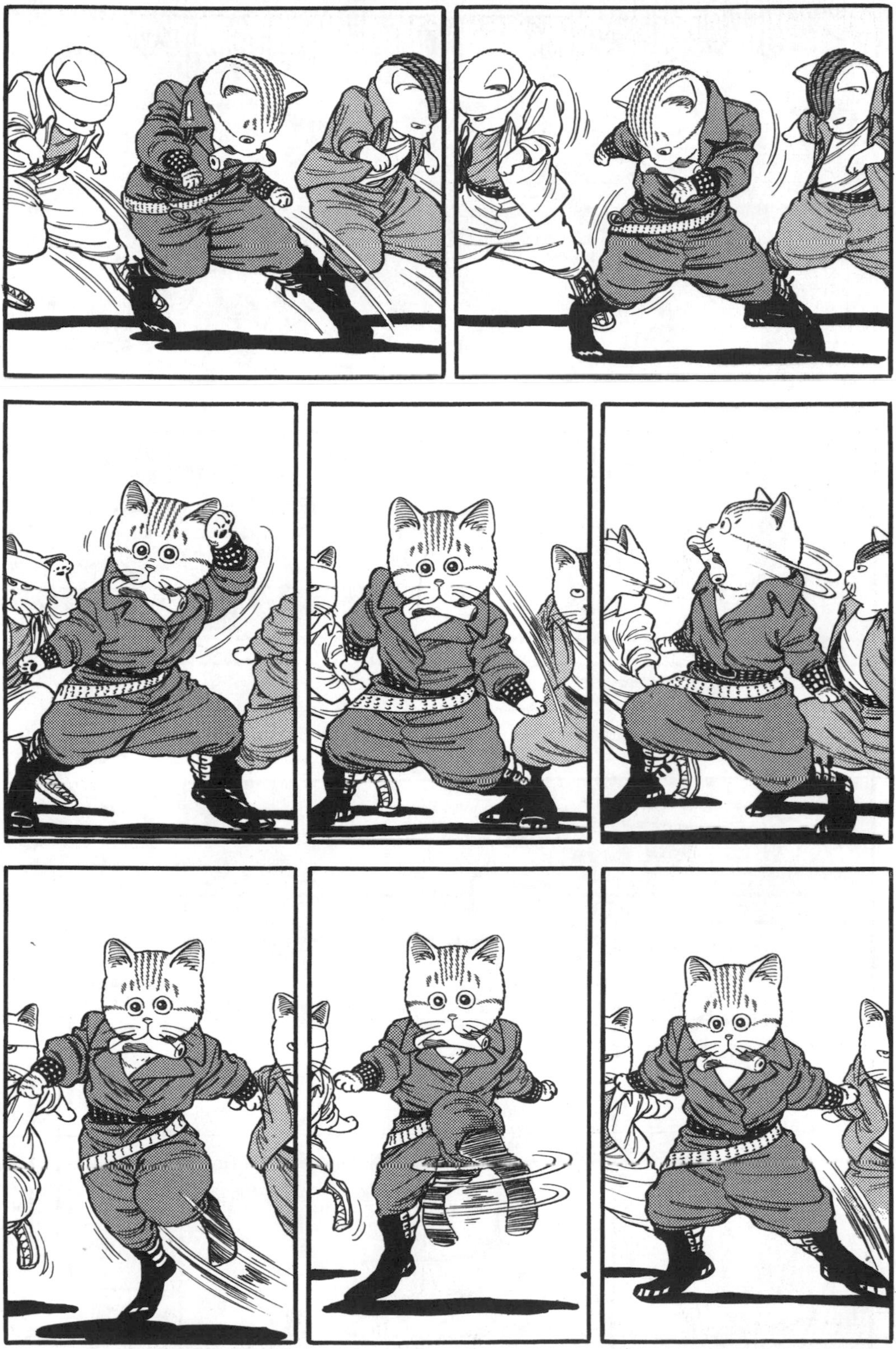

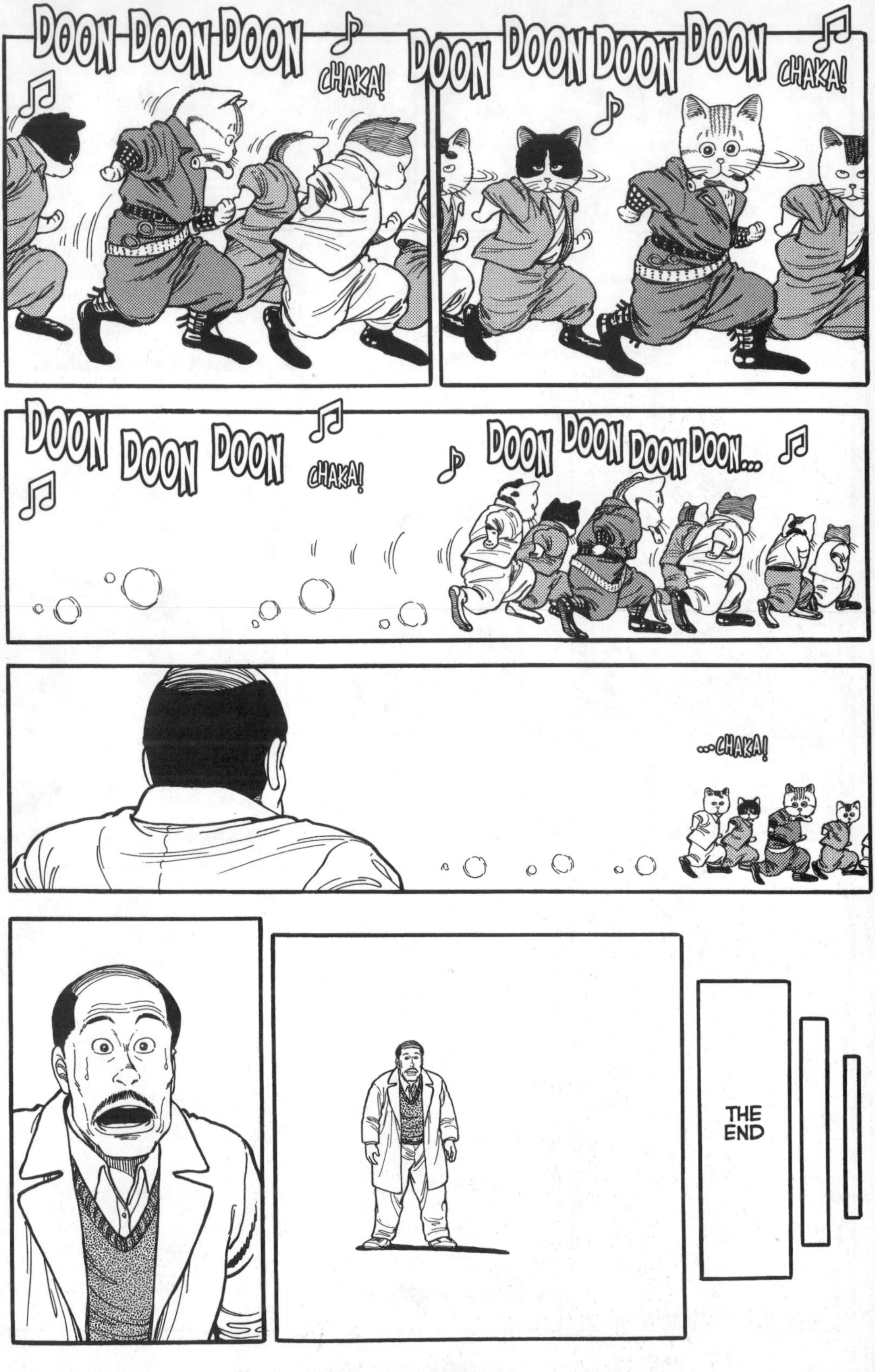
DOON DOON DOON
CHAKA!
DOON DOON DOON DOON
CHAKA!
DOON DOON DOON
CHAKA!
DOON DOON DOON DOON...
...CHAKA!
THE END

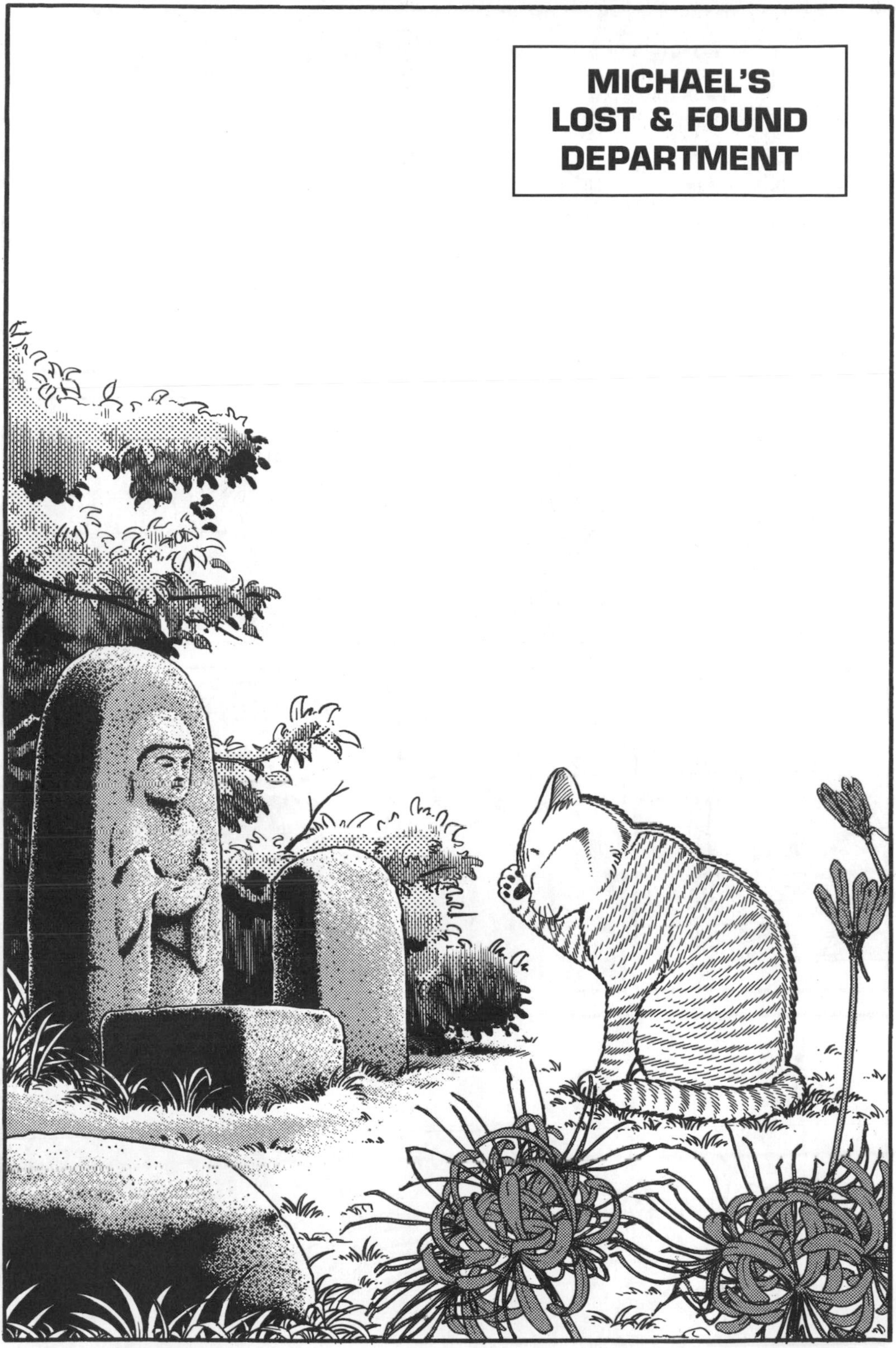
MICHAEL'S
LOST & FOUND
DEPARTMENT

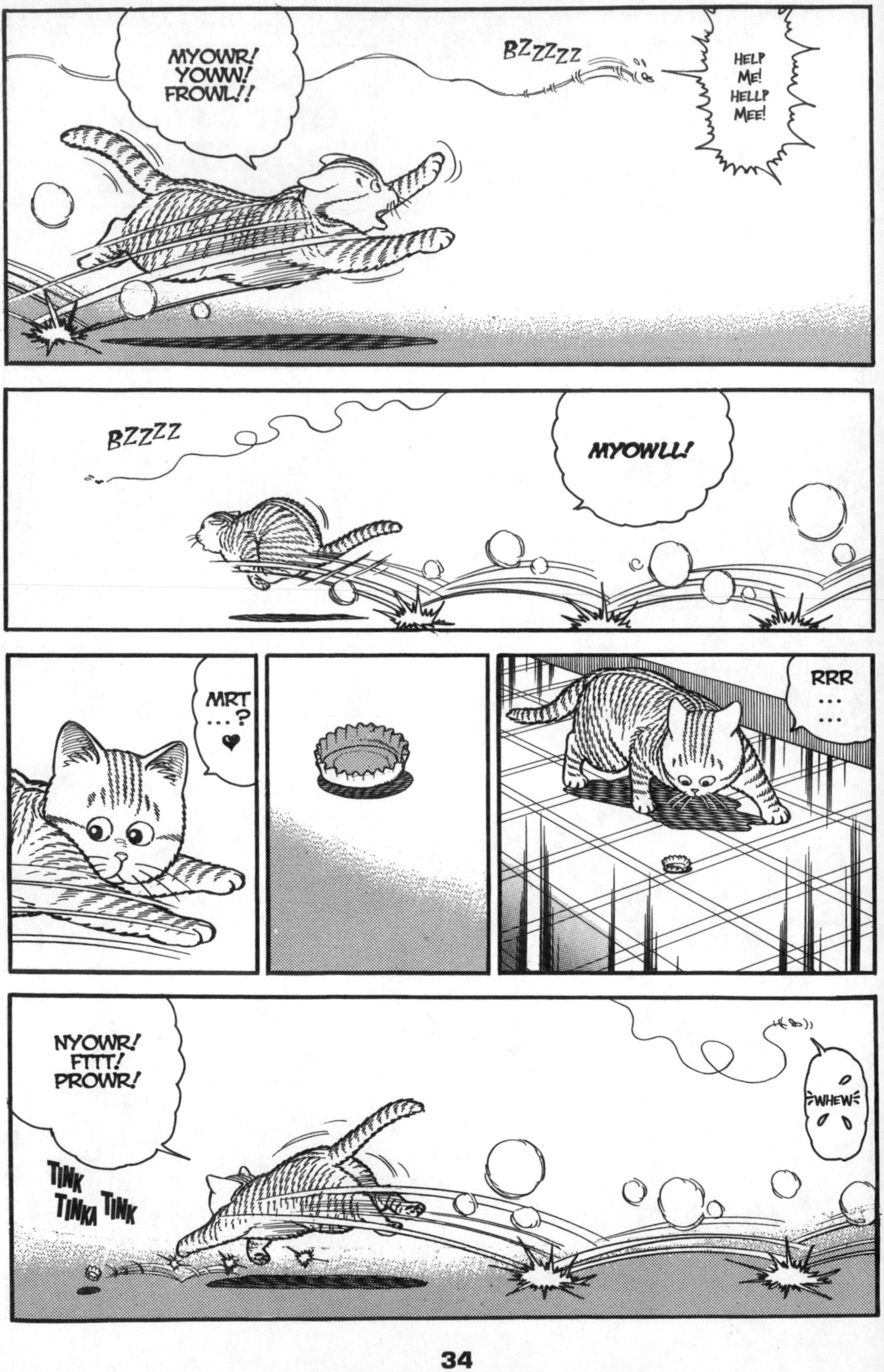
MYOWR! YOWW! FROWL!!
BZZZZZ
HELP ME! HELLP MEE!
BZZZZ
MYOWLL!
MRT ...? ♥
RRR ... ...
NYOWR! FTTT! PROWR!
TINK TINKA TINK
WHEW

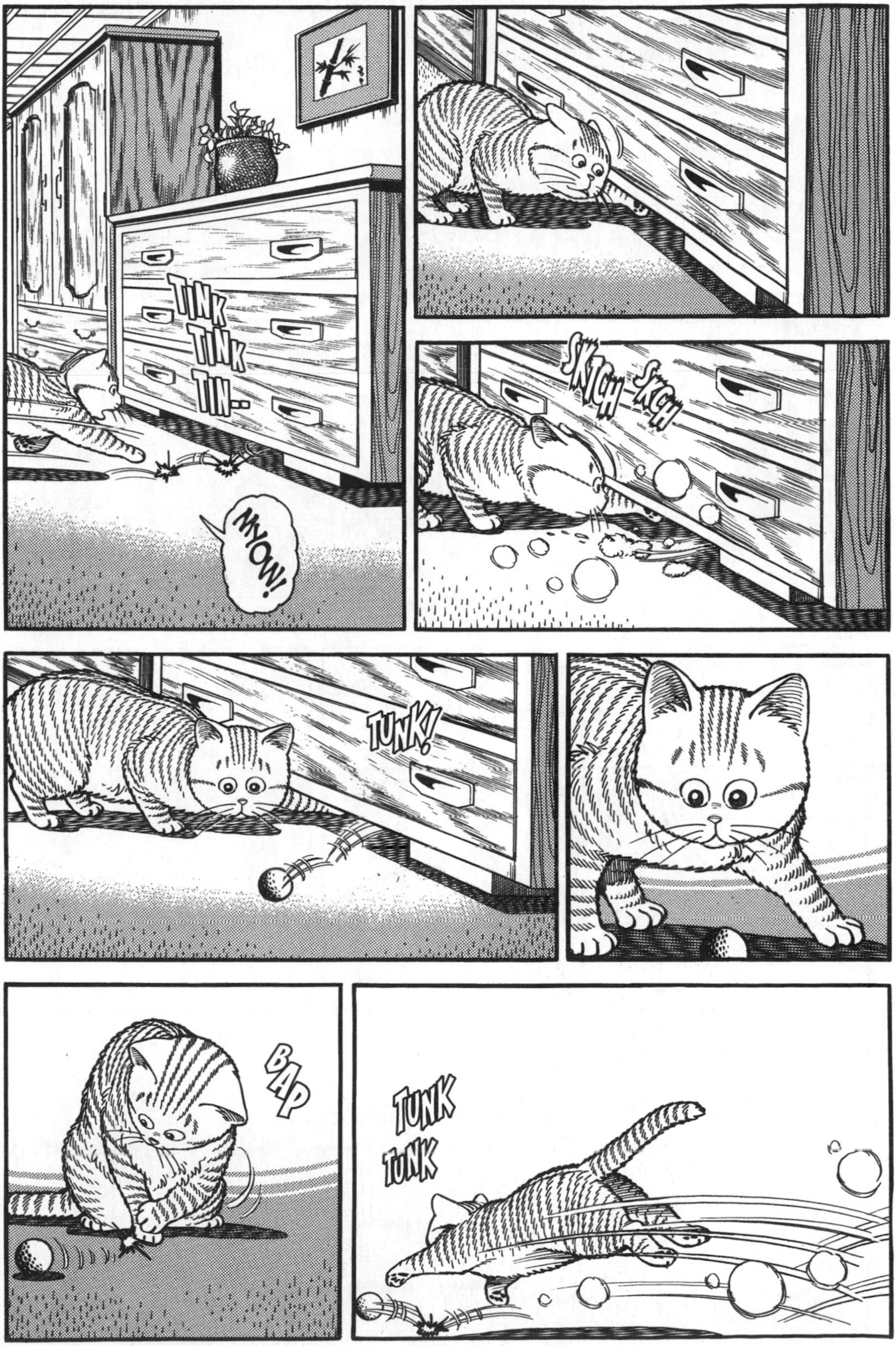
TINK
TINK
TIN..
MYOW!
SKTCH
SKCH
TUNK!
BAP
TUNK
TUNK

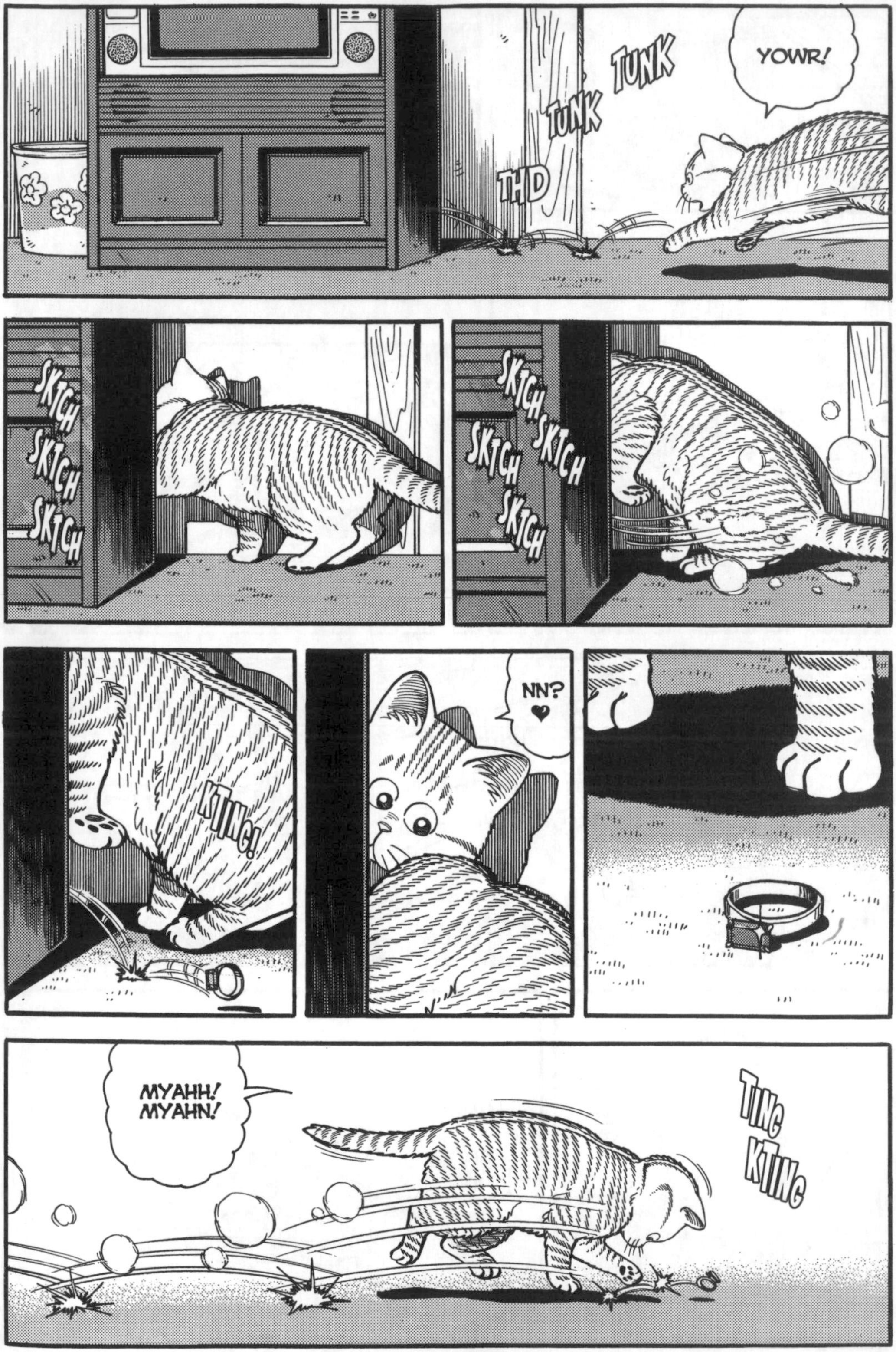
THD
TUNK
TUNK
YOWR!
SKTCH
SKTCH
SKTCH
SKTCH SKTCH
SKTCH
SKTCH
KTING!
NN? ❤
MYAHH! MYAHN!
TING
KTING

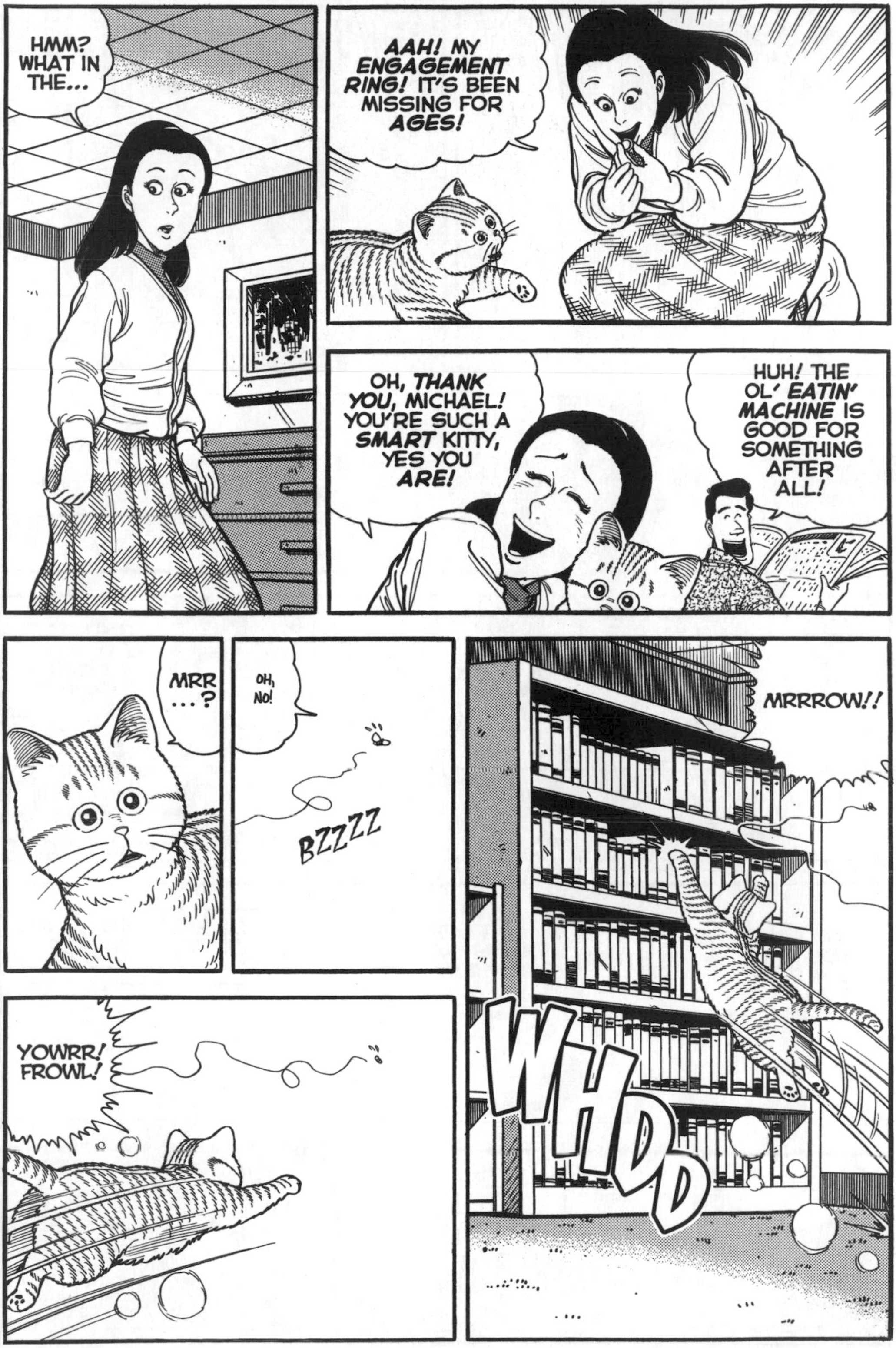
HMM? WHAT IN THE...
AAH! MY ENGAGEMENT RING! IT'S BEEN MISSING FOR AGES!
OH, THANK YOU, MICHAEL! YOU'RE SUCH A SMART KITTY, YES YOU ARE!
HUH! THE OL' EATIN' MACHINE IS GOOD FOR SOMETHING AFTER ALL!
MRR ...?
OH, NO!
BZZZZ
MRRROW!!
WHDD
YOWRR! FROWL!

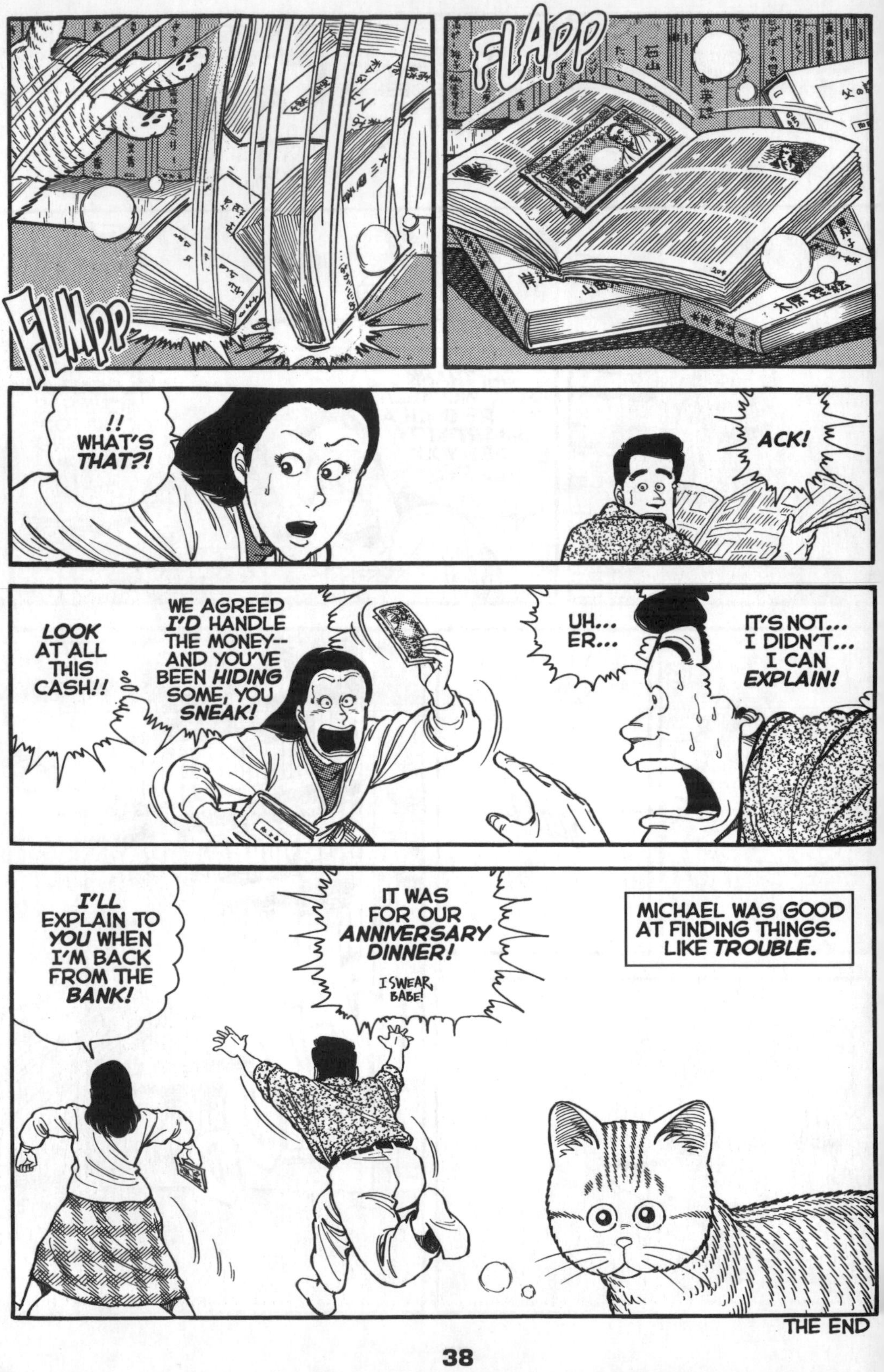
FLMPP
FLAPP
!! WHAT'S THAT?!
ACK!
LOOK AT ALL THIS CASH!!
WE AGREED I'D HANDLE THE MONEY-- AND YOU'VE BEEN HIDING SOME, YOU SNEAK!
UH... ER...
IT'S NOT... I DIDN'T... I CAN EXPLAIN!
I'LL EXPLAIN TO YOU WHEN I'M BACK FROM THE BANK!
IT WAS FOR OUR ANNIVERSARY DINNER!
I SWEAR, BABE!
MICHAEL WAS GOOD AT FINDING THINGS. LIKE TROUBLE.

THE END

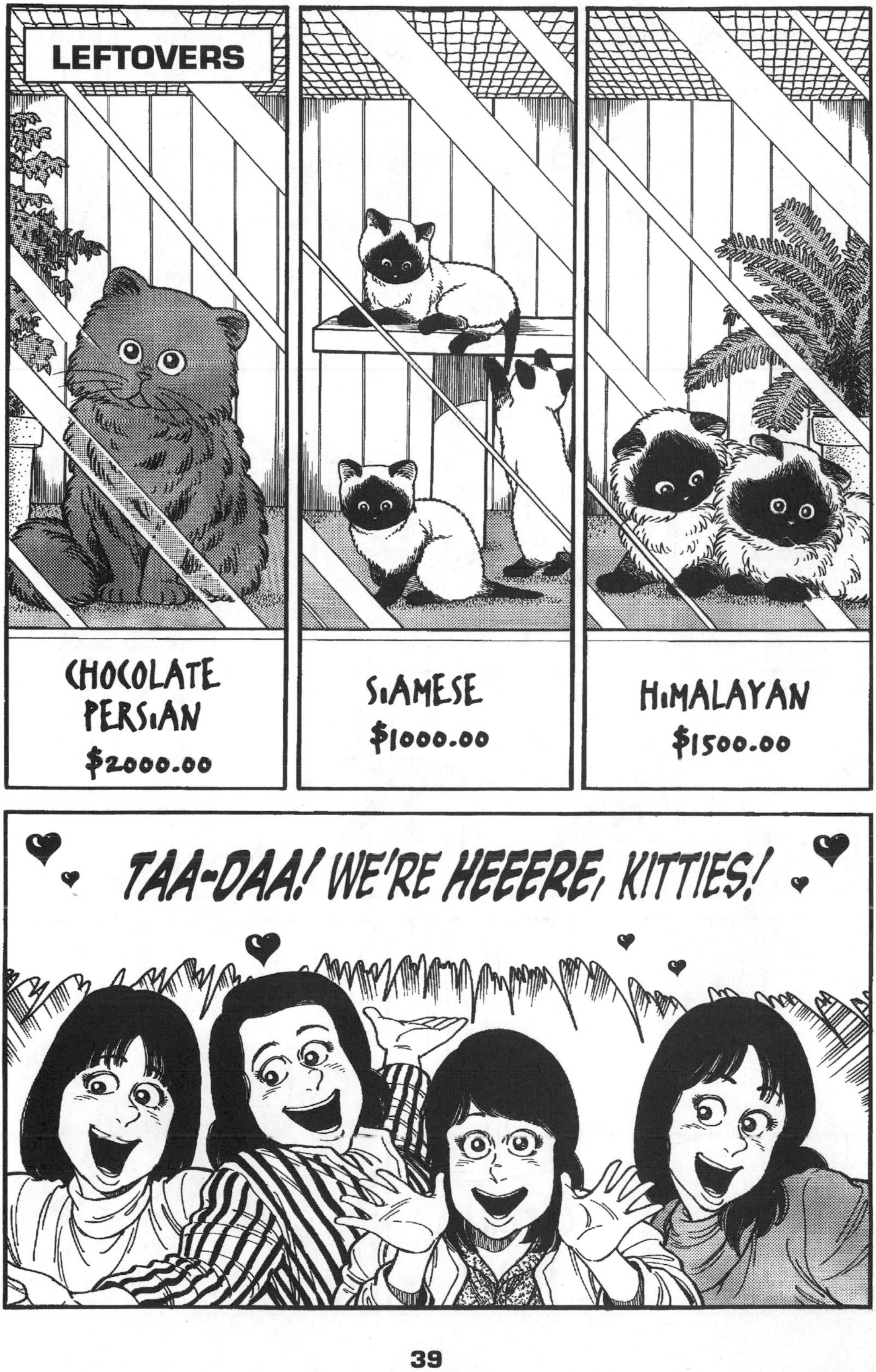

LEFTOVERS
CHOCOLATE PERSIAN
$2000.00
SIAMESE
$1000.00
HIMALAYAN
$1500.00
TAA-DAA! WE'RE HEEERE, KITTIES!

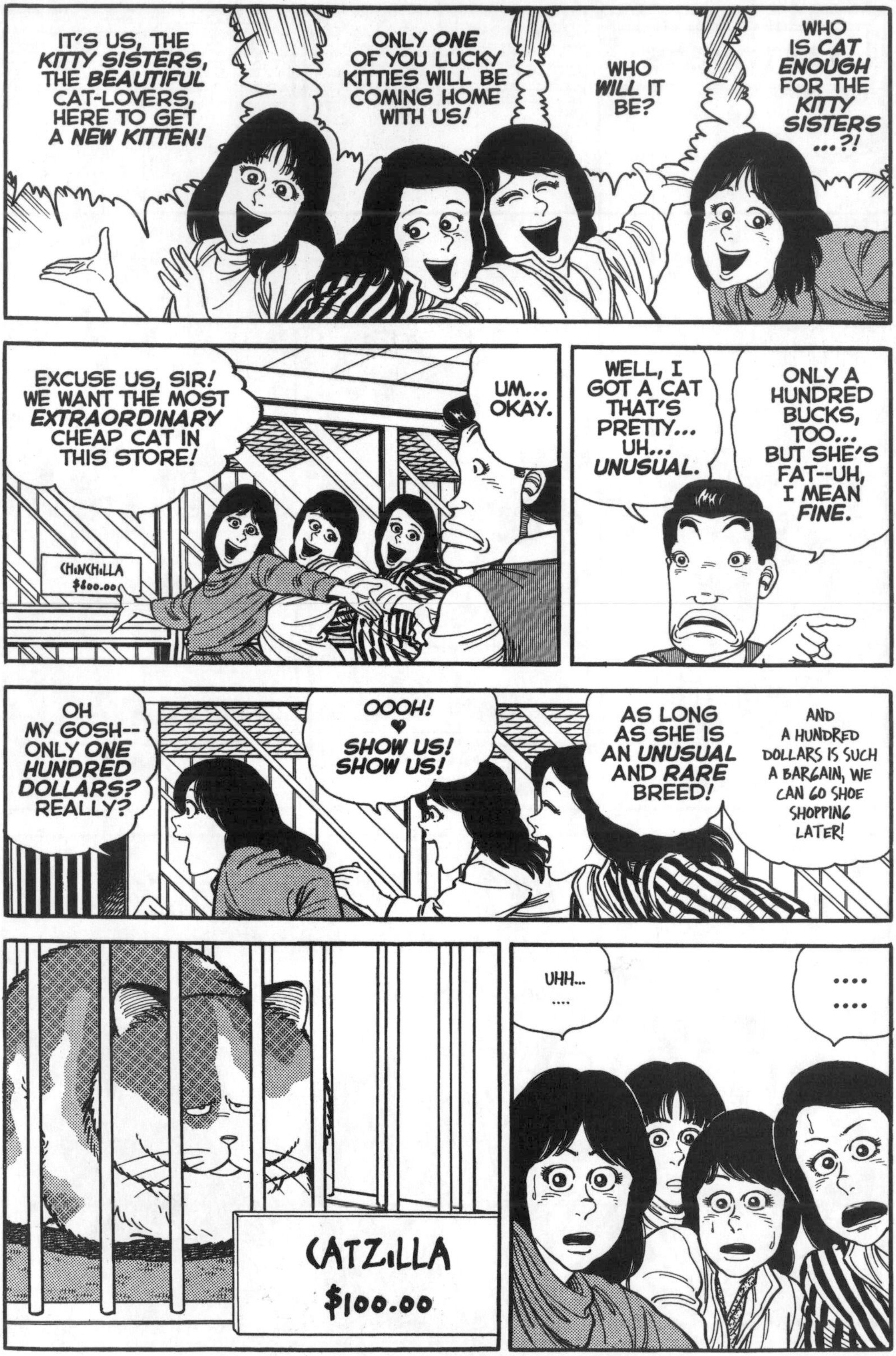

IT'S US, THE KITTY SISTERS, THE BEAUTIFUL CAT-LOVERS, HERE TO GET A NEW KITTEN!
ONLY ONE OF YOU LUCKY KITTIES WILL BE COMING HOME WITH US!
WHO WILL IT BE?
WHO IS CAT ENOUGH FOR THE KITTY SISTERS ...?!
EXCUSE US, SIR! WE WANT THE MOST EXTRAORDINARY CHEAP CAT IN THIS STORE!
UM... OKAY.
CHINCHILLA $600.00
WELL, I GOT A CAT THAT'S PRETTY... UH... UNUSUAL.
ONLY A HUNDRED BUCKS, TOO... BUT SHE'S FAT--UH, I MEAN FINE.
OH MY GOSH-- ONLY ONE HUNDRED DOLLARS? REALLY?
OOOH! ♥ SHOW US! SHOW US!
AS LONG AS SHE IS AN UNUSUAL AND RARE BREED!
AND A HUNDRED DOLLARS IS SUCH A BARGAIN, WE CAN GO SHOE SHOPPING LATER!
CATZILLA $100.00
UHH... ....
....

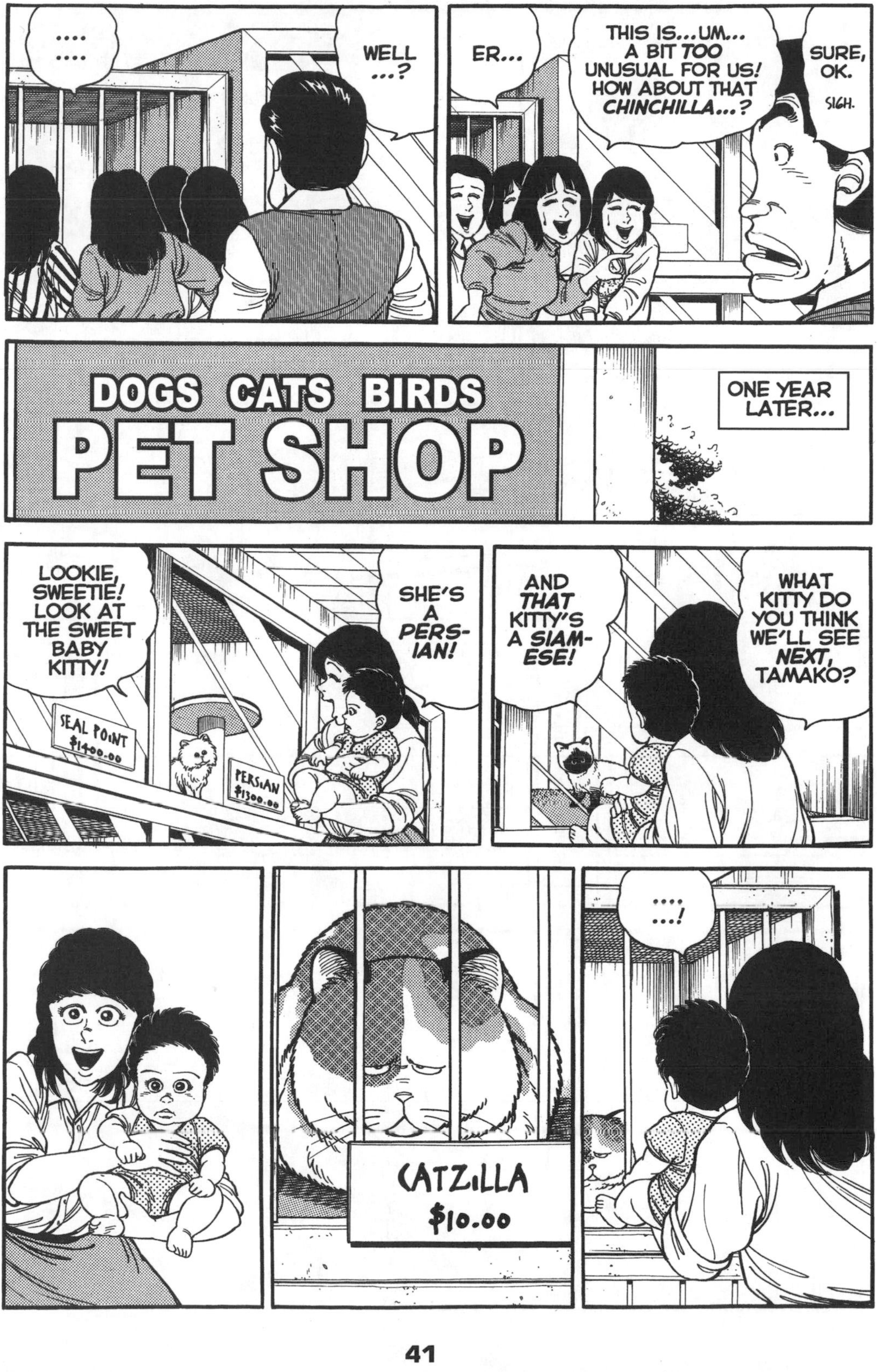
....
....
WELL ...?
ER...
THIS IS...UM... A BIT TOO UNUSUAL FOR US! HOW ABOUT THAT CHINCHILLA...?
SURE, OK.
SIGH.
DOGS CATS BIRDS
PET SHOP
ONE YEAR LATER...
LOOKIE, SWEETIE! LOOK AT THE SWEET BABY KITTY!
SEAL POINT $1400.00
PERSIAN $1300.00
SHE'S A PERSIAN!
AND THAT KITTY'S A SIAMESE!
WHAT KITTY DO YOU THINK WE'LL SEE NEXT, TAMAKO?
CATZILLA $10.00
....,
...!

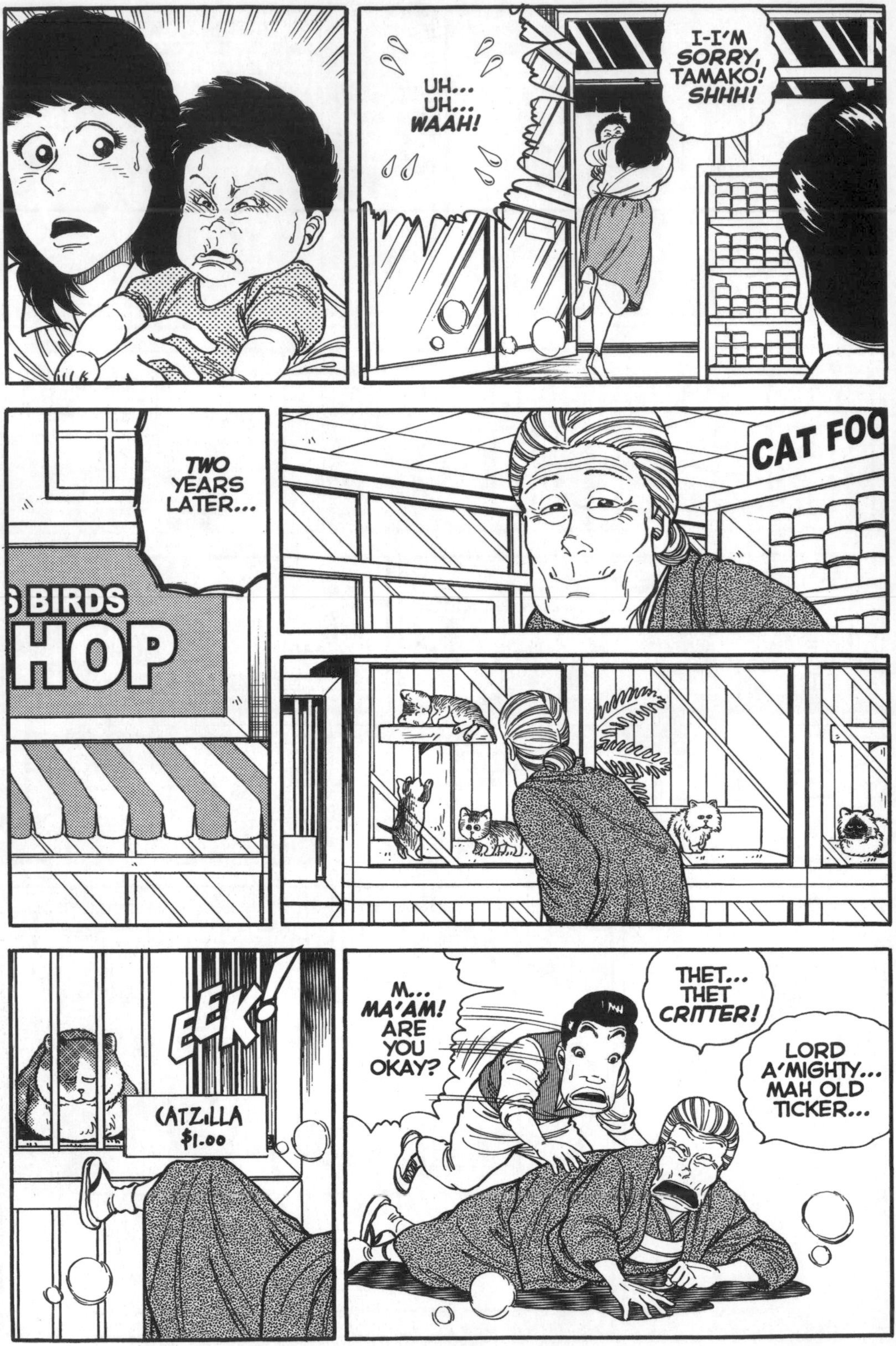
UH... UH... WAAH!
I-I'M SORRY, TAMAKO! SHHH!
TWO YEARS LATER...
S BIRDS
HOP
CAT FOO
EEK!
CATZILLA
$1.00
M... MA'AM! ARE YOU OKAY?
THET... THET CRITTER!
LORD A'MIGHTY... MAH OLD TICKER...

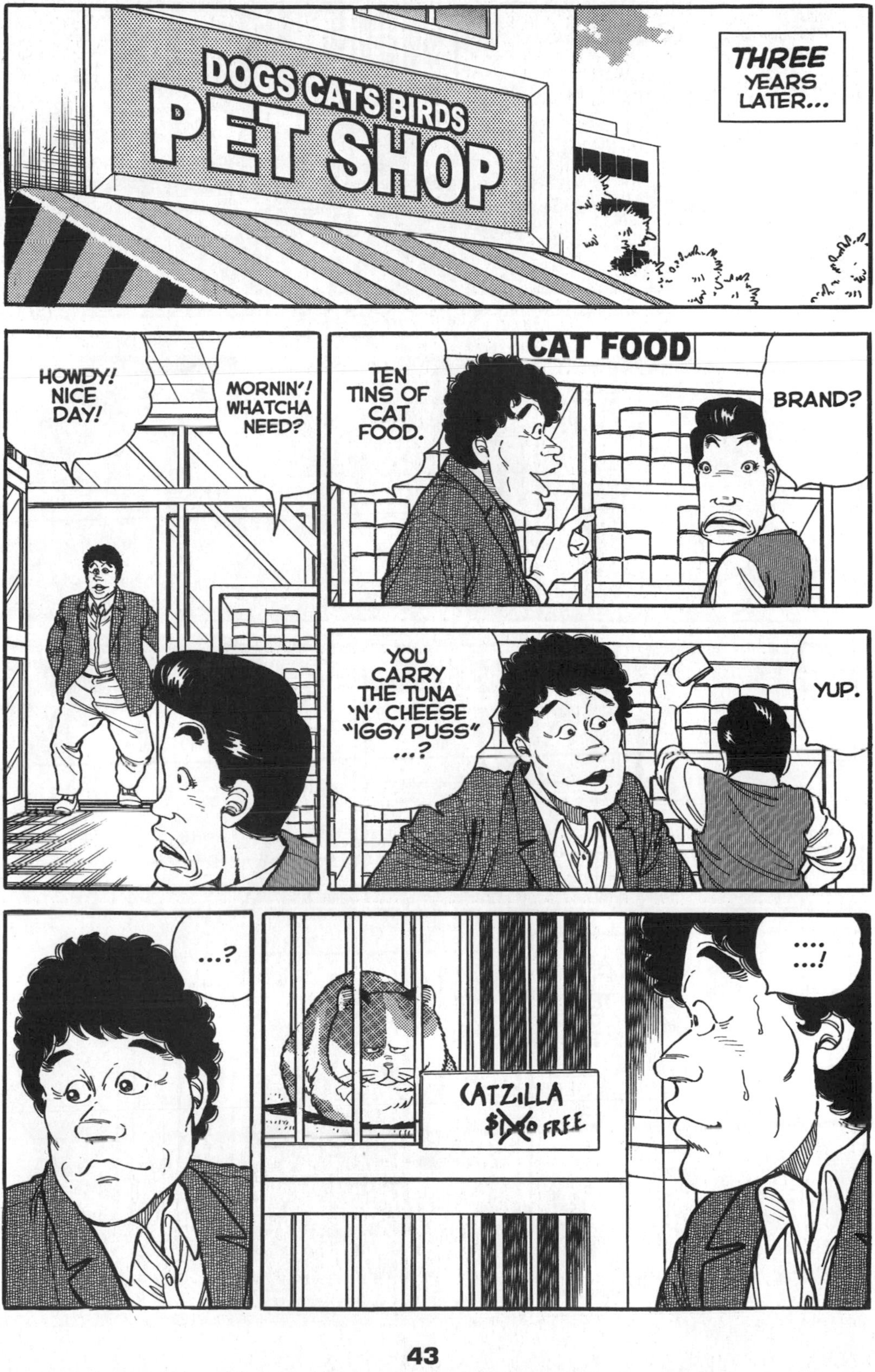
DOGS CATS BIRDS
PET SHOP
THREE YEARS LATER...
HOWDY! NICE DAY!
MORNIN'! WHATCHA NEED?
TEN TINS OF CAT FOOD.
CAT FOOD
BRAND?
YOU CARRY THE TUNA 'N' CHEESE "IGGY PUSS" ...?
YUP.
...?
CATZILLA
FREE
...
...!

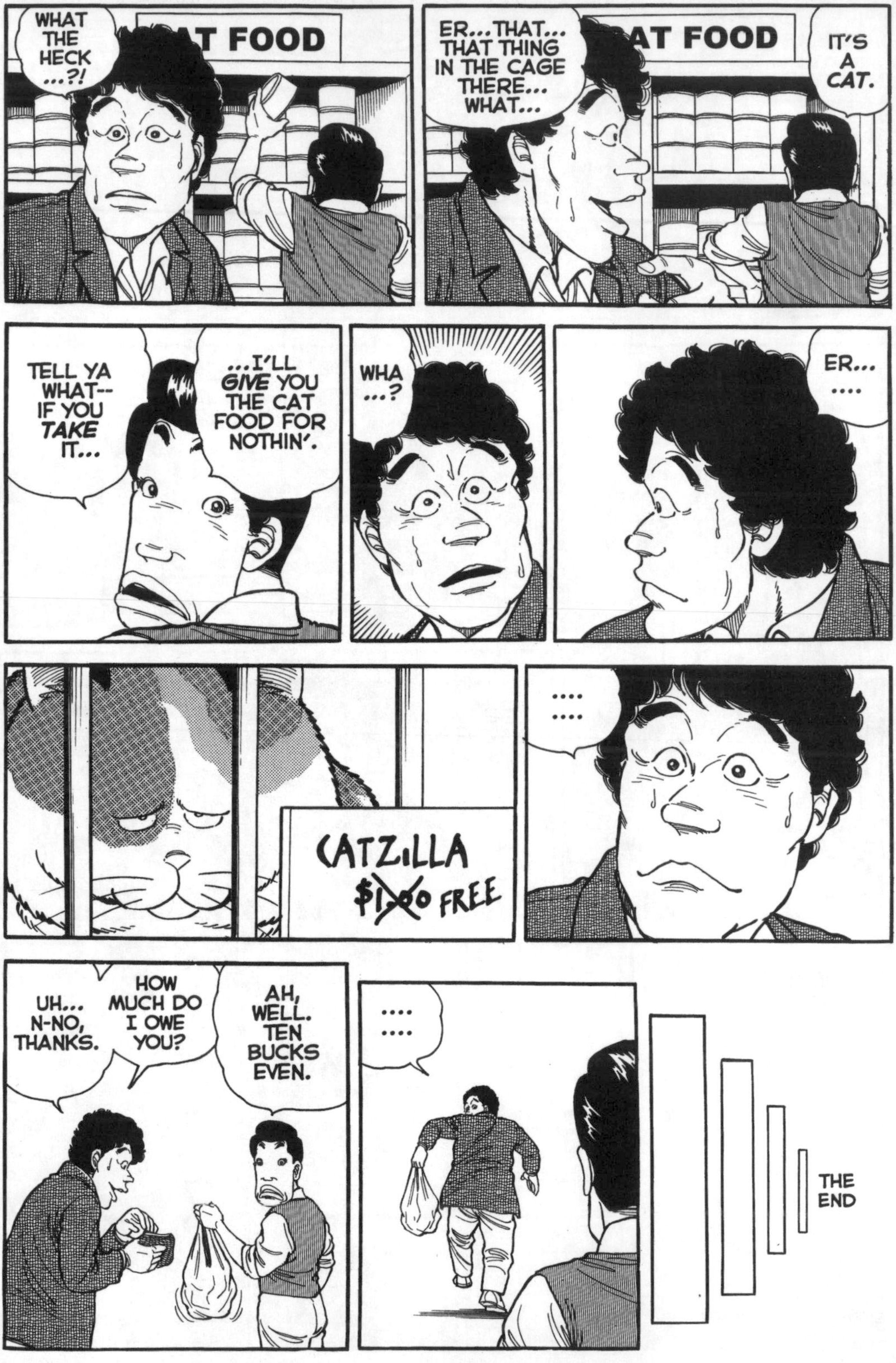

WHAT THE HECK ...?!
CAT FOOD
ER... THAT... THAT THING IN THE CAGE THERE... WHAT...
IT'S A CAT.
TELL YA WHAT-- IF YOU TAKE IT...
...I'LL GIVE YOU THE CAT FOOD FOR NOTHIN'.
WHA ...?
ER... ....
CATZILLA
$1.00 FREE
....
UH... N-NO, THANKS.
HOW MUCH DO I OWE YOU?
AH, WELL. TEN BUCKS EVEN.
....
THE END

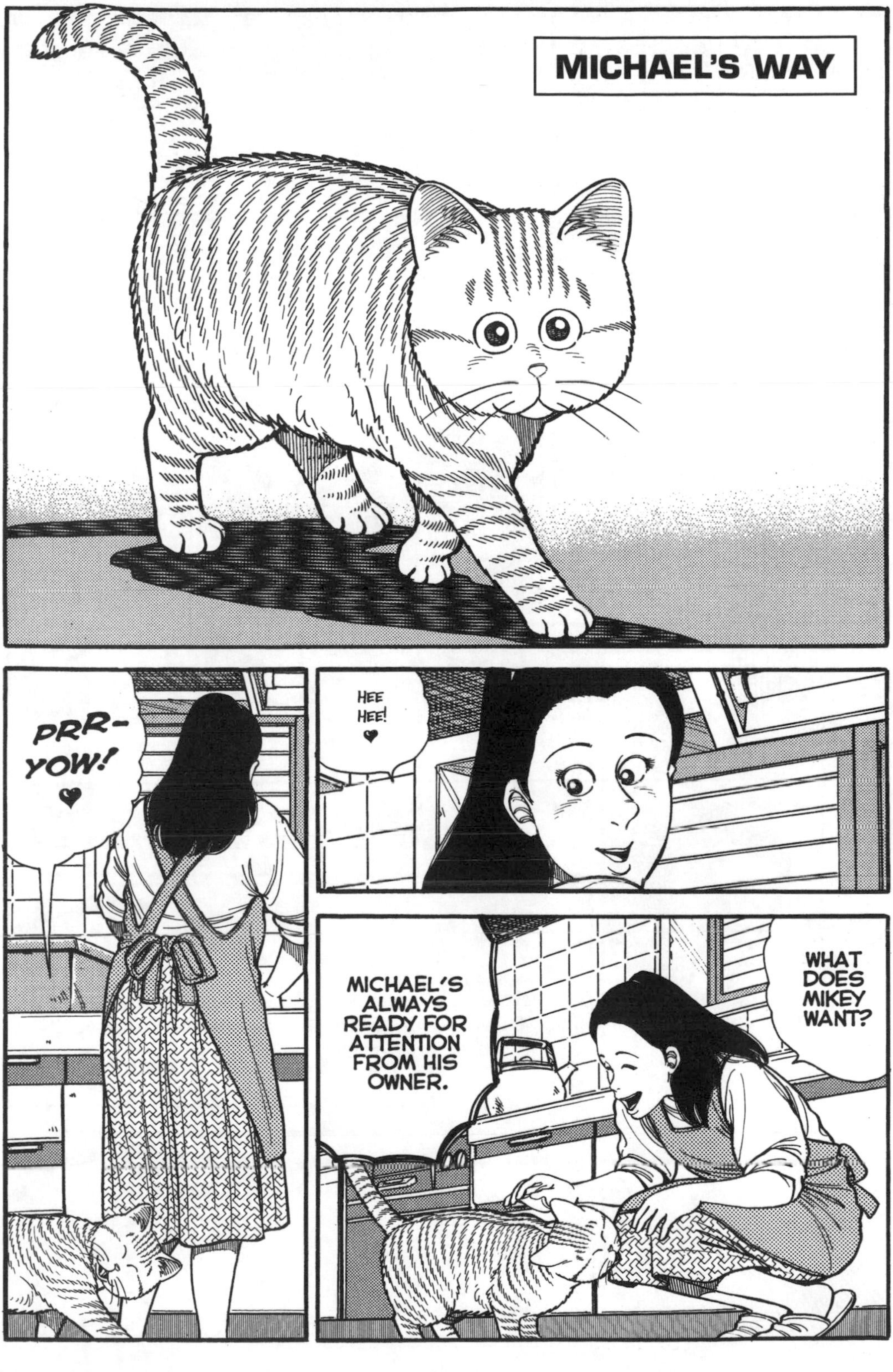
MICHAEL'S WAY
PRR-YOW! ♥
HEE HEE! ♥
MICHAEL'S ALWAYS READY FOR ATTENTION FROM HIS OWNER.
WHAT DOES MIKEY WANT?

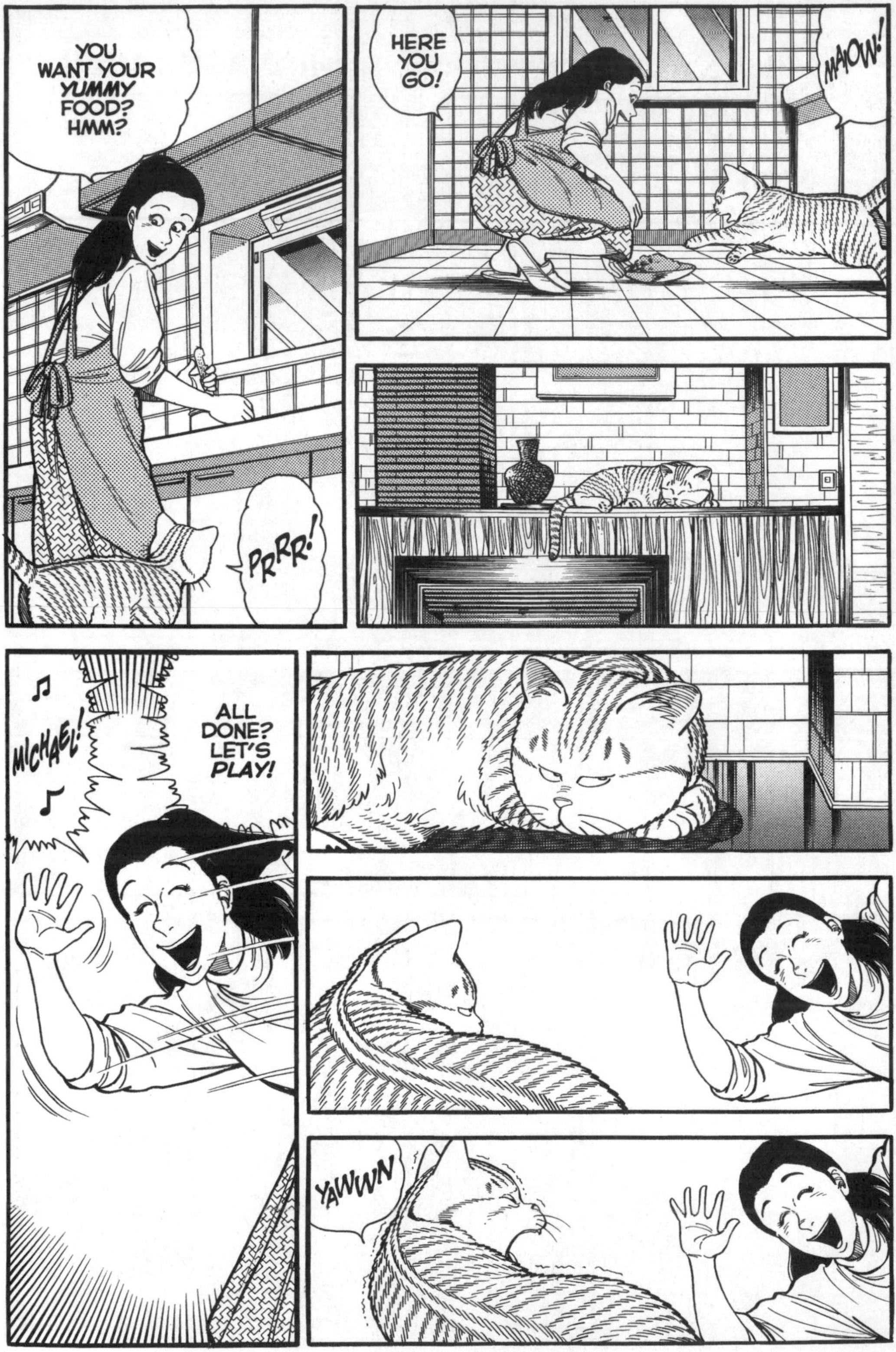

YOU WANT YOUR YUMMY FOOD? HMM?
PRRR!
HERE YOU GO!
MAIOW!
MICHAEL!
ALL DONE? LET'S PLAY!
YAWWN

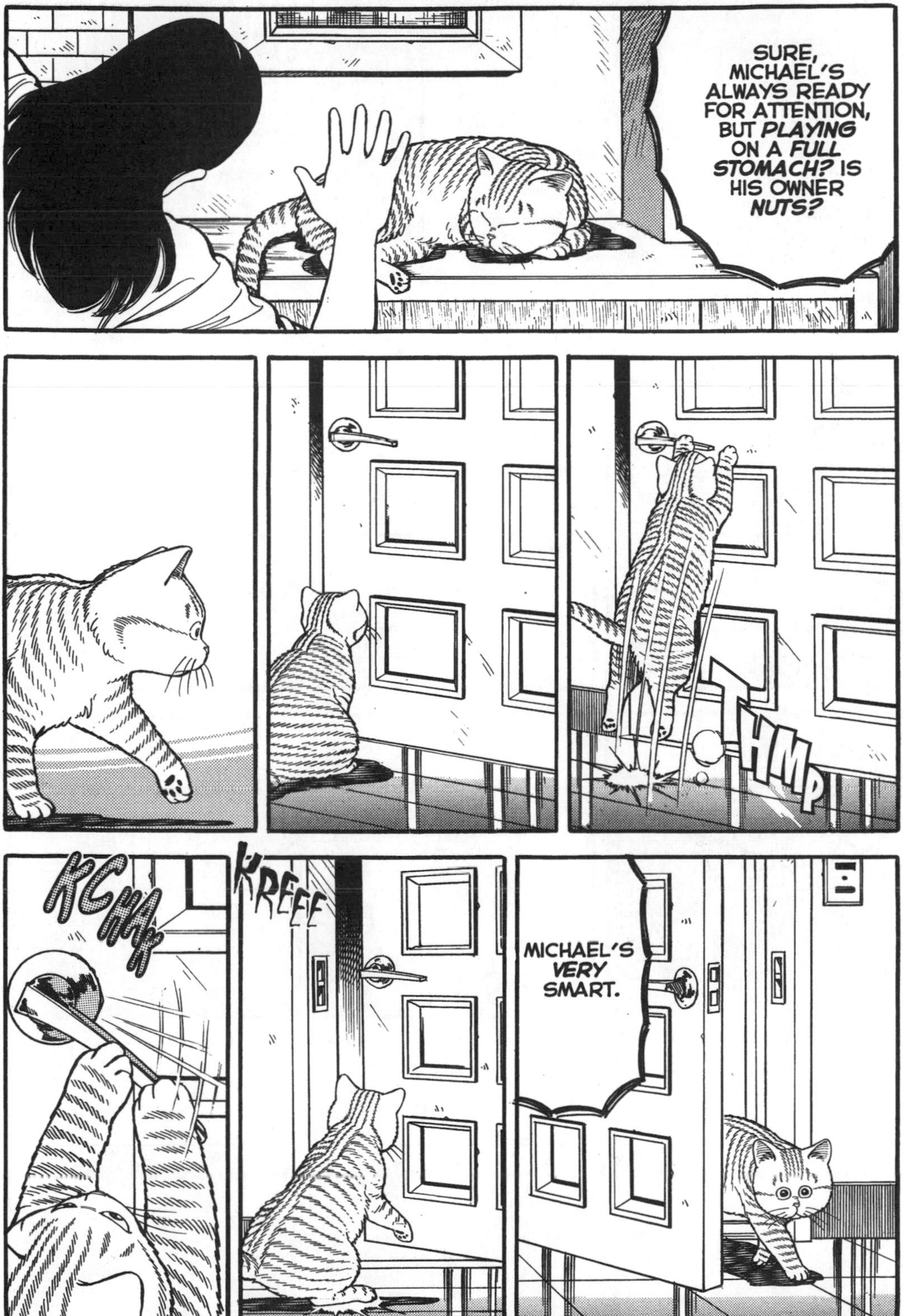
SURE, MICHAEL'S ALWAYS READY FOR ATTENTION, BUT *PLAYING* ON A *FULL STOMACH?* IS HIS OWNER *NUTS?*
THMP
KCHAK
KREEE
MICHAEL'S *VERY* SMART.

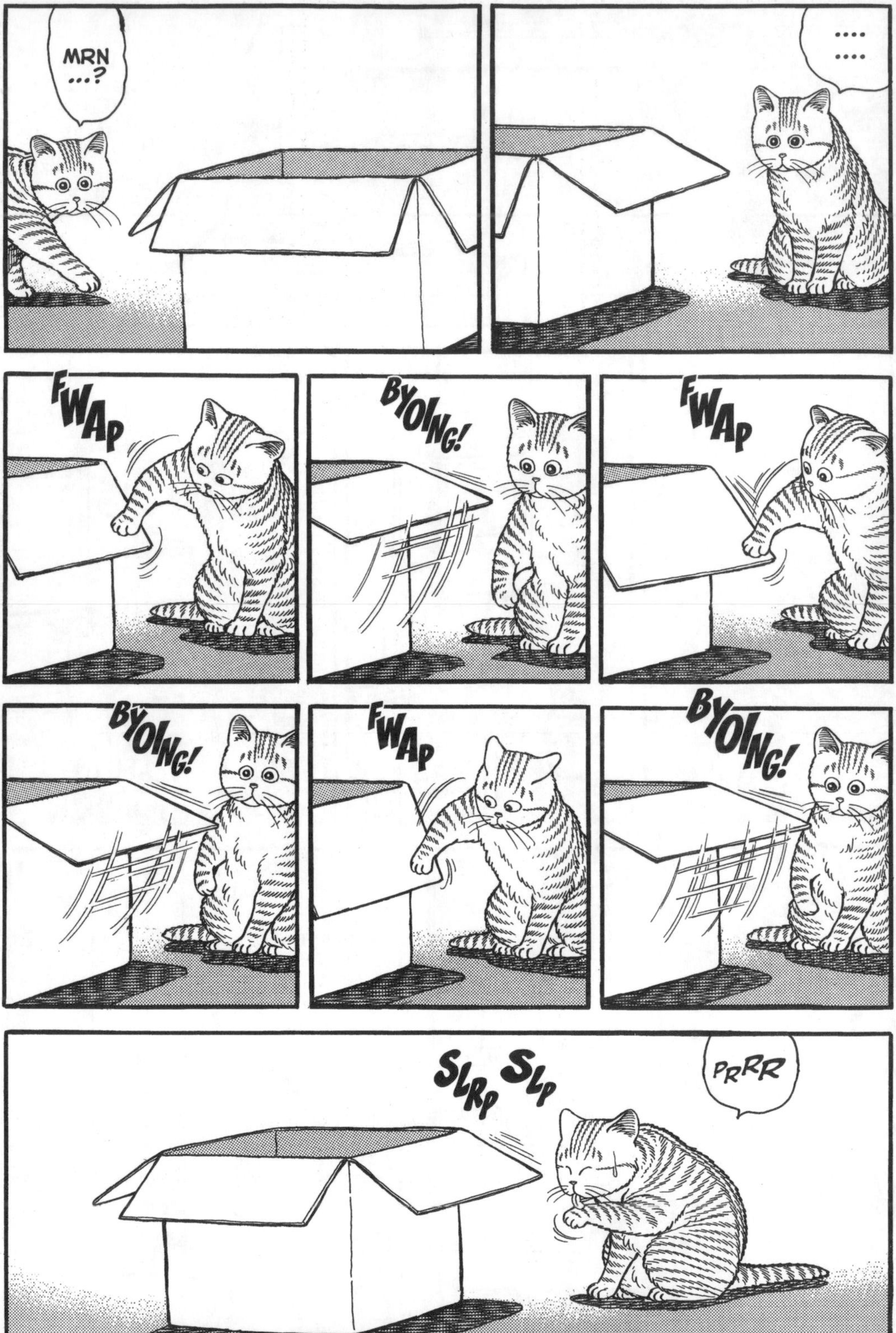
MRN ...?
....
FWAP
BYOING!
FWAP
BYOING!
FWAP
BYOING!
SLRP SLP
PRRR

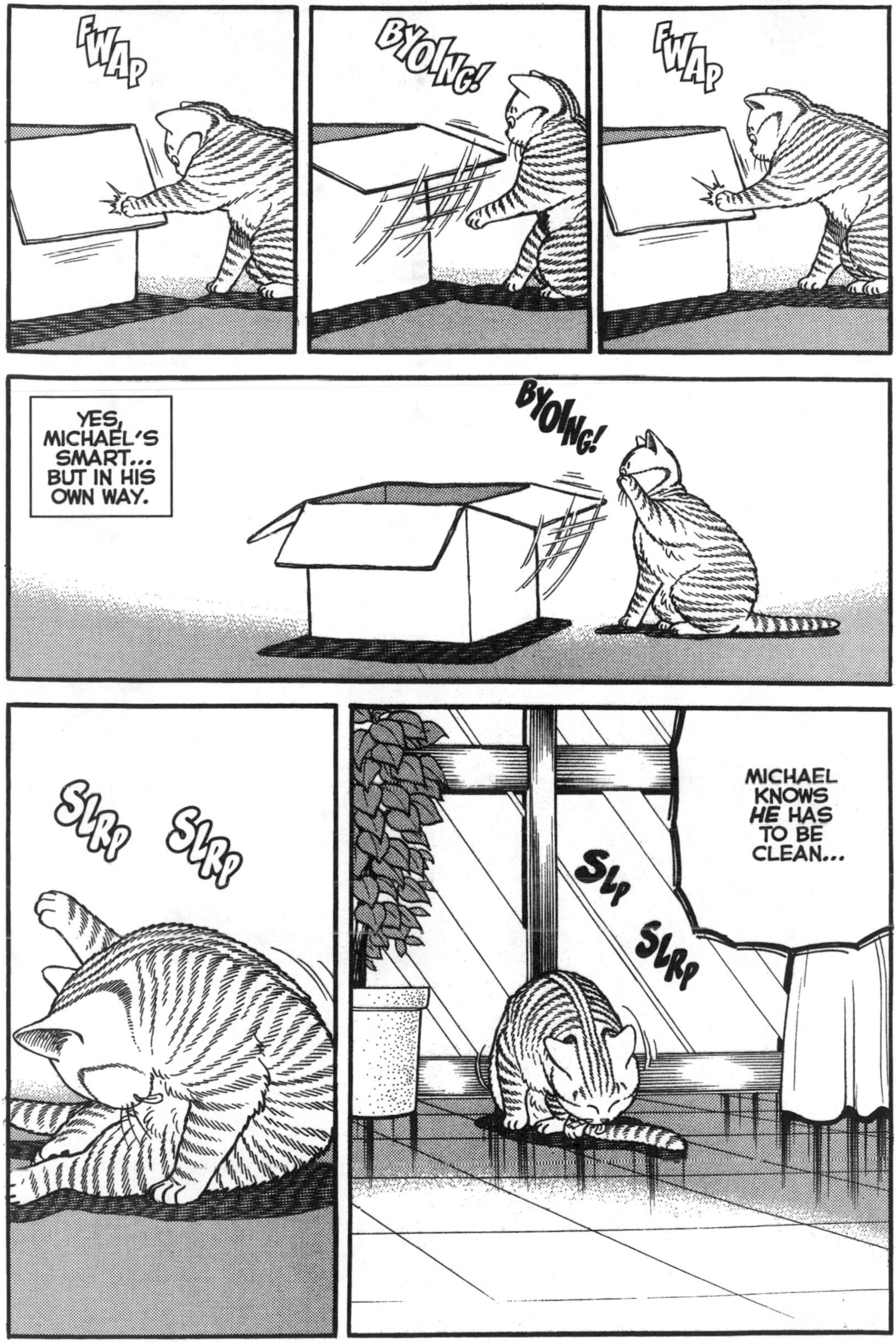
FWAP
BYOING!
FWAP
YES, MICHAEL'S SMART... BUT IN HIS OWN WAY.
BYOING!
SLRP
SLRP
MICHAEL KNOWS HE HAS TO BE CLEAN...
SLP
SLRP

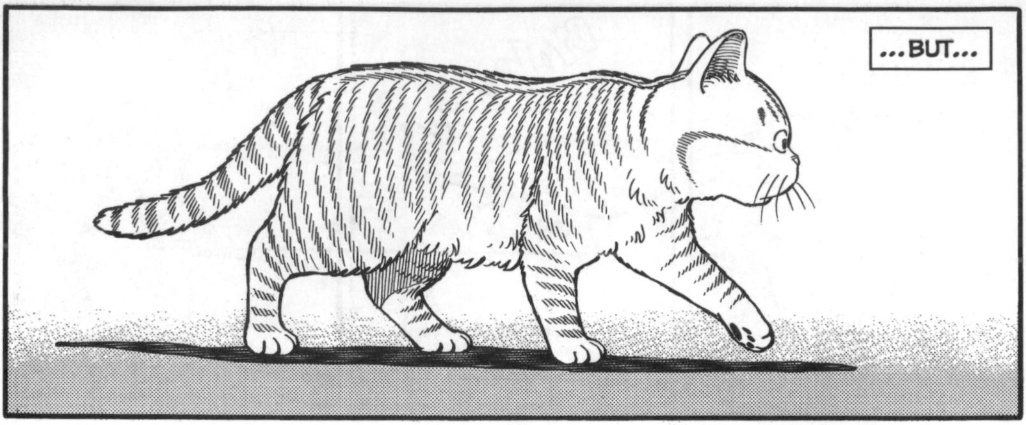
...BUT...

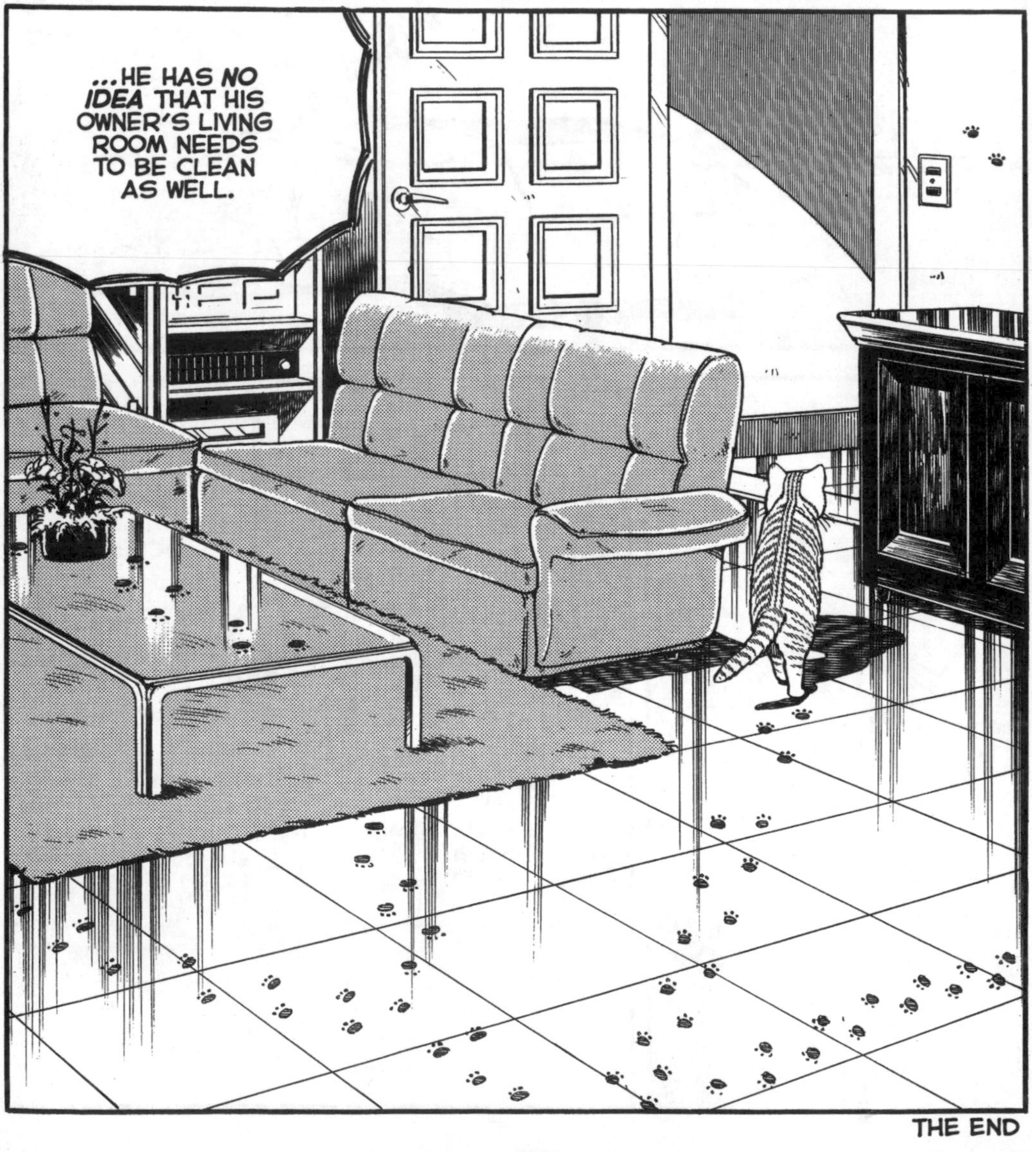
...HE HAS NO IDEA THAT HIS OWNER'S LIVING ROOM NEEDS TO BE CLEAN AS WELL.

THE END

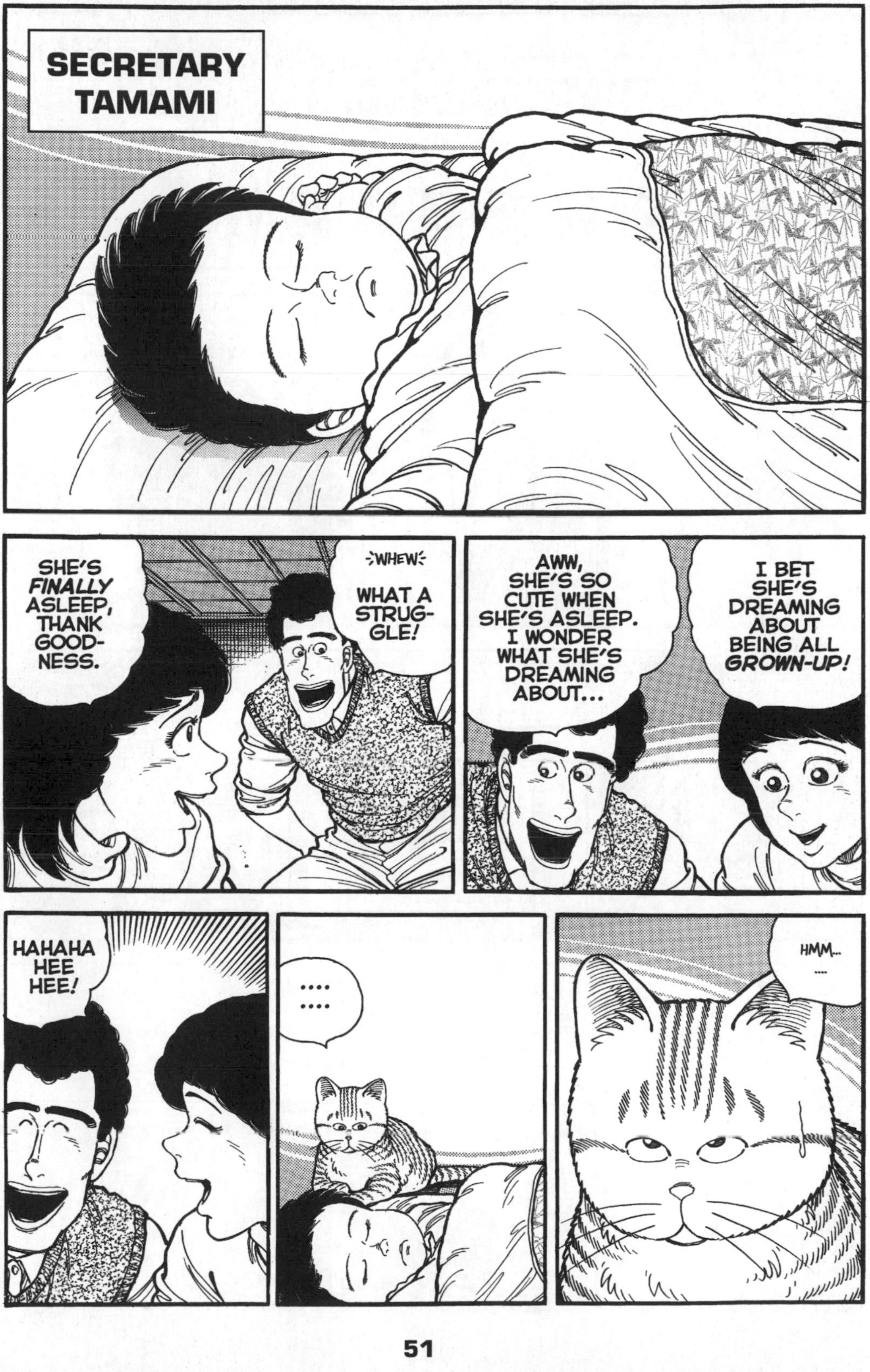
SECRETARY TAMAMI
SHE'S *FINALLY* ASLEEP, THANK GOOD-NESS.
WHEW
WHAT A STRUG-GLE!
AWW, SHE'S SO CUTE WHEN SHE'S ASLEEP. I WONDER WHAT SHE'S DREAMING ABOUT...
I BET SHE'S DREAMING ABOUT BEING ALL *GROWN-UP*!
HAHAHA HEE HEE!
....
....
HMM...
....

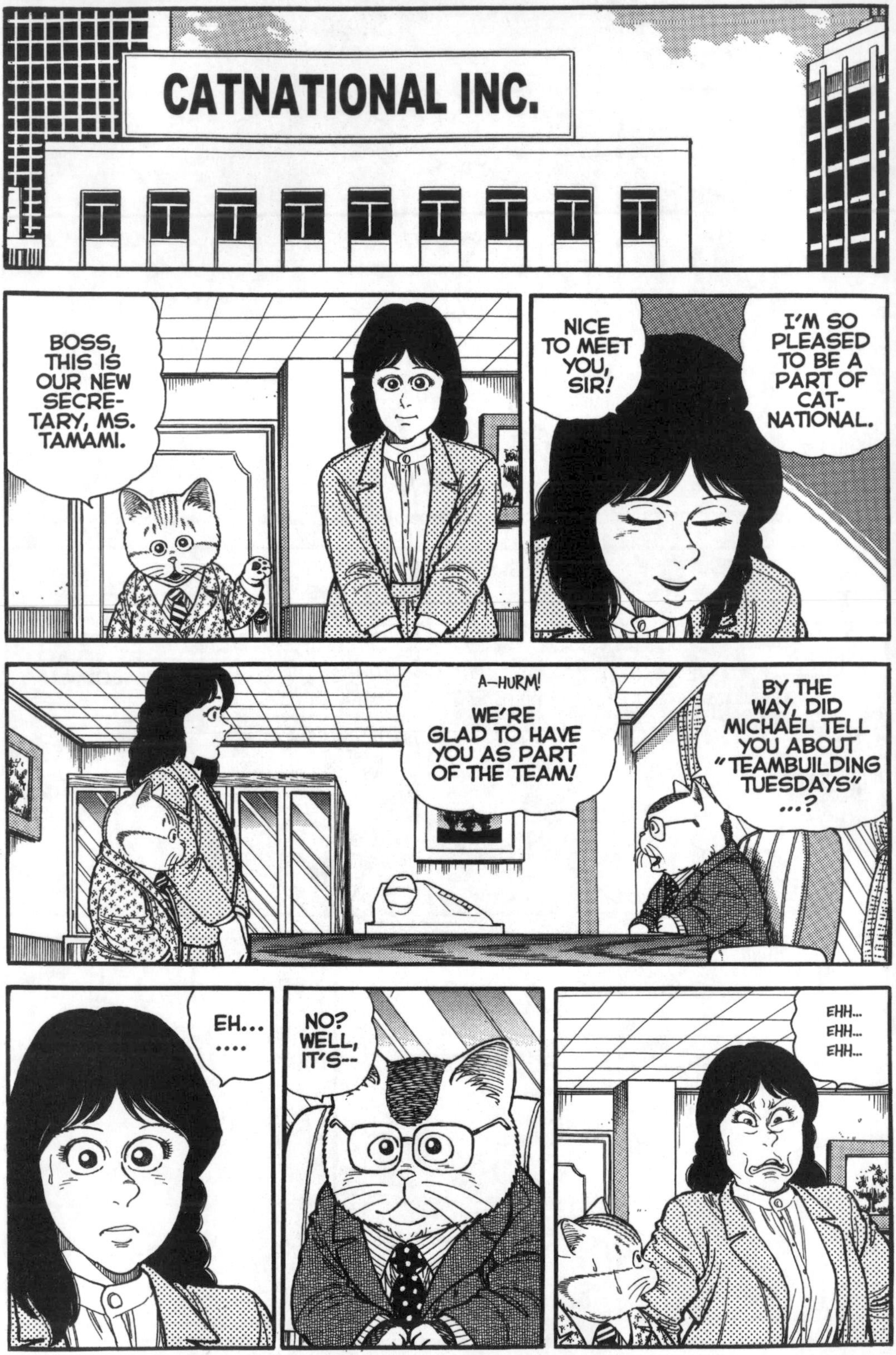
CATNATIONAL INC.
BOSS, THIS IS OUR NEW SECRETARY, MS. TAMAMI.
NICE TO MEET YOU, SIR!
I'M SO PLEASED TO BE A PART OF CATNATIONAL.
A-HURM!
WE'RE GLAD TO HAVE YOU AS PART OF THE TEAM!
BY THE WAY, DID MICHAEL TELL YOU ABOUT "TEAMBUILDING TUESDAYS" ...?
EH... ....
NO? WELL, IT'S--
EHH... EHH... EHH...

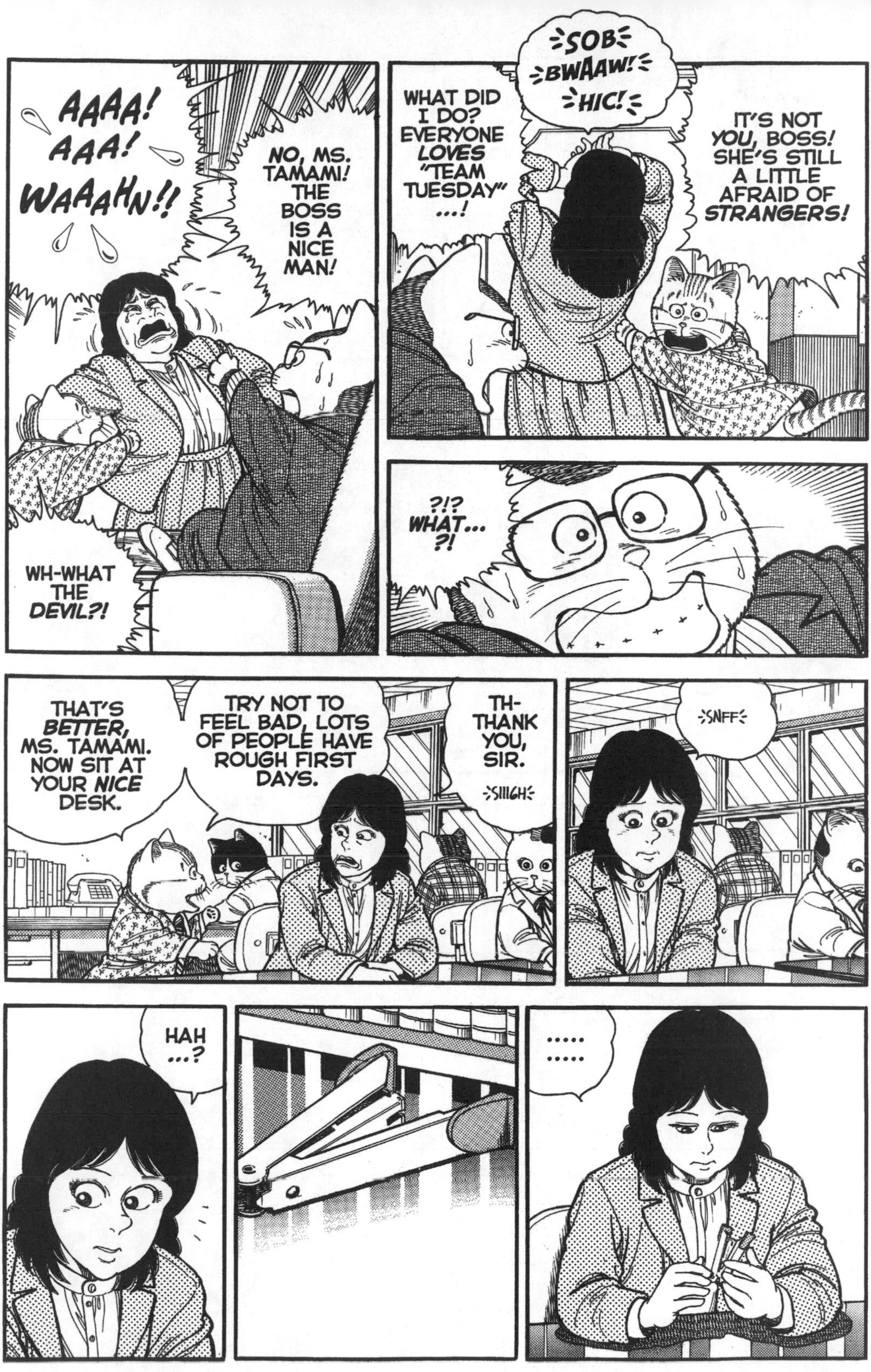
AAAA! AAA! WAAAAHN!!
NO, MS. TAMAMI! THE BOSS IS A NICE MAN!
WH-WHAT THE DEVIL?!
SOB BWAAW! HIC!
WHAT DID I DO? EVERYONE LOVES "TEAM TUESDAY" ...!
IT'S NOT YOU, BOSS! SHE'S STILL A LITTLE AFRAID OF STRANGERS!
?!? WHAT... ?!
TH- THANK YOU, SIR.
SIIIGH
TRY NOT TO FEEL BAD, LOTS OF PEOPLE HAVE ROUGH FIRST DAYS.
THAT'S BETTER, MS. TAMAMI. NOW SIT AT YOUR NICE DESK.
SNFF
HAH ...?
.....
.....

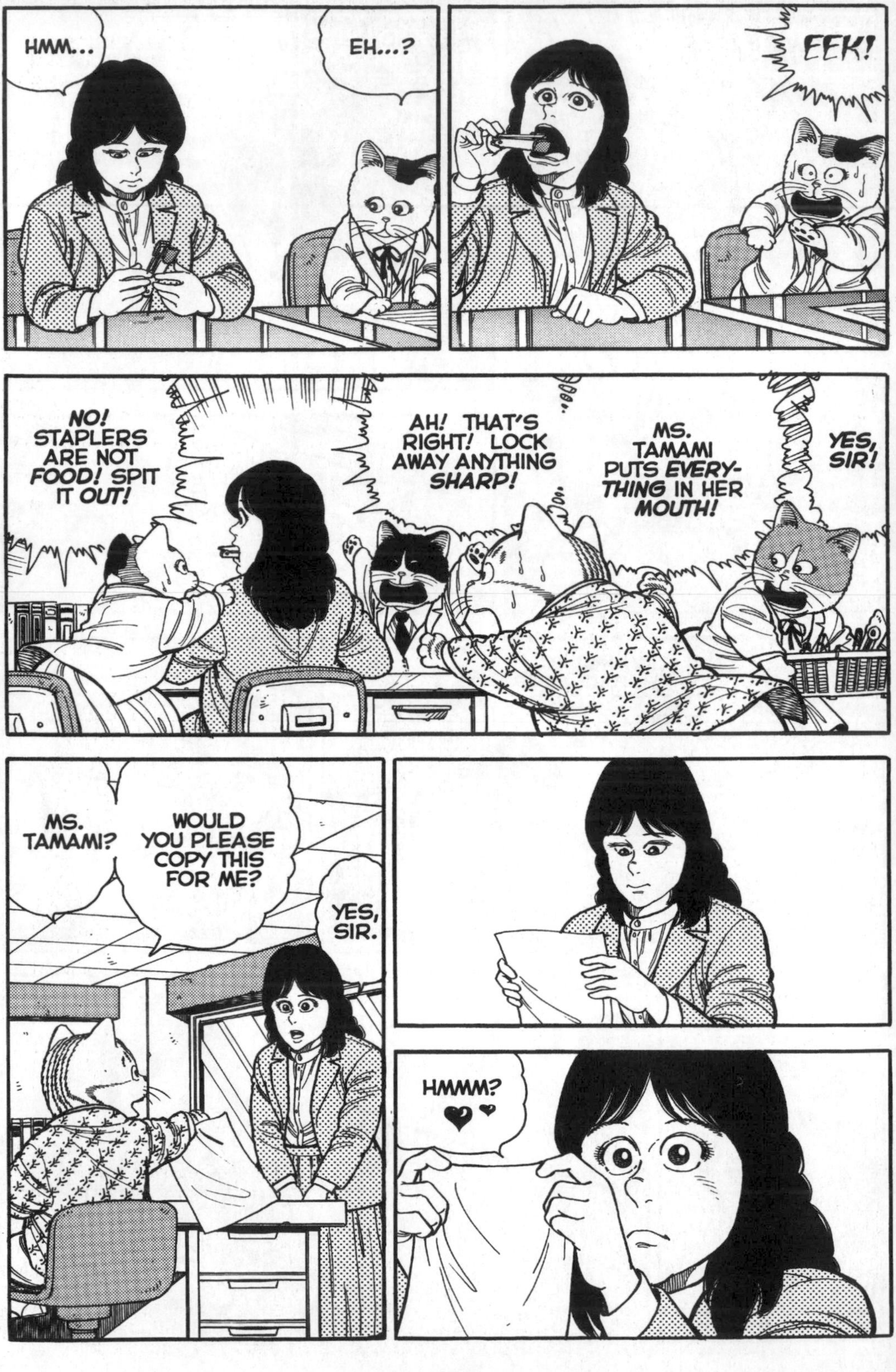
HMM...
EH...?
EEK!
NO! STAPLERS ARE NOT FOOD! SPIT IT OUT!
AH! THAT'S RIGHT! LOCK AWAY ANYTHING SHARP!
MS. TAMAMI PUTS EVERYTHING IN HER MOUTH!
YES, SIR!
MS. TAMAMI?
WOULD YOU PLEASE COPY THIS FOR ME?
YES, SIR.
HMMM?

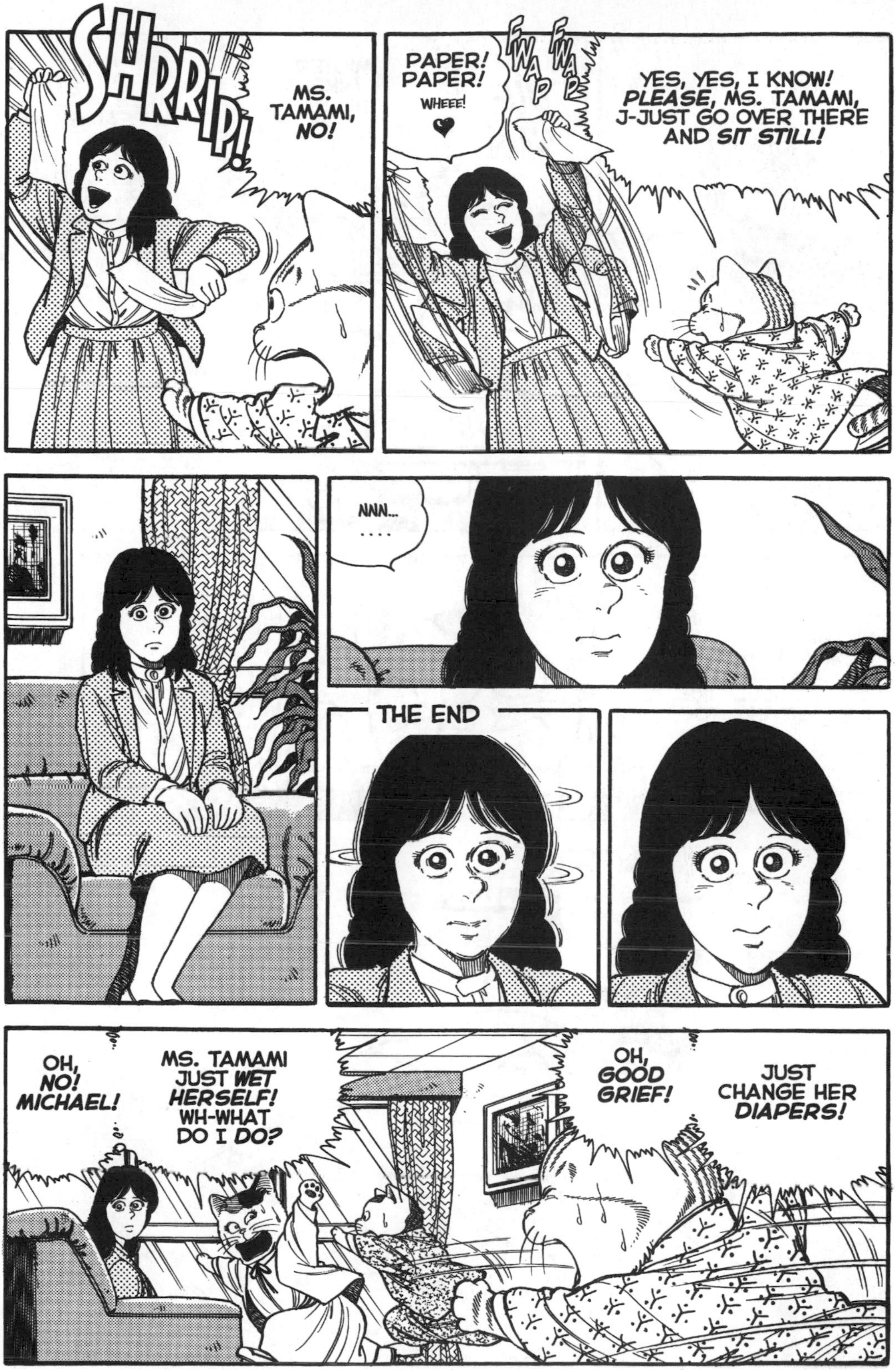
SHRRIP!
MS. TAMAMI, NO!
PAPER! PAPER!
WHEEE!
FWAP FWAP
YES, YES, I KNOW! PLEASE, MS. TAMAMI, J-JUST GO OVER THERE AND SIT STILL!
NNN... ....
THE END
OH, NO! MICHAEL!
MS. TAMAMI JUST WET HERSELF! WH-WHAT DO I DO?
OH, GOOD GRIEF!
JUST CHANGE HER DIAPERS!

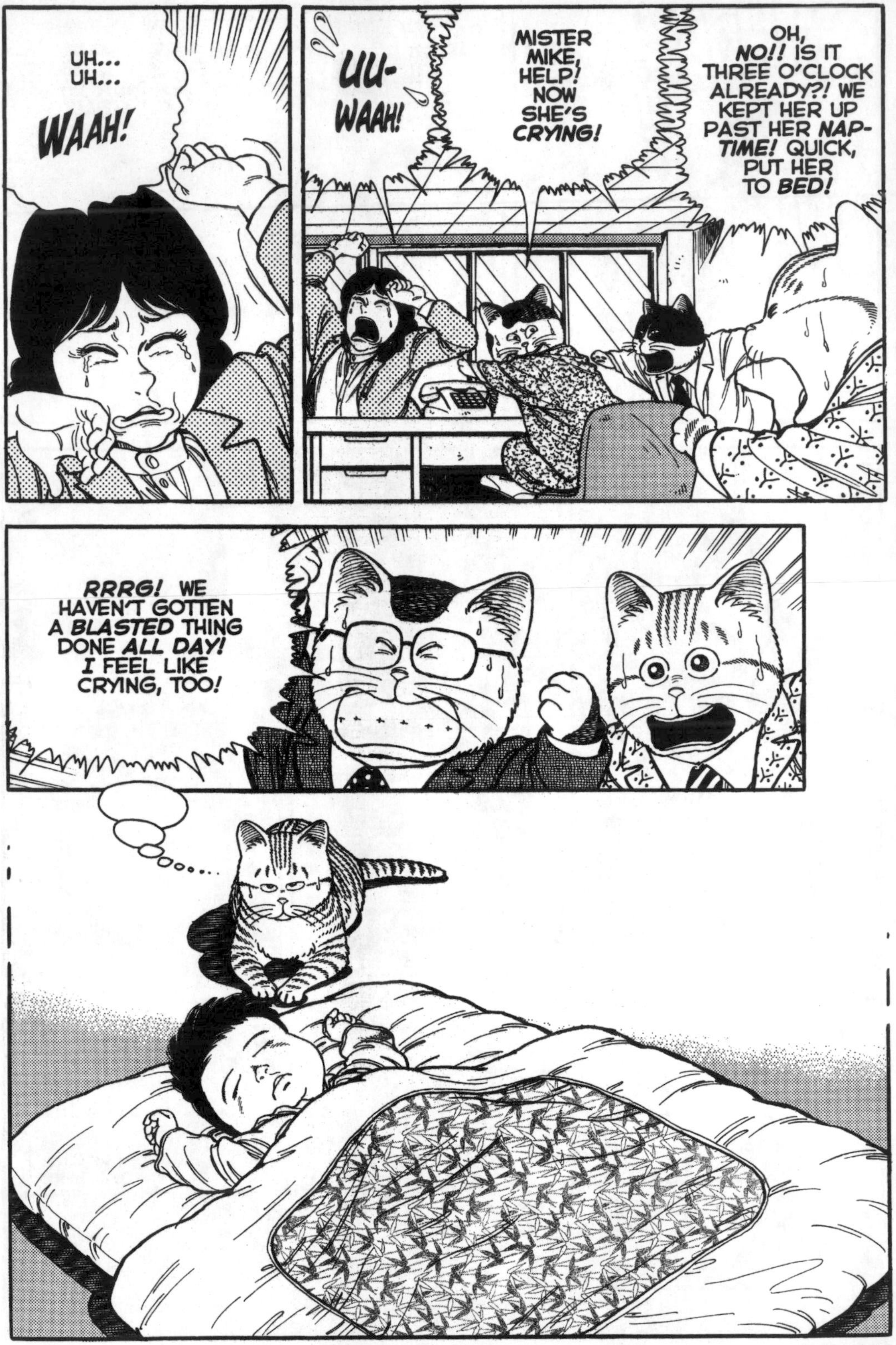
UH... UH...
WAAH!
OH, NO!! IS IT THREE O'CLOCK ALREADY?! WE KEPT HER UP PAST HER NAP-TIME! QUICK, PUT HER TO BED!
MISTER MIKE, HELP! NOW SHE'S CRYING!
UU-WAAH!
RRRG! WE HAVEN'T GOTTEN A BLASTED THING DONE ALL DAY! I FEEL LIKE CRYING, TOO!

THE END

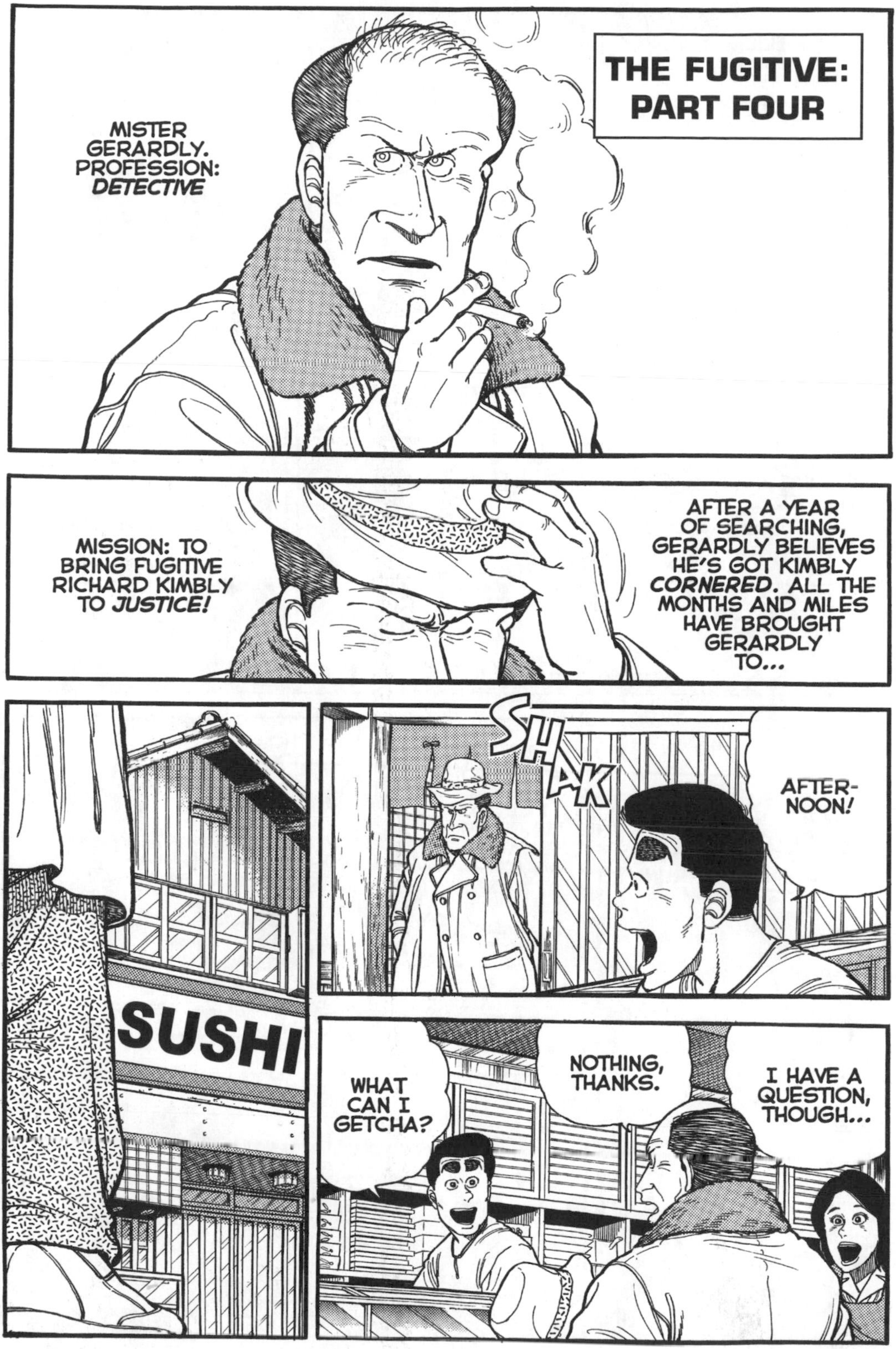
THE FUGITIVE: PART FOUR
MISTER GERARDLY. PROFESSION: *DETECTIVE*
MISSION: TO BRING FUGITIVE RICHARD KIMBLY TO *JUSTICE!*
AFTER A YEAR OF SEARCHING, GERARDLY BELIEVES HE'S GOT KIMBLY *CORNERED*. ALL THE MONTHS AND MILES HAVE BROUGHT GERARDLY TO...
SUSHI
SHAK
AFTER-NOON!
WHAT CAN I GETCHA?
NOTHING, THANKS.
I HAVE A QUESTION, THOUGH...

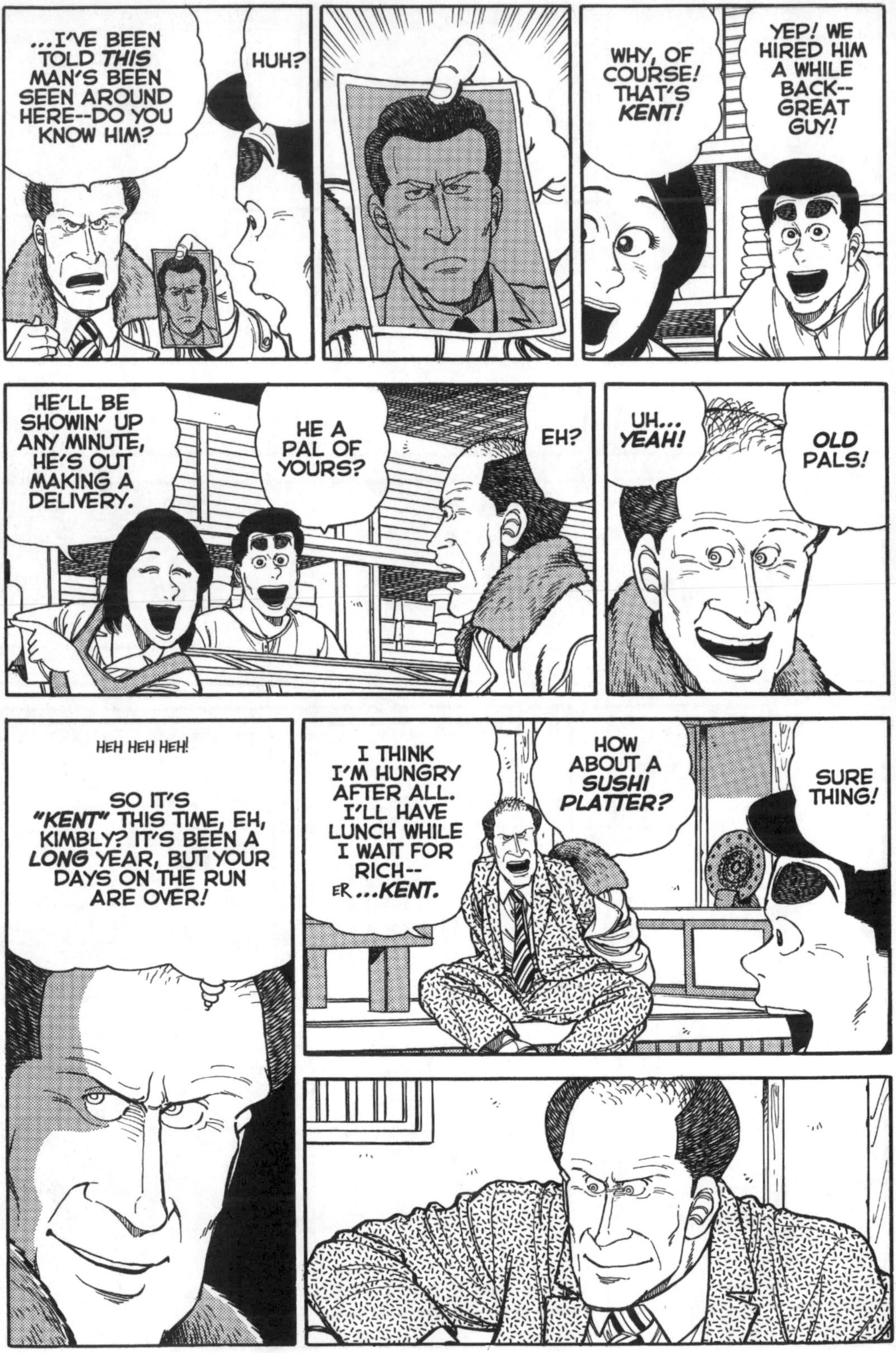
...I'VE BEEN TOLD THIS MAN'S BEEN SEEN AROUND HERE--DO YOU KNOW HIM?
HUH?
WHY, OF COURSE! THAT'S KENT!
YEP! WE HIRED HIM A WHILE BACK--GREAT GUY!
HE'LL BE SHOWIN' UP ANY MINUTE, HE'S OUT MAKING A DELIVERY.
HE A PAL OF YOURS?
EH?
UH... YEAH!
OLD PALS!
HEH HEH HEH!
SO IT'S "KENT" THIS TIME, EH, KIMBLY? IT'S BEEN A LONG YEAR, BUT YOUR DAYS ON THE RUN ARE OVER!
I THINK I'M HUNGRY AFTER ALL. I'LL HAVE LUNCH WHILE I WAIT FOR RICH-- ER ...KENT.
HOW ABOUT A SUSHI PLATTER?
SURE THING!

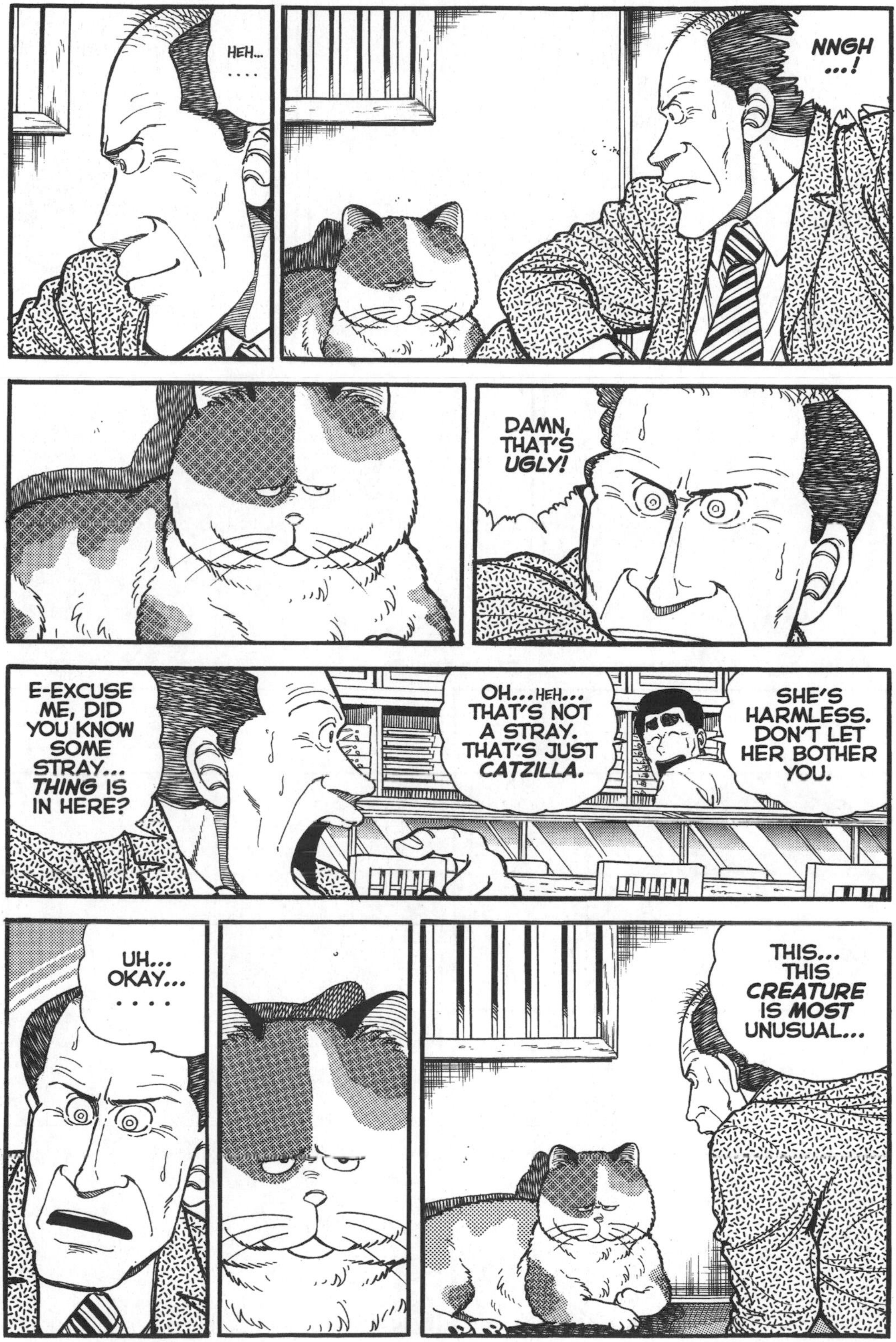
HEH... ....
NNGH ...!
DAMN, THAT'S UGLY!
E-EXCUSE ME, DID YOU KNOW SOME STRAY... THING IS IN HERE?
OH... HEH... THAT'S NOT A STRAY. THAT'S JUST CATZILLA.
SHE'S HARMLESS. DON'T LET HER BOTHER YOU.
UH... OKAY... ....
THIS... THIS CREATURE IS MOST UNUSUAL...

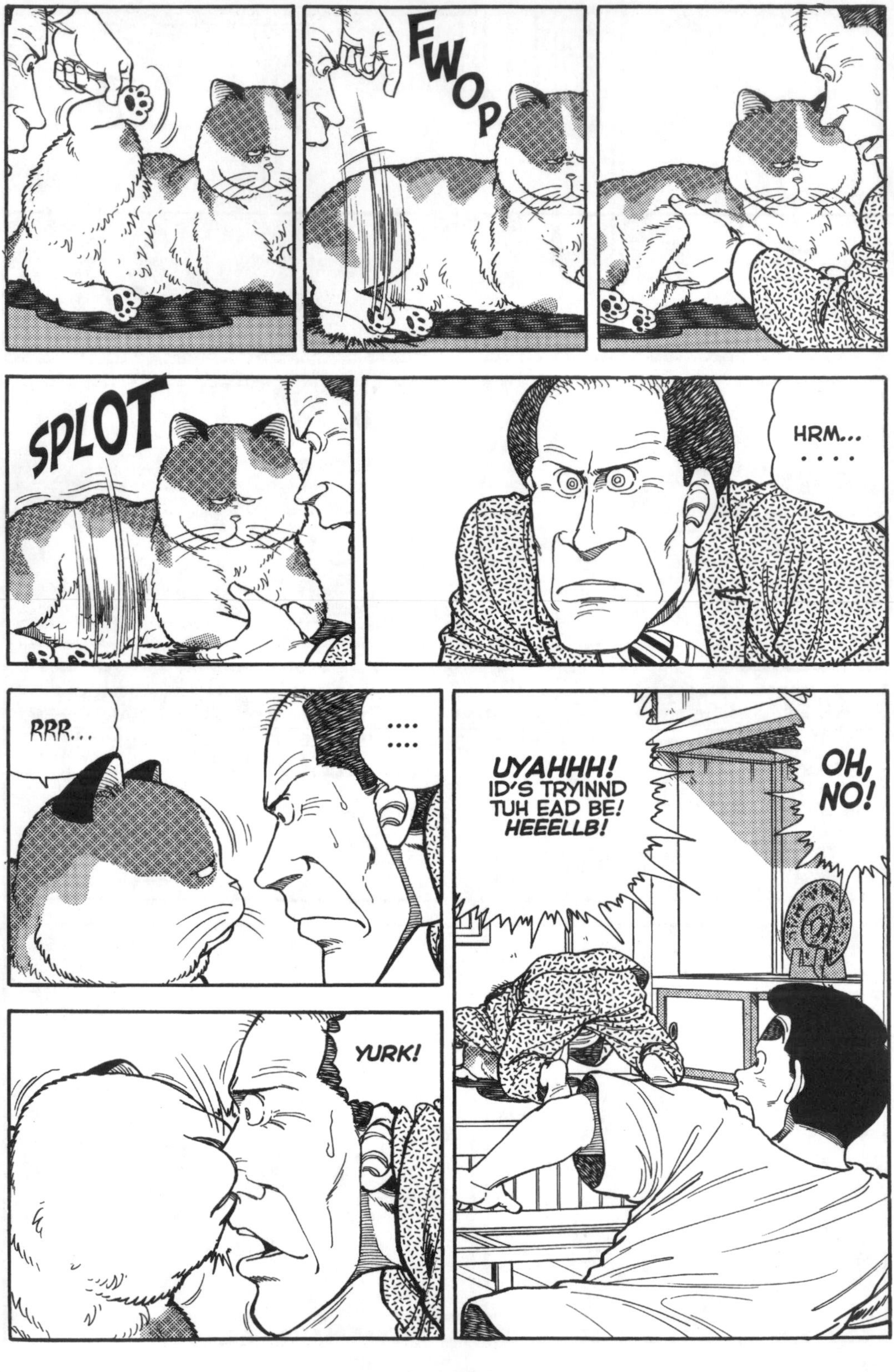
FWOP
SPLOT
HRM... ....
RRR...
....
UYAHHH! ID'S TRYINND TUH EAD BE! HEEELLB!
OH, NO!
YURK!

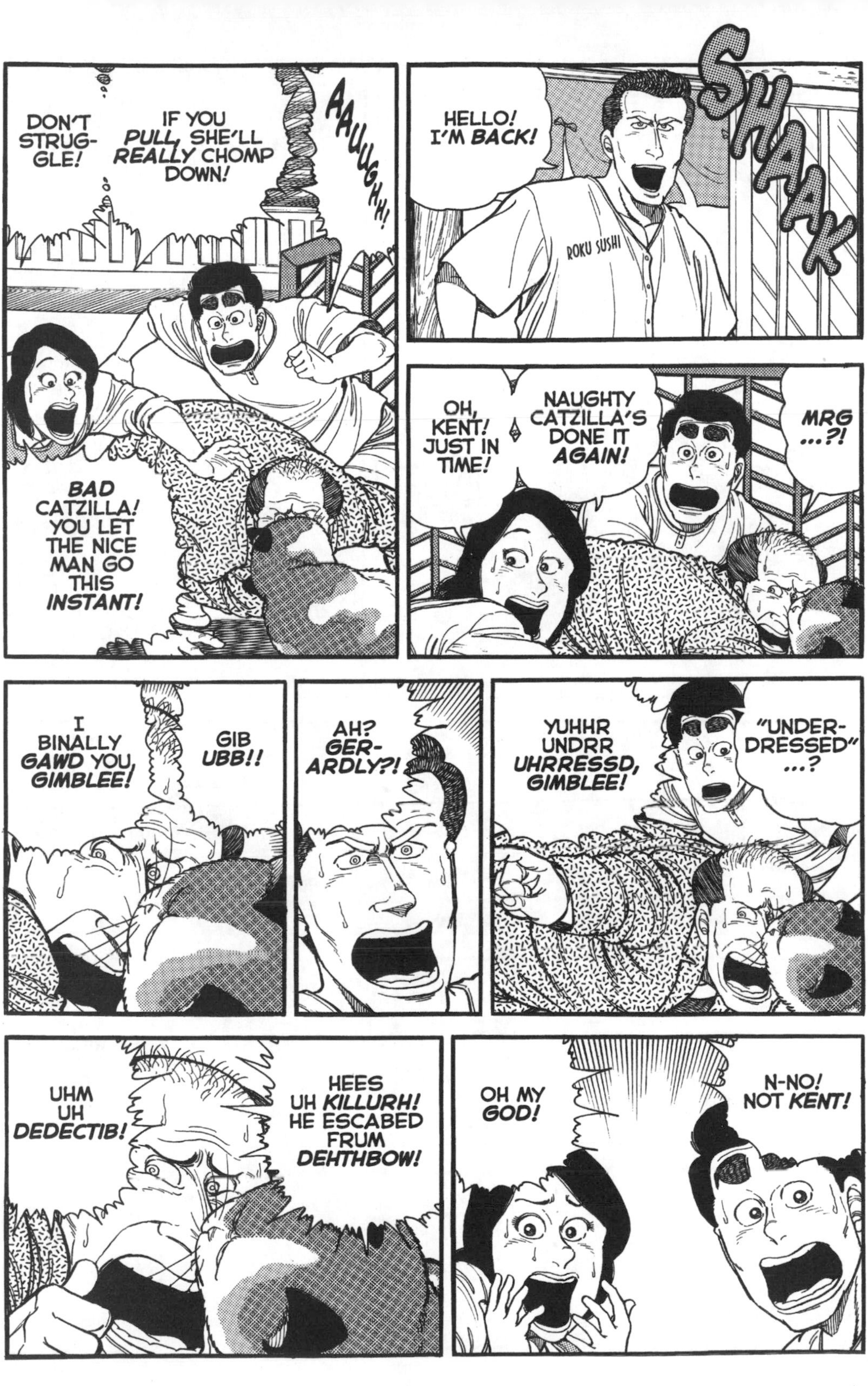
DON'T STRUG-GLE!
IF YOU PULL, SHE'LL REALLY CHOMP DOWN!
AAAUUGHH!
BAD CATZILLA! YOU LET THE NICE MAN GO THIS INSTANT!
SHAAAK
HELLO! I'M BACK!
ROKU SUSHI
OH, KENT! JUST IN TIME!
NAUGHTY CATZILLA'S DONE IT AGAIN!
MRG ...?!
I BINALLY GAWD YOU, GIMBLEE!
GIB UBB!!
AH? GER-ARDLY?!
YUHHR UNDRR UHRRESSD, GIMBLEE!
"UNDER-DRESSED" ...?
UHM UH DEDECTIB!
HEES UH KILLURH! HE ESCABED FRUM DEHTHBOW!
OH MY GOD!
N-NO! NOT KENT!

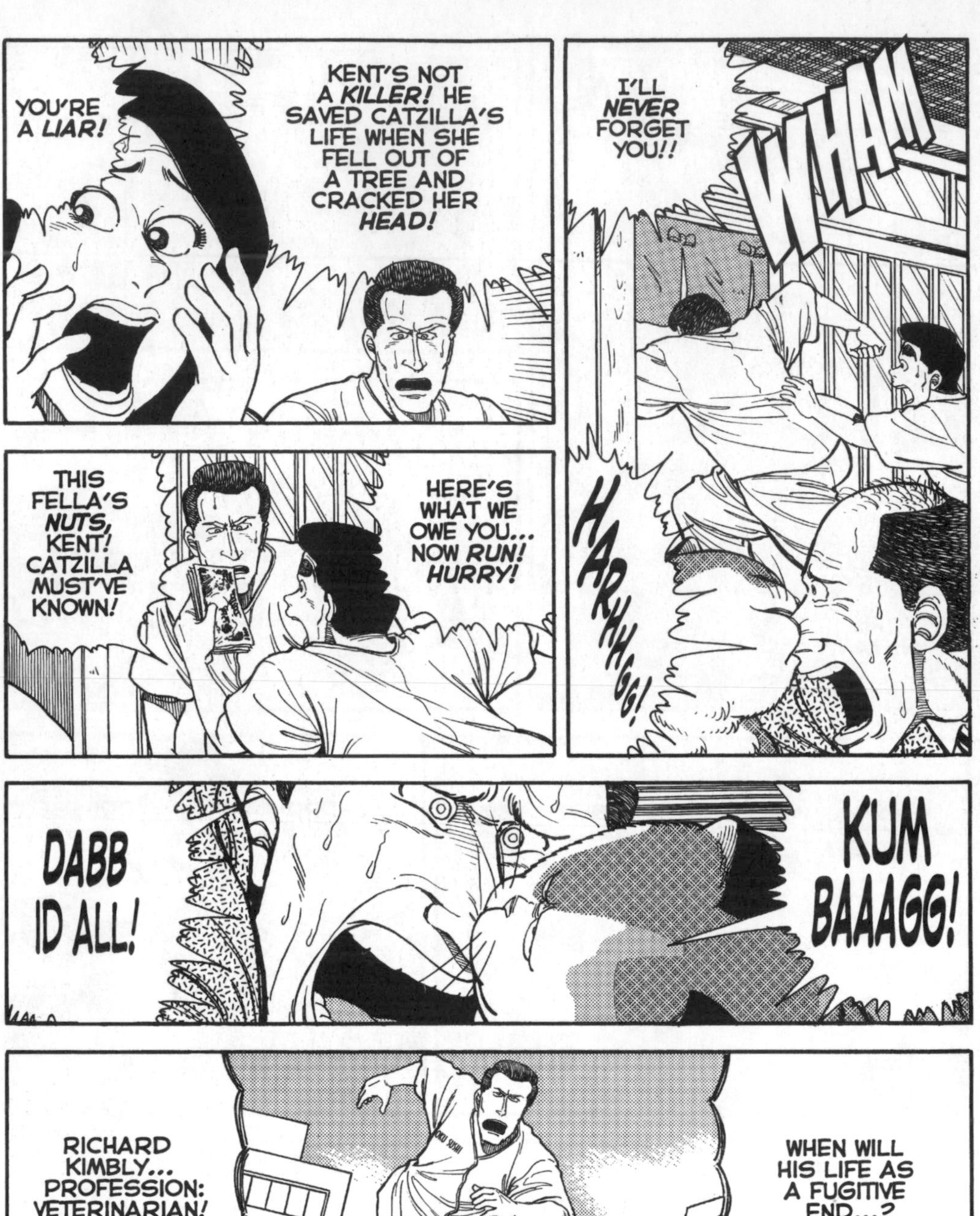
YOU'RE A LIAR!
KENT'S NOT A KILLER! HE SAVED CATZILLA'S LIFE WHEN SHE FELL OUT OF A TREE AND CRACKED HER HEAD!
I'LL NEVER FORGET YOU!!
WHAM
THIS FELLA'S NUTS, KENT! CATZILLA MUST'VE KNOWN!
HERE'S WHAT WE OWE YOU... NOW RUN! HURRY!
HARHHGG!
DABB ID ALL!
KUM BAAAGG!
RICHARD KIMBLY... PROFESSION: VETERINARIAN!
WHEN WILL HIS LIFE AS A FUGITIVE END...?

THE END

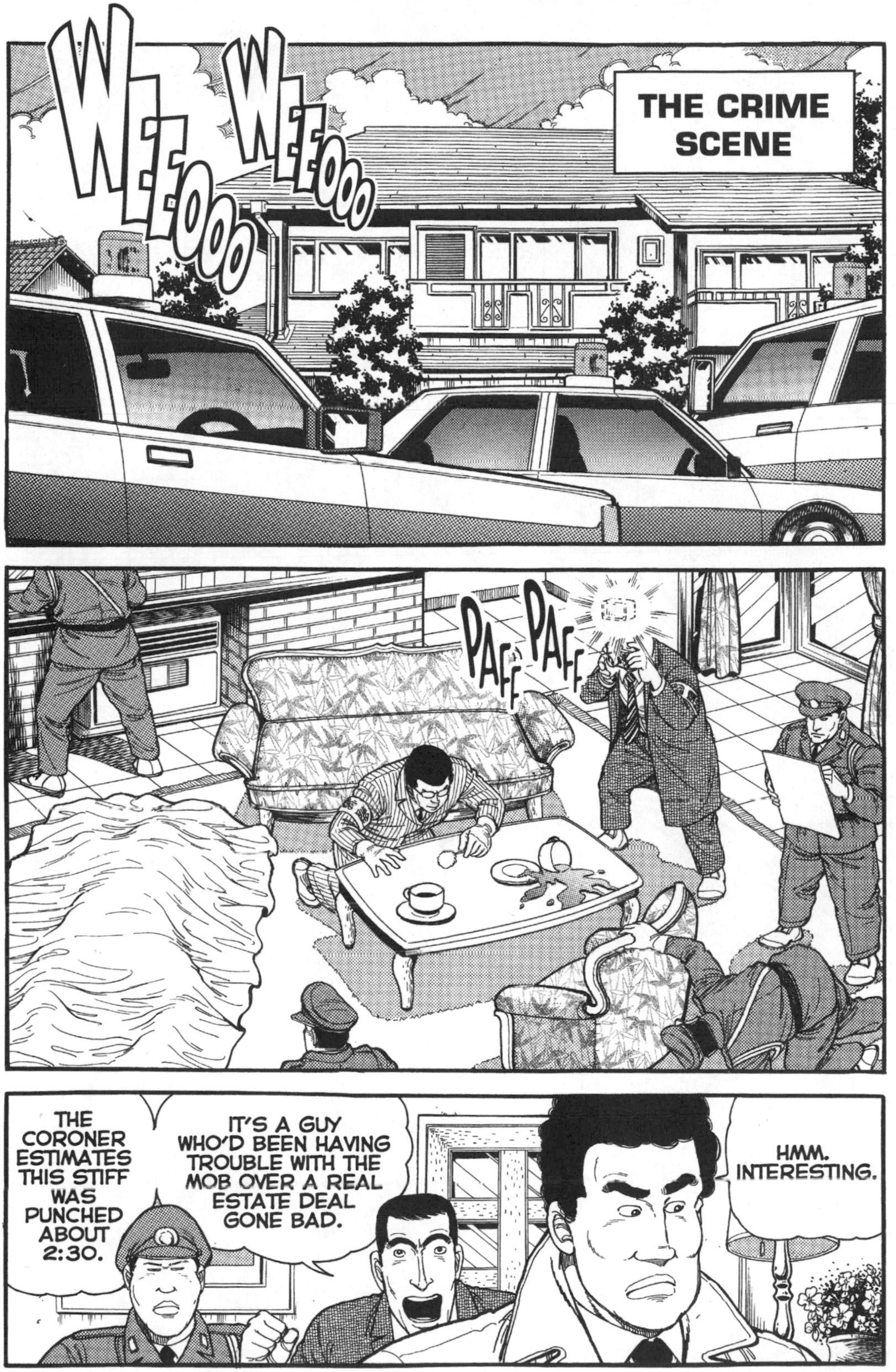
WEE-OOO WEE-OOO
THE CRIME SCENE
PAFF PAFF
THE CORONER ESTIMATES THIS STIFF WAS PUNCHED ABOUT 2:30.
IT'S A GUY WHO'D BEEN HAVING TROUBLE WITH THE MOB OVER A REAL ESTATE DEAL GONE BAD.
HMM. INTERESTING.

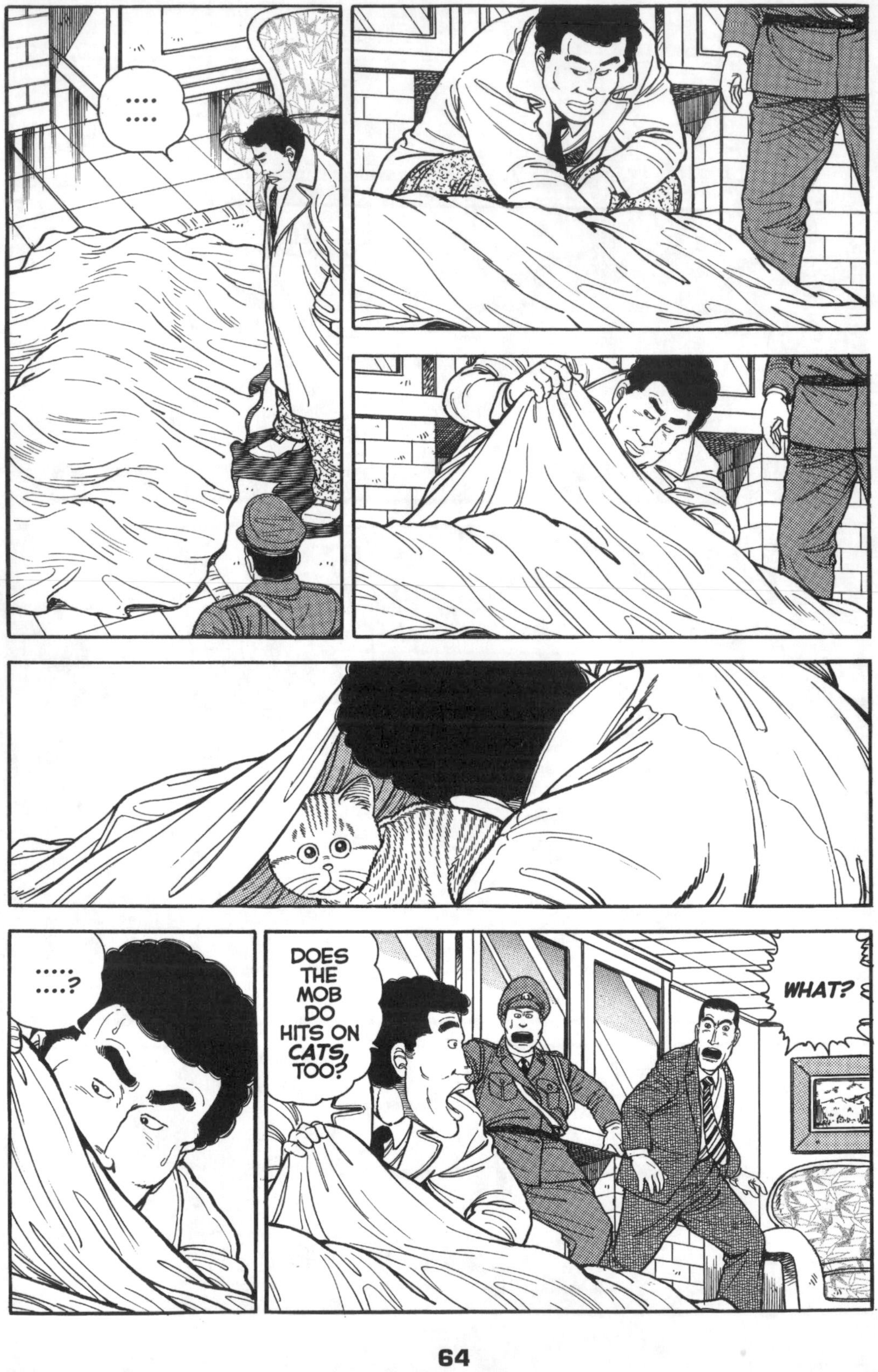
....
....
.....
....?
DOES THE MOB DO HITS ON CATS, TOO?
WHAT?

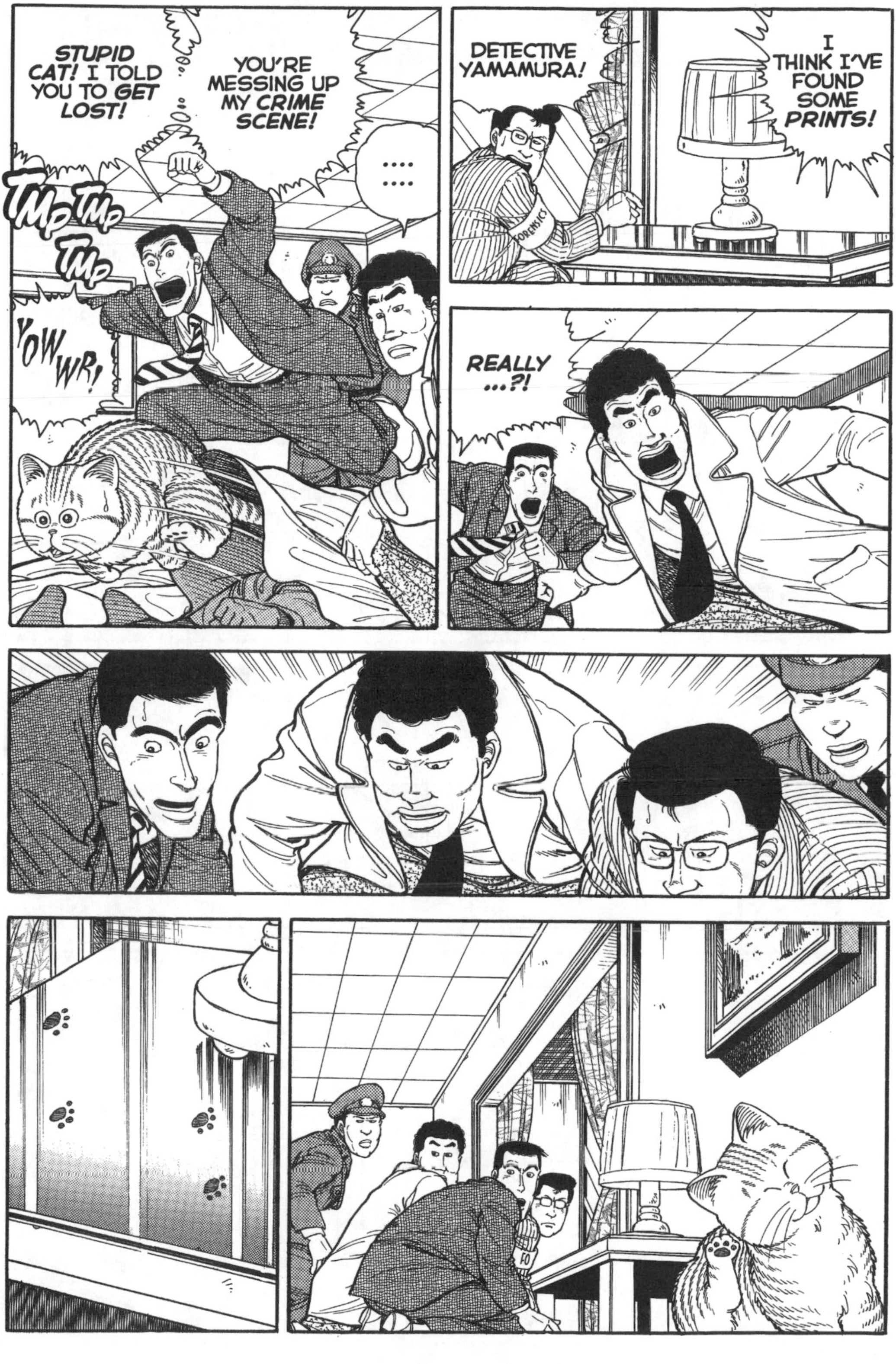
STUPID CAT! I TOLD YOU TO GET LOST!
YOU'RE MESSING UP MY CRIME SCENE!
....
....
TMP TMP TMP
YOWWR!
DETECTIVE YAMAMURA!
I THINK I'VE FOUND SOME PRINTS!
FORENSICS
REALLY ...?!

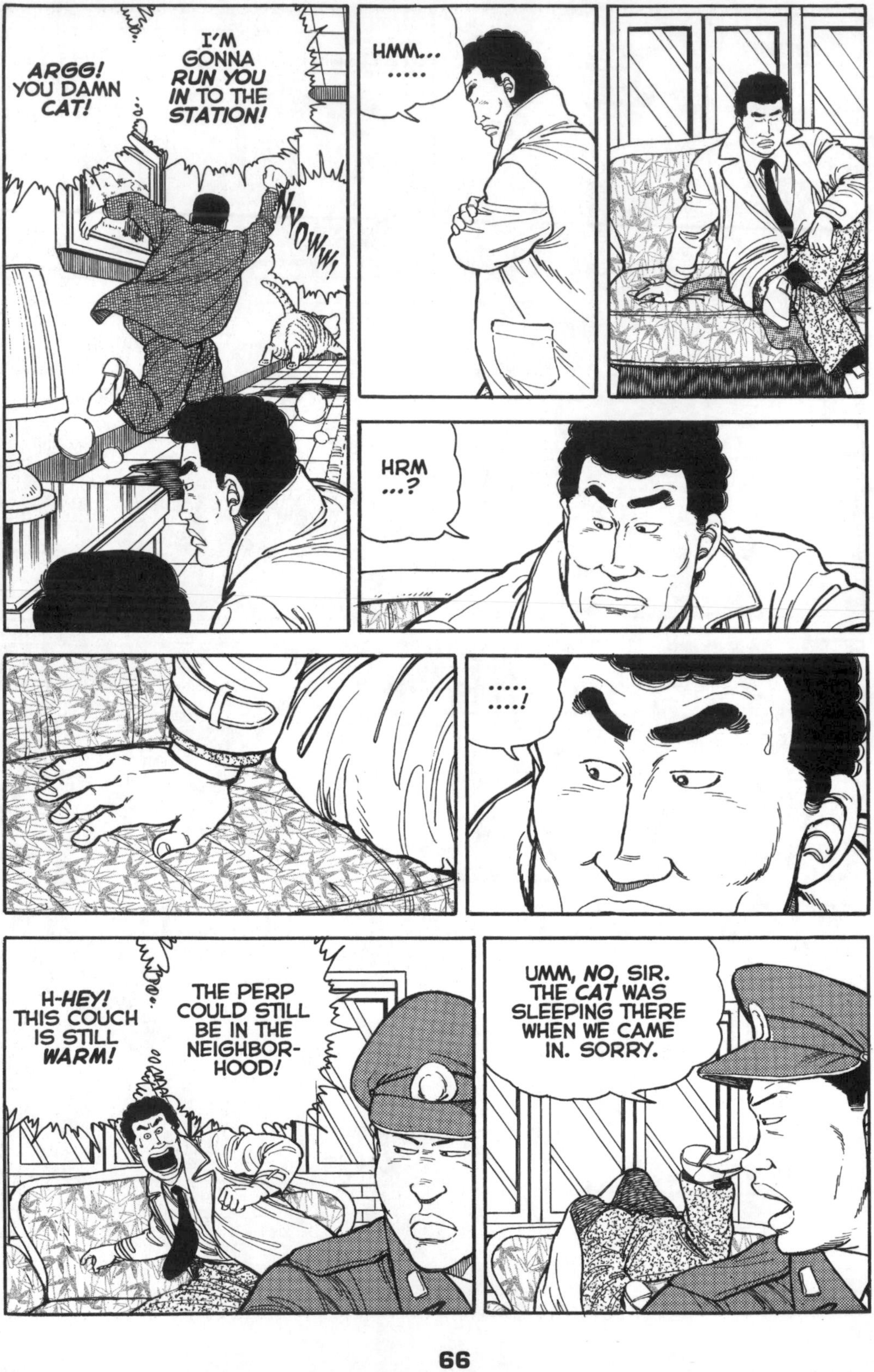
ARGG! YOU DAMN CAT!
I'M GONNA RUN YOU IN TO THE STATION!
NYOWW!
HMM... ......
HRM ...?
H-HEY! THIS COUCH IS STILL WARM!
THE PERP COULD STILL BE IN THE NEIGHBOR-HOOD!
UMM, NO, SIR. THE CAT WAS SLEEPING THERE WHEN WE CAME IN. SORRY.

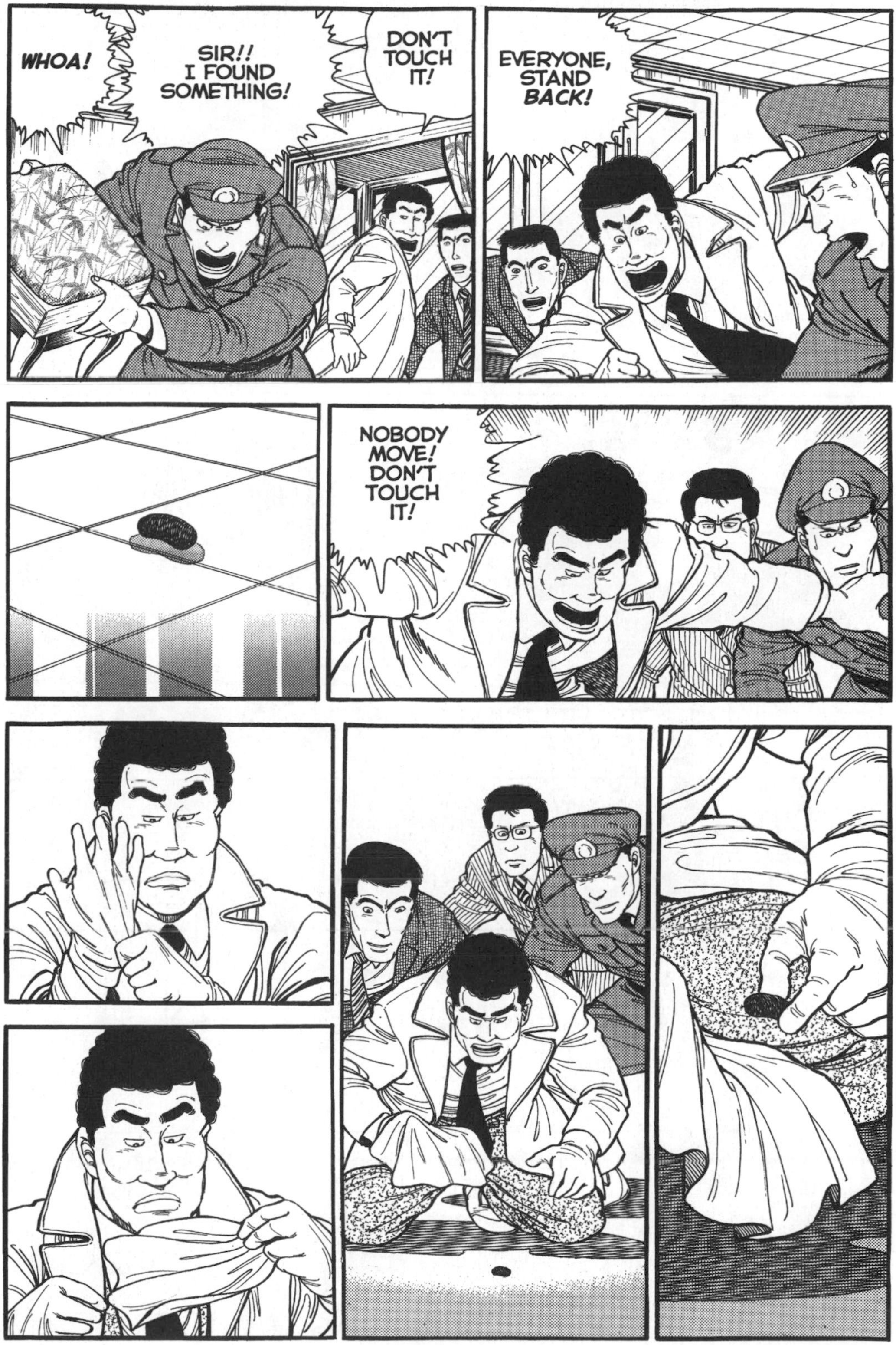
WHOA!
SIR!! I FOUND SOMETHING!
DON'T TOUCH IT!
EVERYONE, STAND BACK!
NOBODY MOVE! DON'T TOUCH IT!

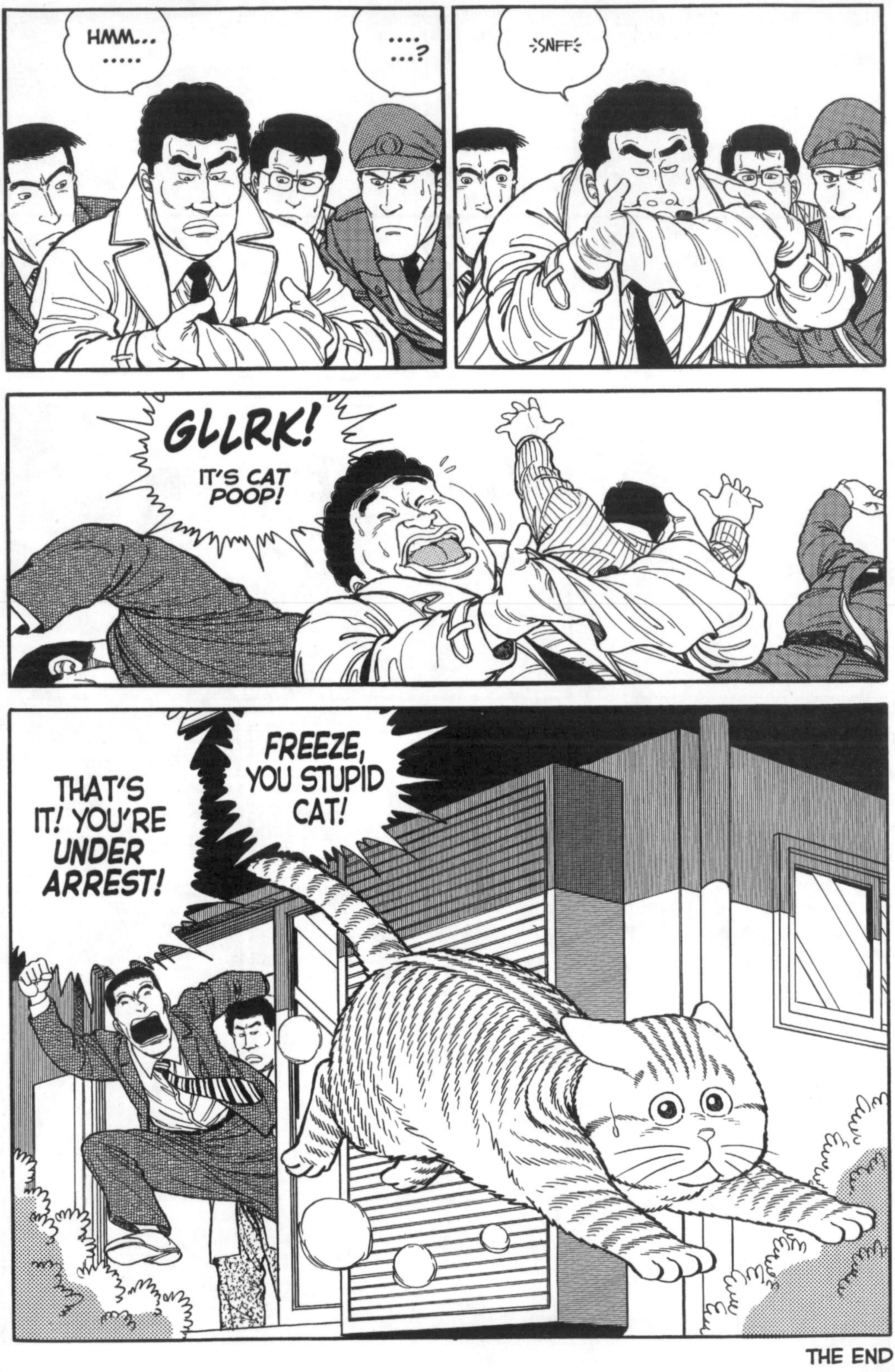
HMM...
.....
....
...?
SNFF
GLLRK!
IT'S CAT POOP!
THAT'S IT! YOU'RE UNDER ARREST!
FREEZE, YOU STUPID CAT!
THE END

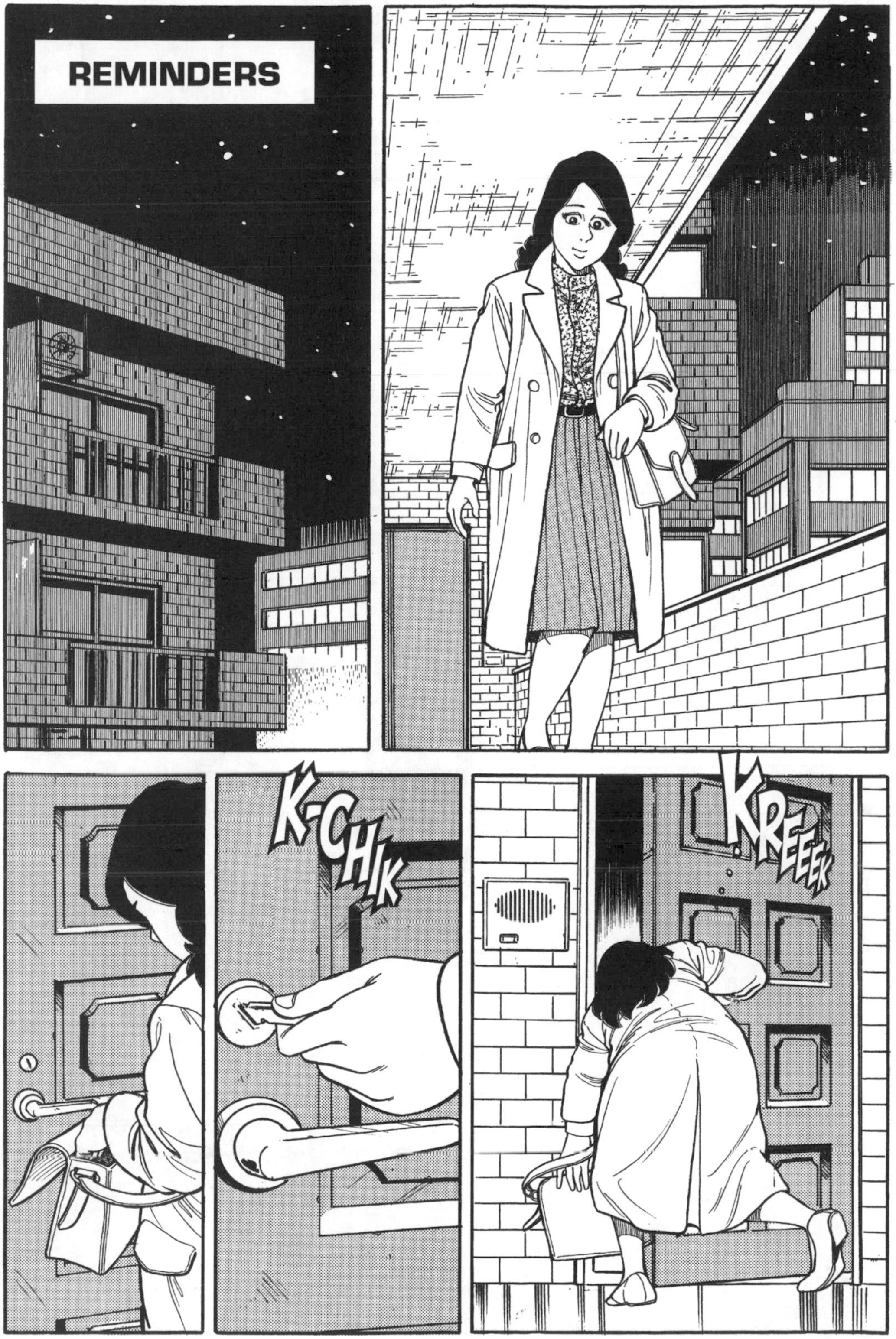
REMINDERS
K-CHIK
KREEEK

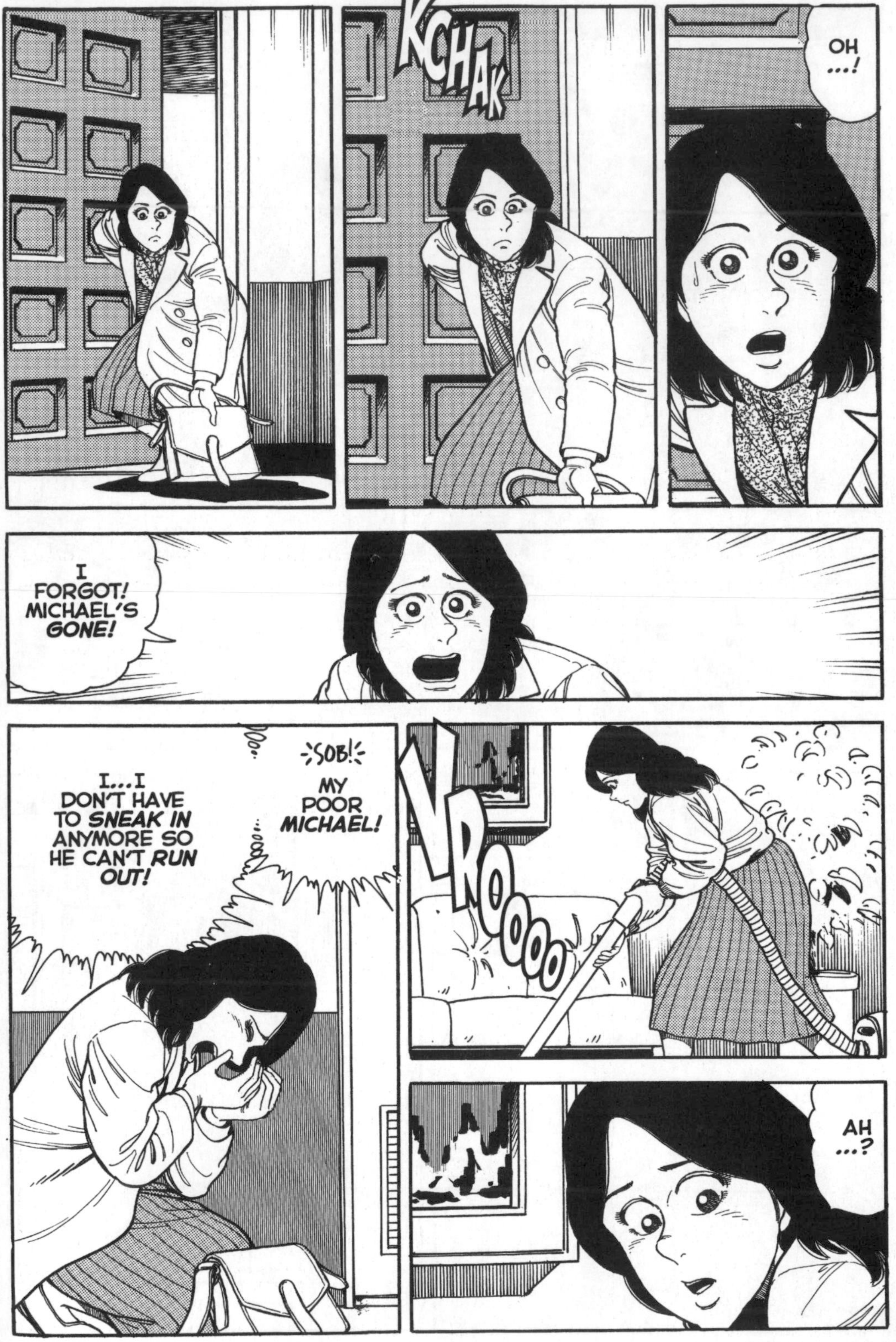
KCHAK
OH ...!
I FORGOT! MICHAEL'S GONE!
I...I DON'T HAVE TO SNEAK IN ANYMORE SO HE CAN'T RUN OUT!
SOB!
MY POOR MICHAEL!
VROOOOO
AH ...?

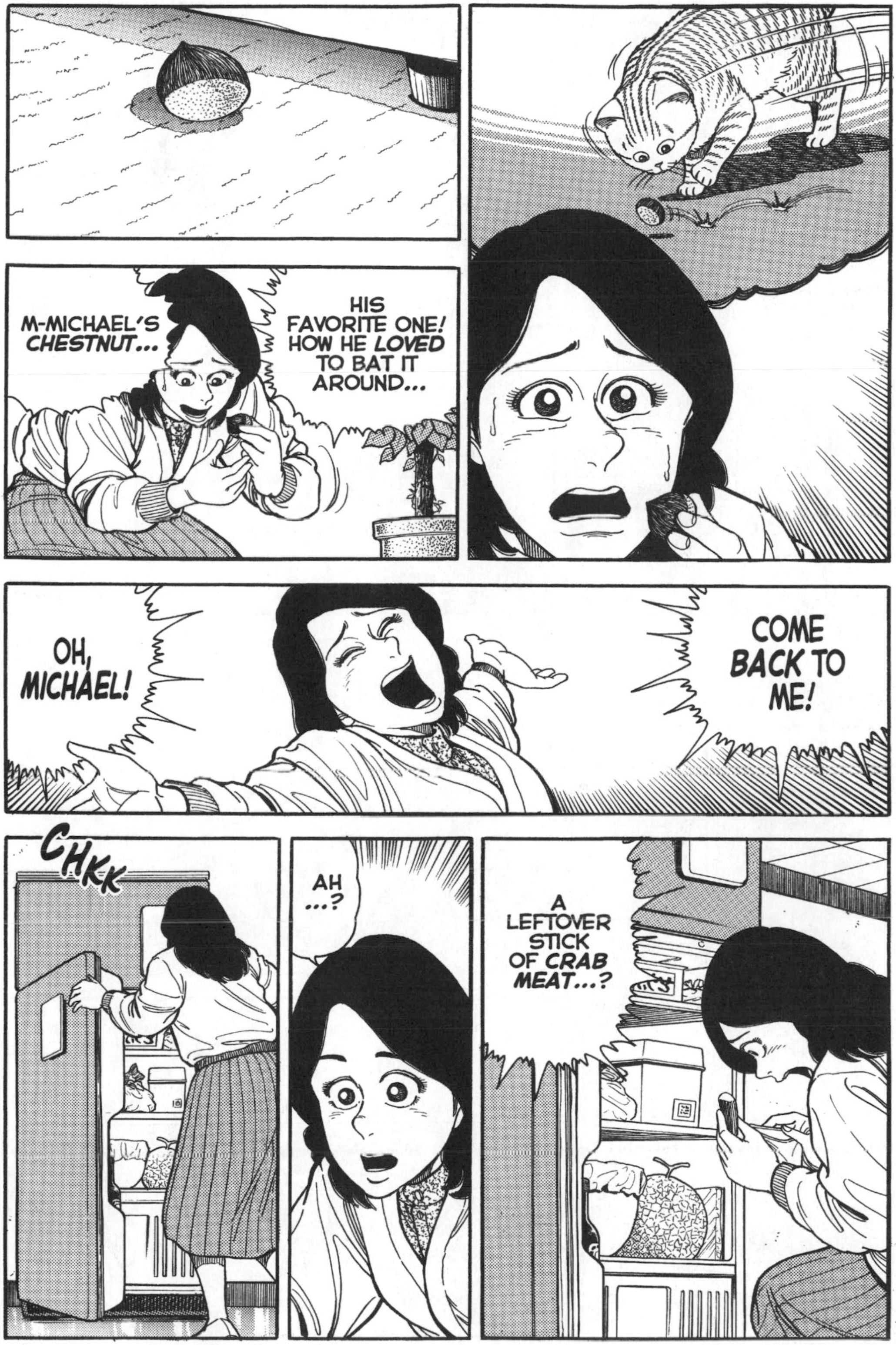
M-MICHAEL'S *CHESTNUT...*
HIS FAVORITE ONE! HOW HE *LOVED* TO BAT IT AROUND...
OH, **MICHAEL!**
COME **BACK** TO **ME!**
CHKK
AH ...?
A LEFTOVER STICK OF *CRAB MEAT...?*

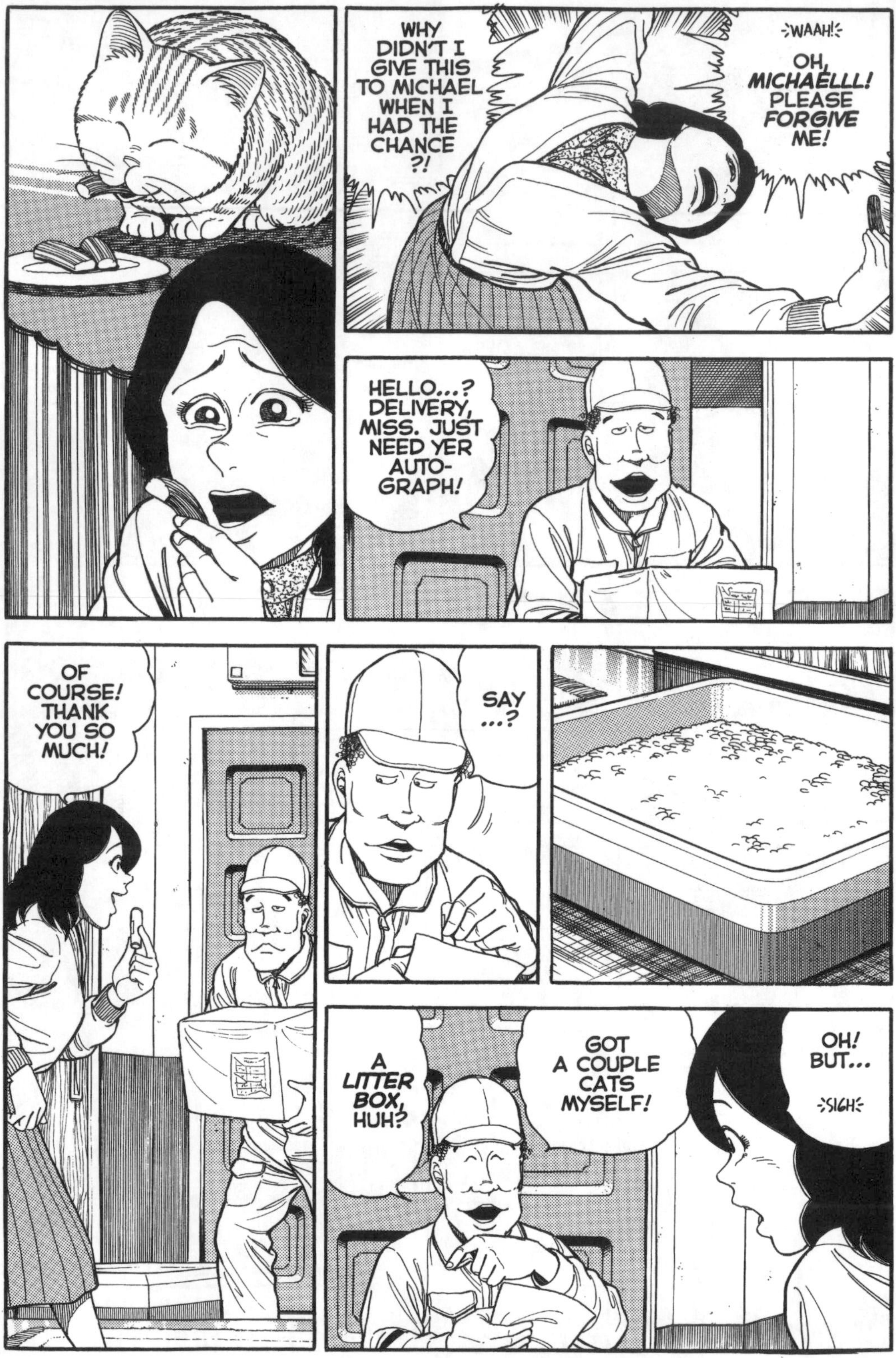

WHY DIDN'T I GIVE THIS TO MICHAEL WHEN I HAD THE CHANCE ?!
WAAH!
OH, MICHAELLL! PLEASE FORGIVE ME!
HELLO...? DELIVERY, MISS. JUST NEED YER AUTO-GRAPH!
OF COURSE! THANK YOU SO MUCH!
SAY ...?
A LITTER BOX, HUH?
GOT A COUPLE CATS MYSELF!
OH! BUT...
SIGH

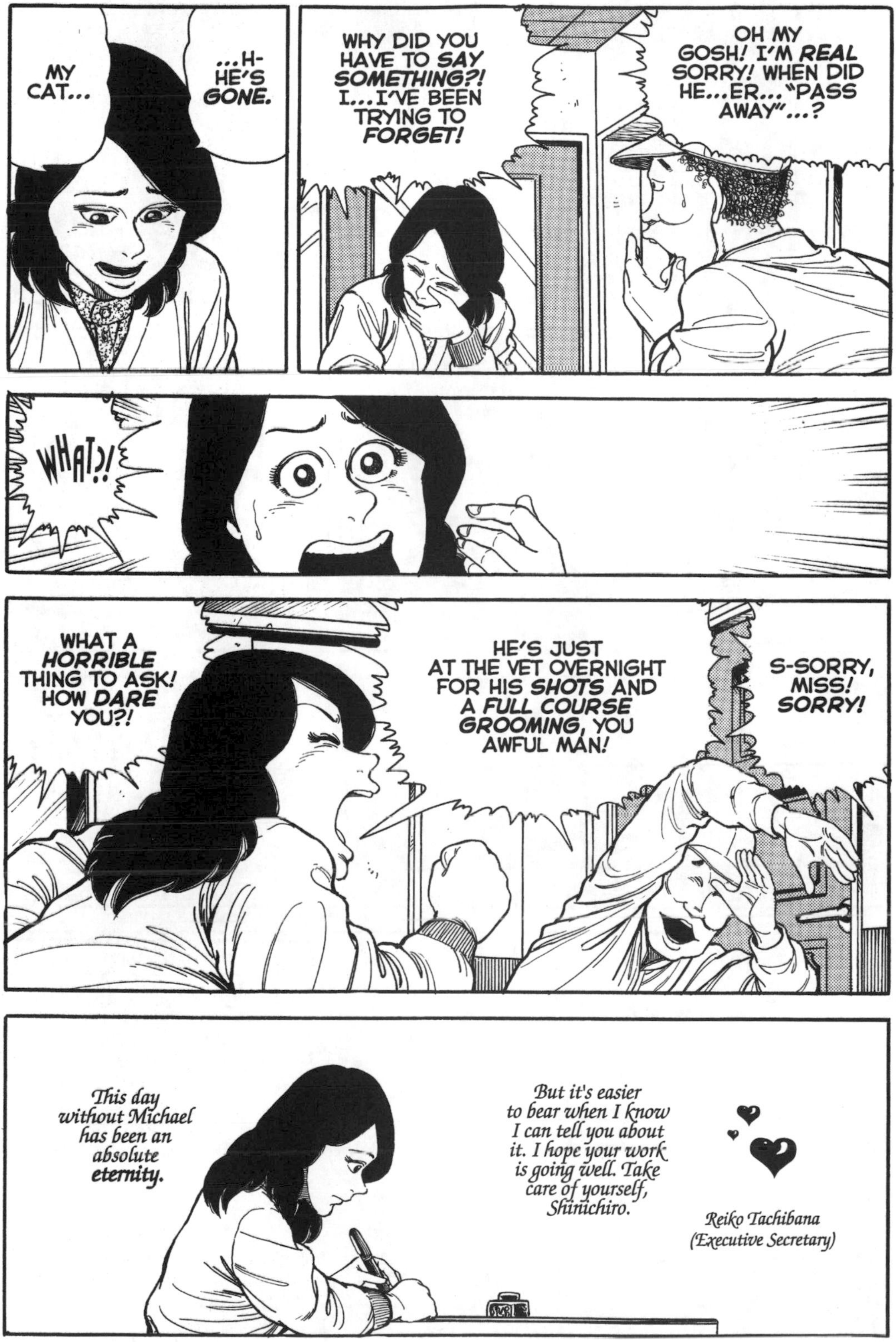
MY CAT...
...H- HE'S GONE.
WHY DID YOU HAVE TO SAY SOMETHING?! I...I'VE BEEN TRYING TO FORGET!
OH MY GOSH! I'M REAL SORRY! WHEN DID HE...ER..."PASS AWAY"...?
WHAT?!
WHAT A HORRIBLE THING TO ASK! HOW DARE YOU?!
HE'S JUST AT THE VET OVERNIGHT FOR HIS SHOTS AND A FULL COURSE GROOMING, YOU AWFUL MAN!
S-SORRY, MISS! SORRY!
This day without Michael has been an absolute eternity.
But it's easier to bear when I know I can tell you about it. I hope your work is going well. Take care of yourself, Shinichiro.
Reiko Tachibana (Executive Secretary)

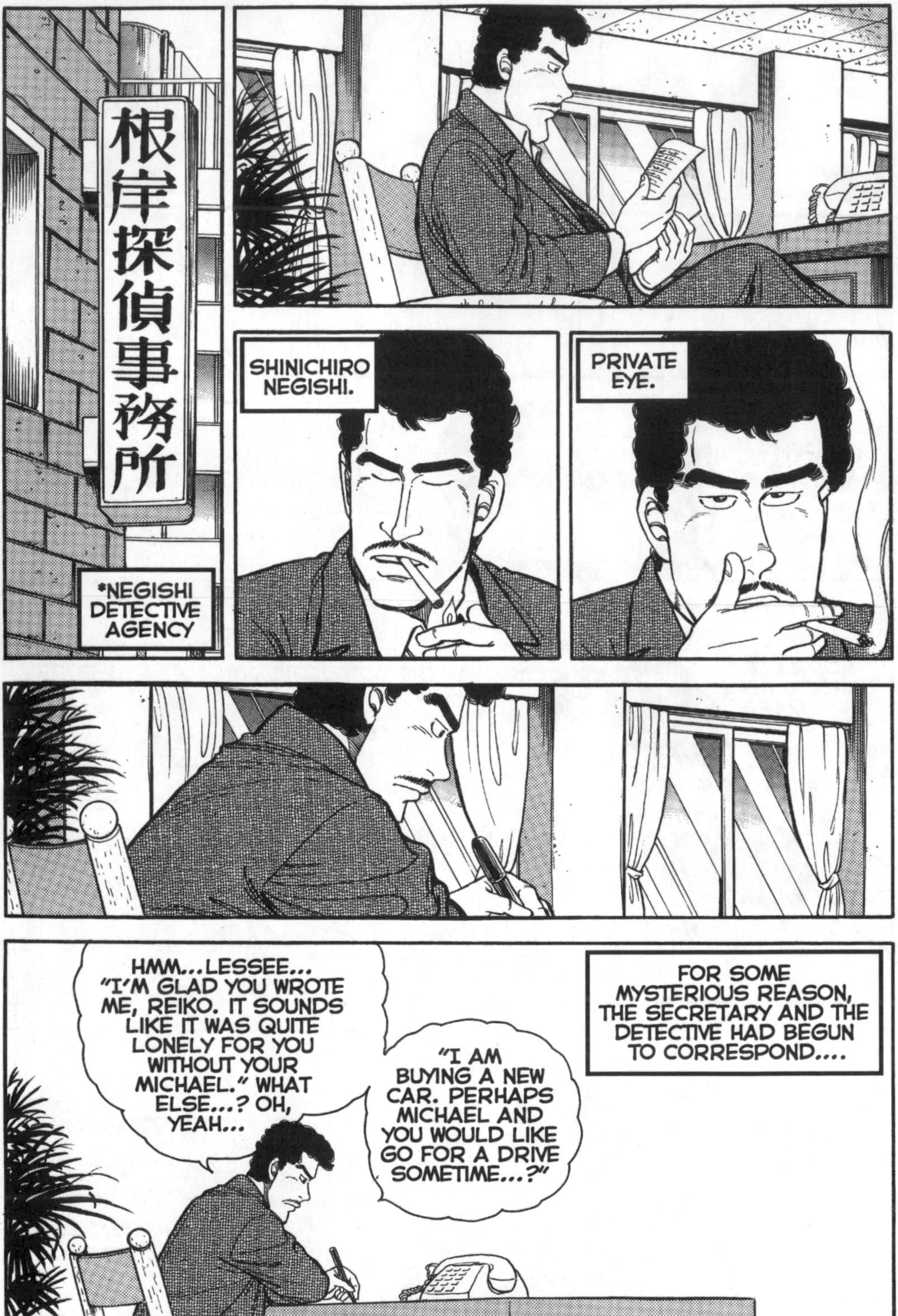
根岸探偵事務所
*NEGISHI DETECTIVE AGENCY
SHINICHIRO NEGISHI.
PRIVATE EYE.
HMM...LESSEE... "I'M GLAD YOU WROTE ME, REIKO. IT SOUNDS LIKE IT WAS QUITE LONELY FOR YOU WITHOUT YOUR MICHAEL." WHAT ELSE...? OH, YEAH...
"I AM BUYING A NEW CAR. PERHAPS MICHAEL AND YOU WOULD LIKE GO FOR A DRIVE SOMETIME...?"
FOR SOME MYSTERIOUS REASON, THE SECRETARY AND THE DETECTIVE HAD BEGUN TO CORRESPOND....

THE END

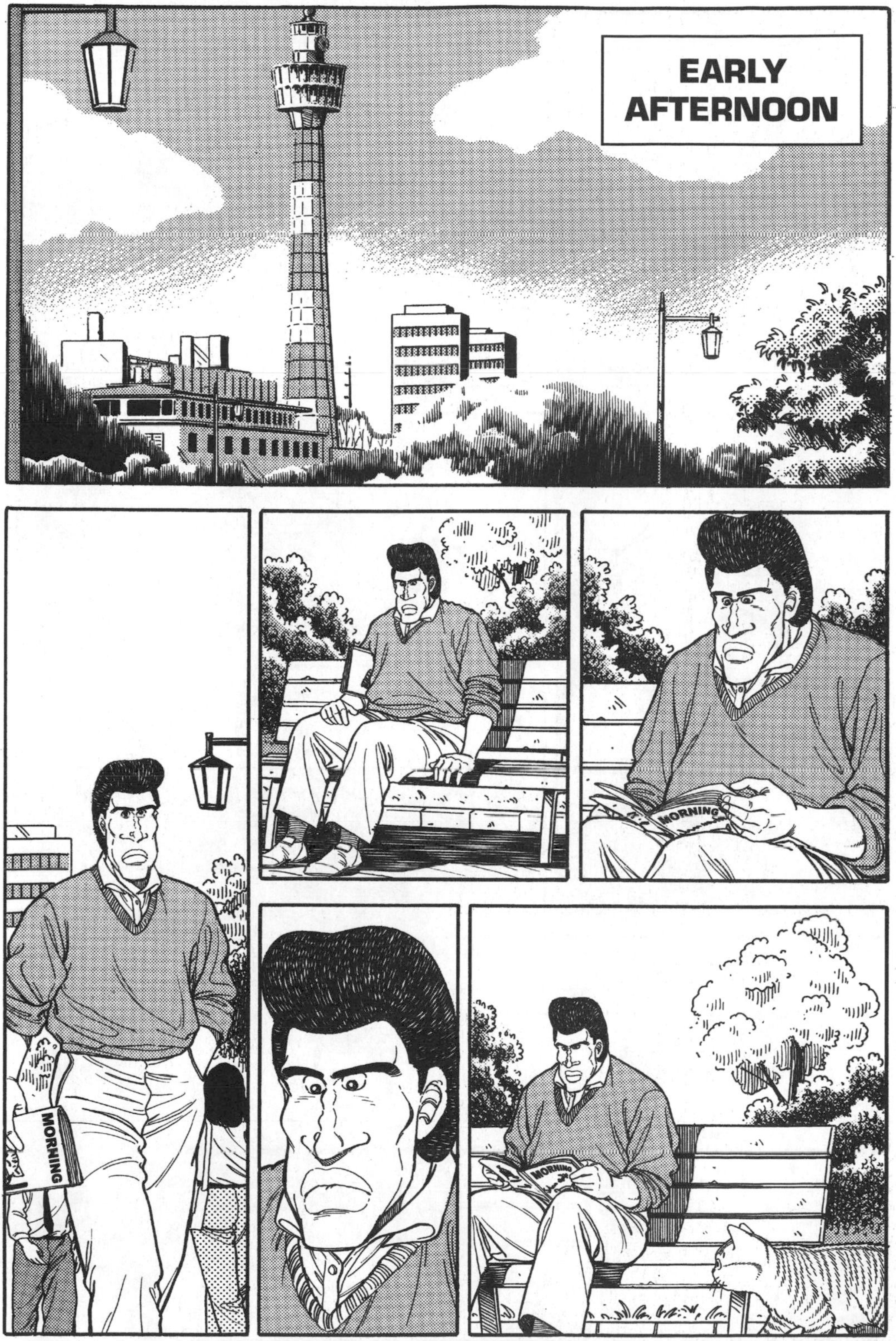
EARLY AFTERNOON
MORNING
MORNING
MORNING

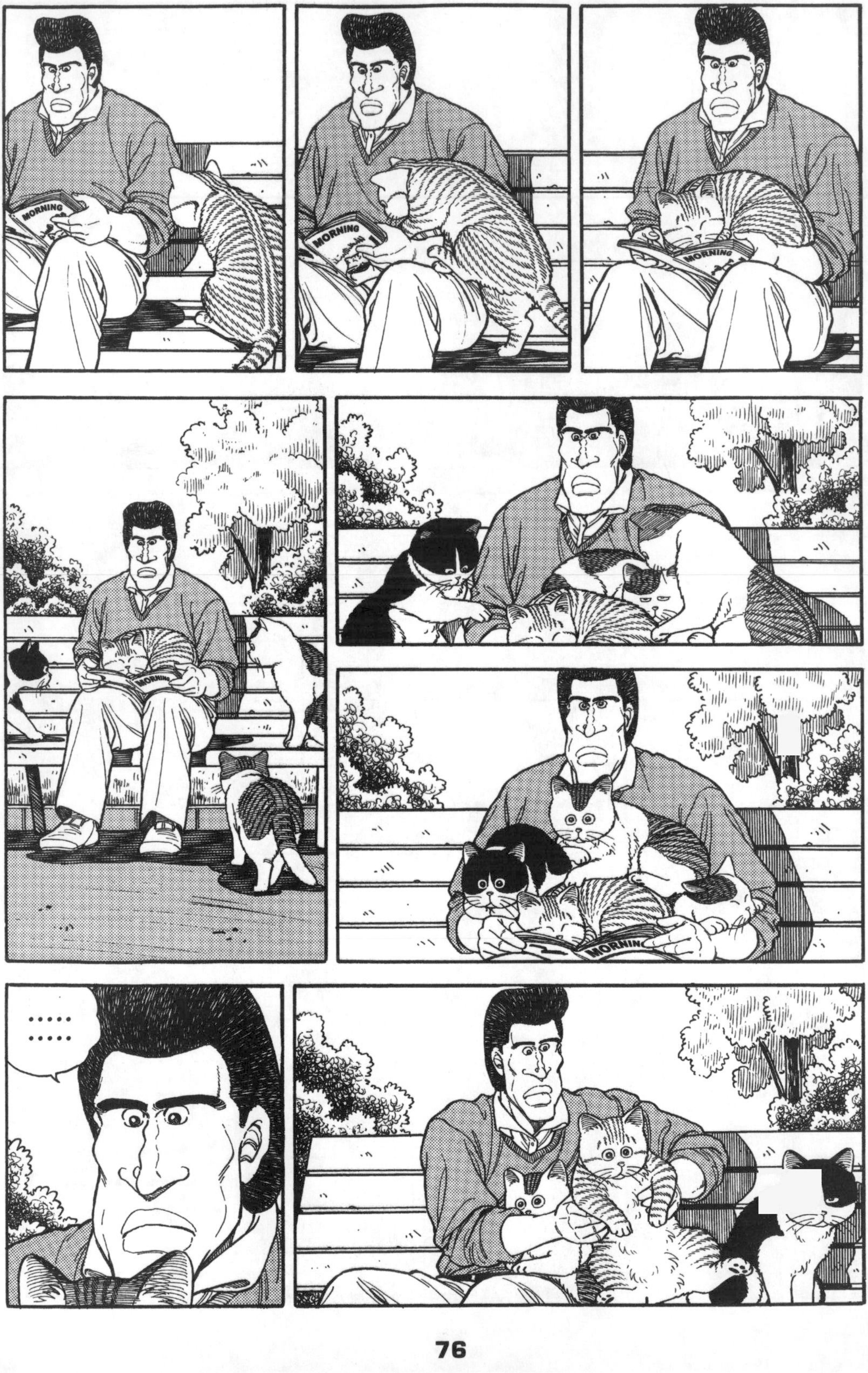
MORNING
MORNING
MORNING
MORNING
MORNING
.....
.....

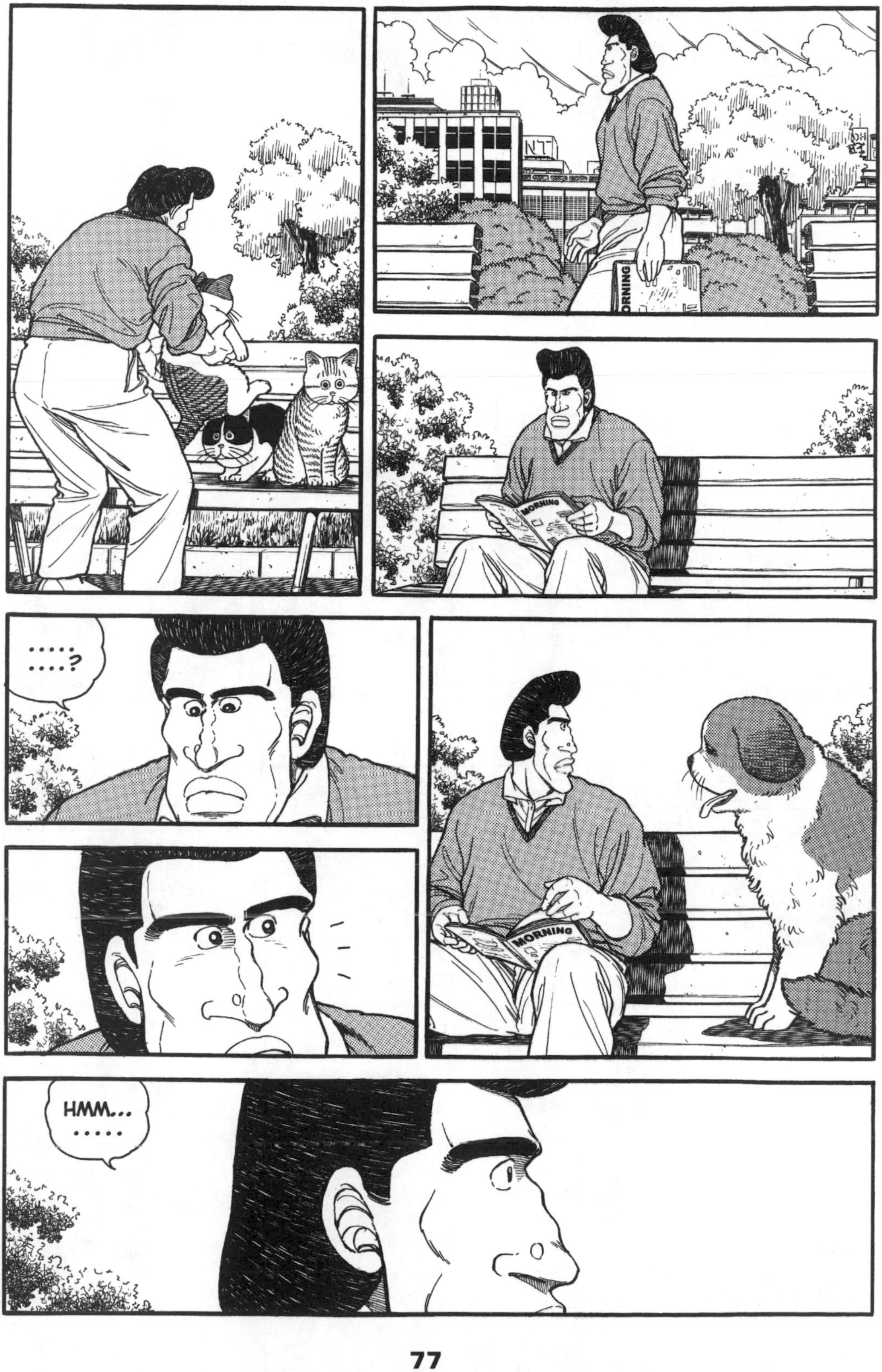
MORNING
MORNING
.....
....?
MORNING
HMM...
......

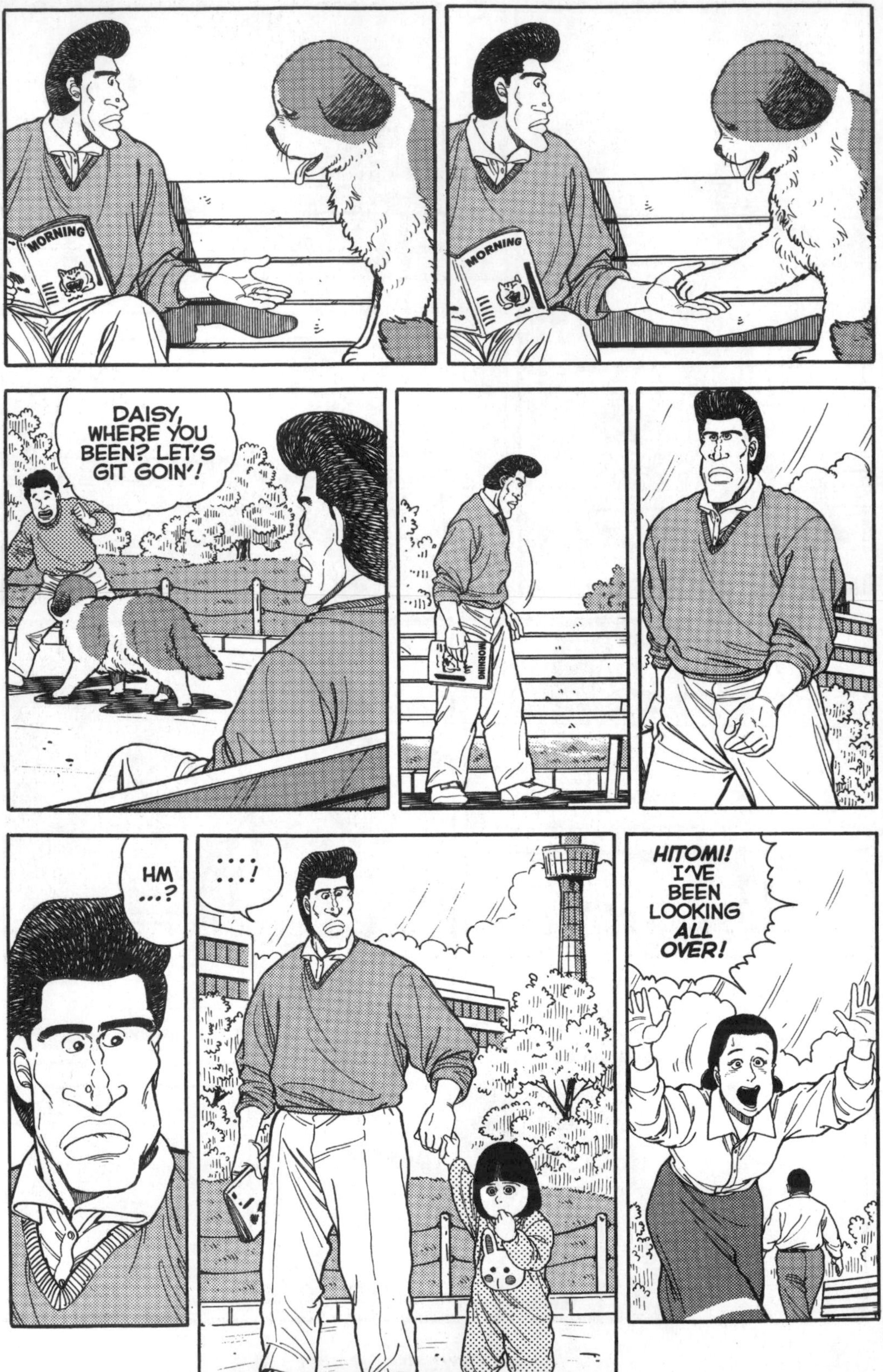
MORNING
MORNING
DAISY, WHERE YOU BEEN? LET'S GIT GOIN'!
MORNING
HM ...?
...; ...!
HITOMI! I'VE BEEN LOOKING ALL OVER!

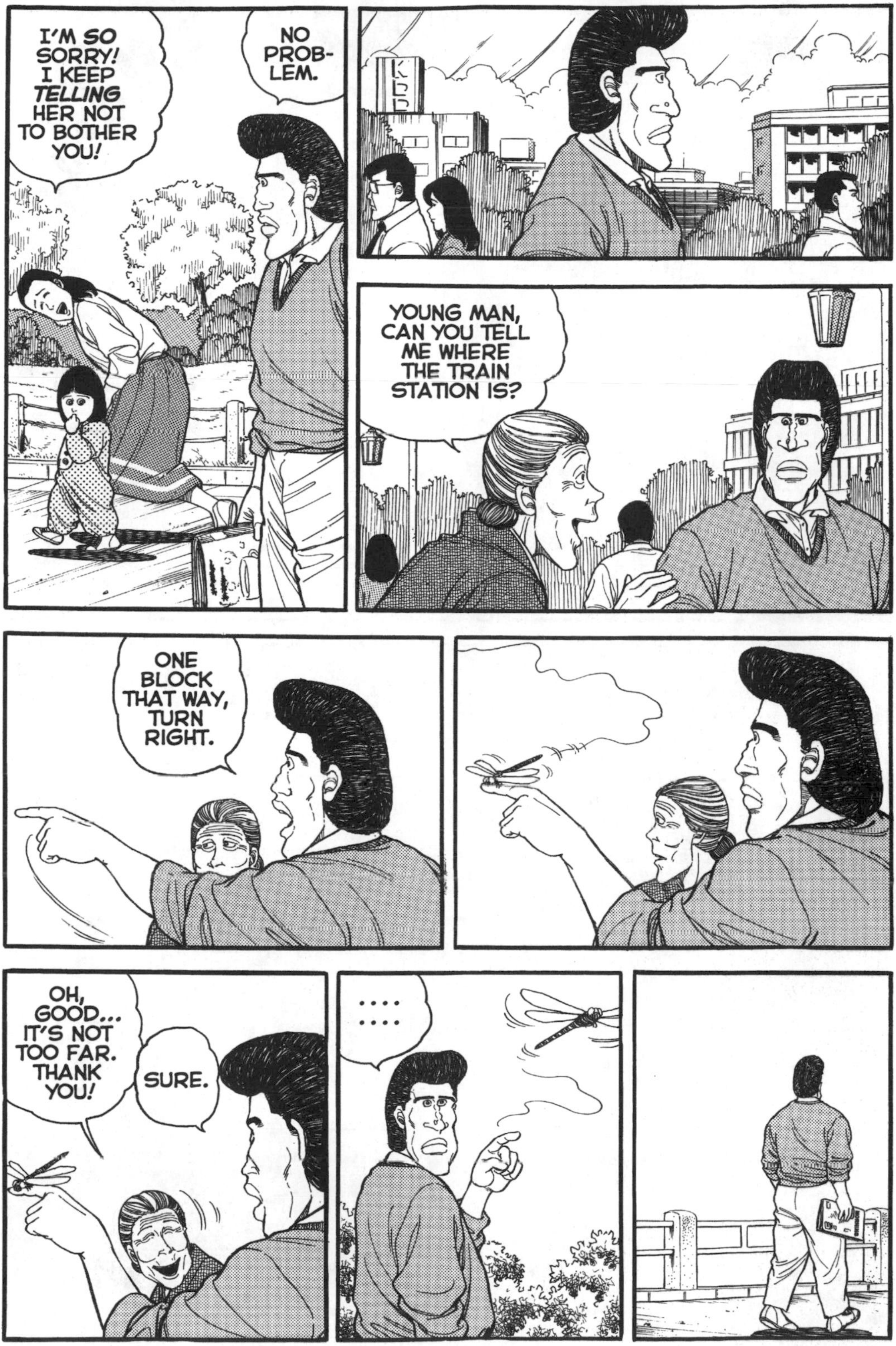
I'M SO SORRY! I KEEP TELLING HER NOT TO BOTHER YOU!
NO PROB-LEM.
YOUNG MAN, CAN YOU TELL ME WHERE THE TRAIN STATION IS?
ONE BLOCK THAT WAY, TURN RIGHT.
OH, GOOD... IT'S NOT TOO FAR. THANK YOU!
SURE.
....
....

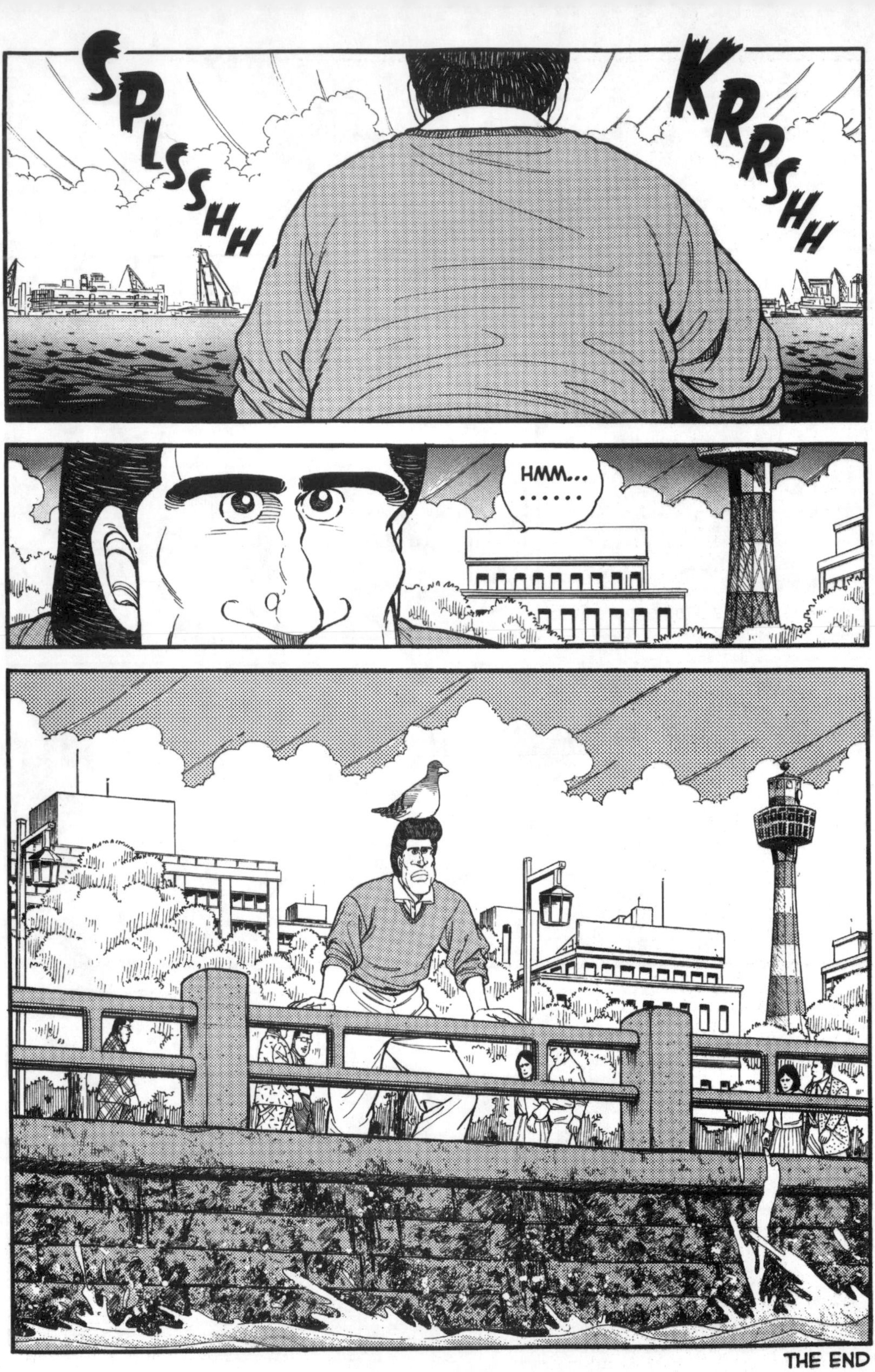
SPLSSHH
KRRSHH
HMM...
......
THE END

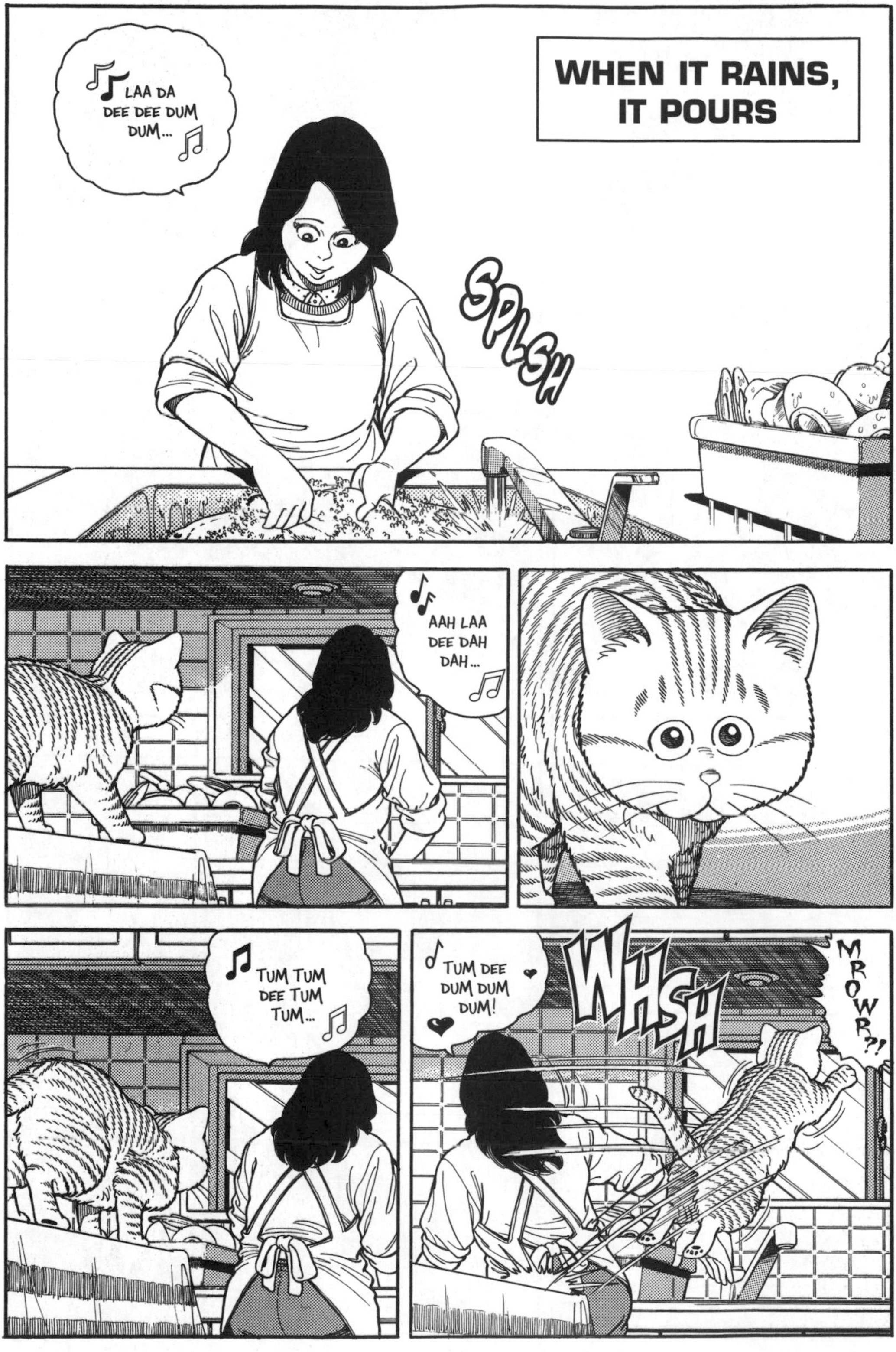

WHEN IT RAINS, IT POURS
LAA DA DEE DEE DUM DUM...
SPLSH
AAH LAA DEE DAH DAH...
TUM TUM DEE TUM TUM...
TUM DEE DUM DUM DUM!
WHSH
MROWR?!

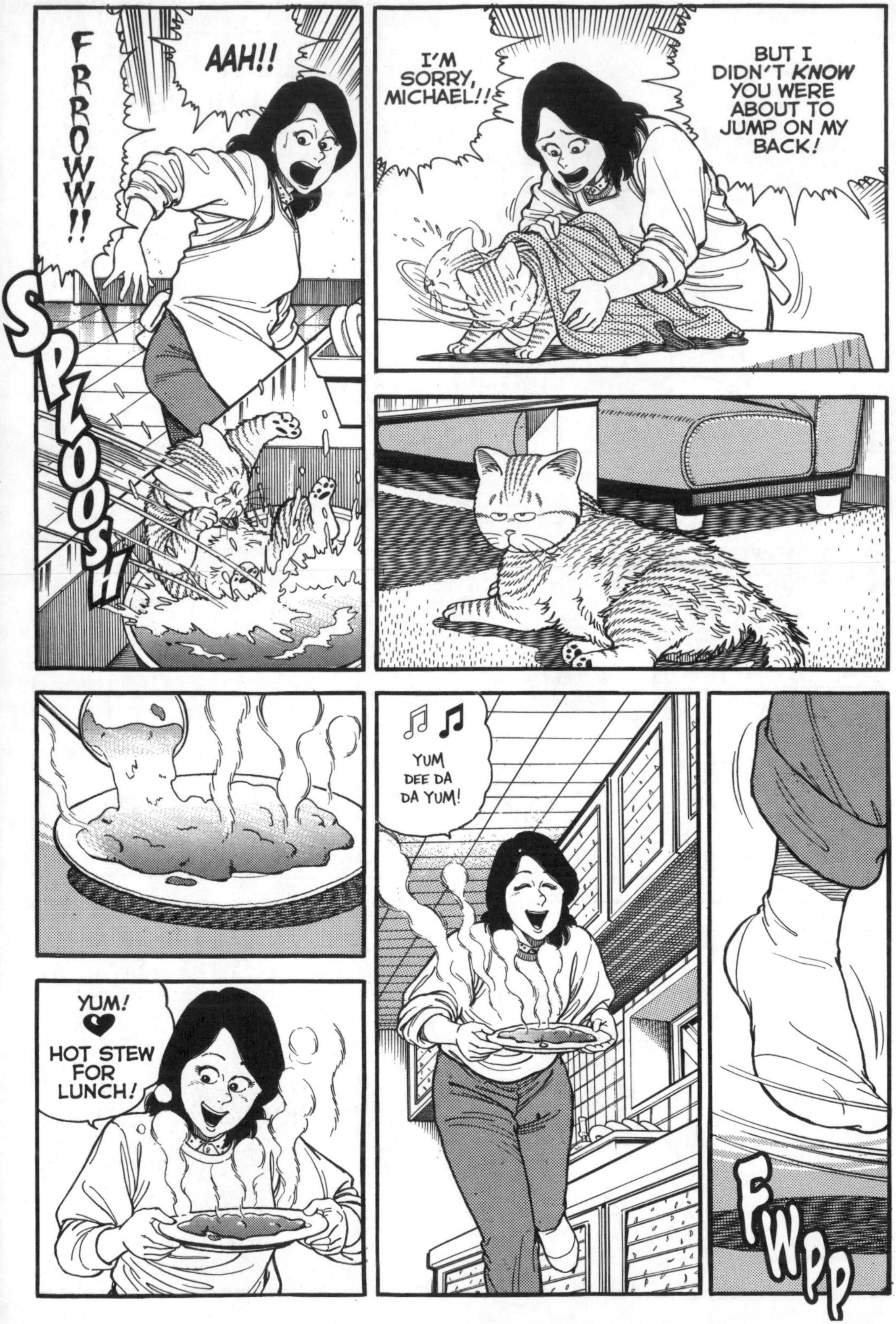

FRROWW!!
AAH!!
SPLOOSH
I'M SORRY, MICHAEL!!
BUT I DIDN'T KNOW YOU WERE ABOUT TO JUMP ON MY BACK!
YUM! HOT STEW FOR LUNCH!
YUM DEE DA DA YUM!
FWPP

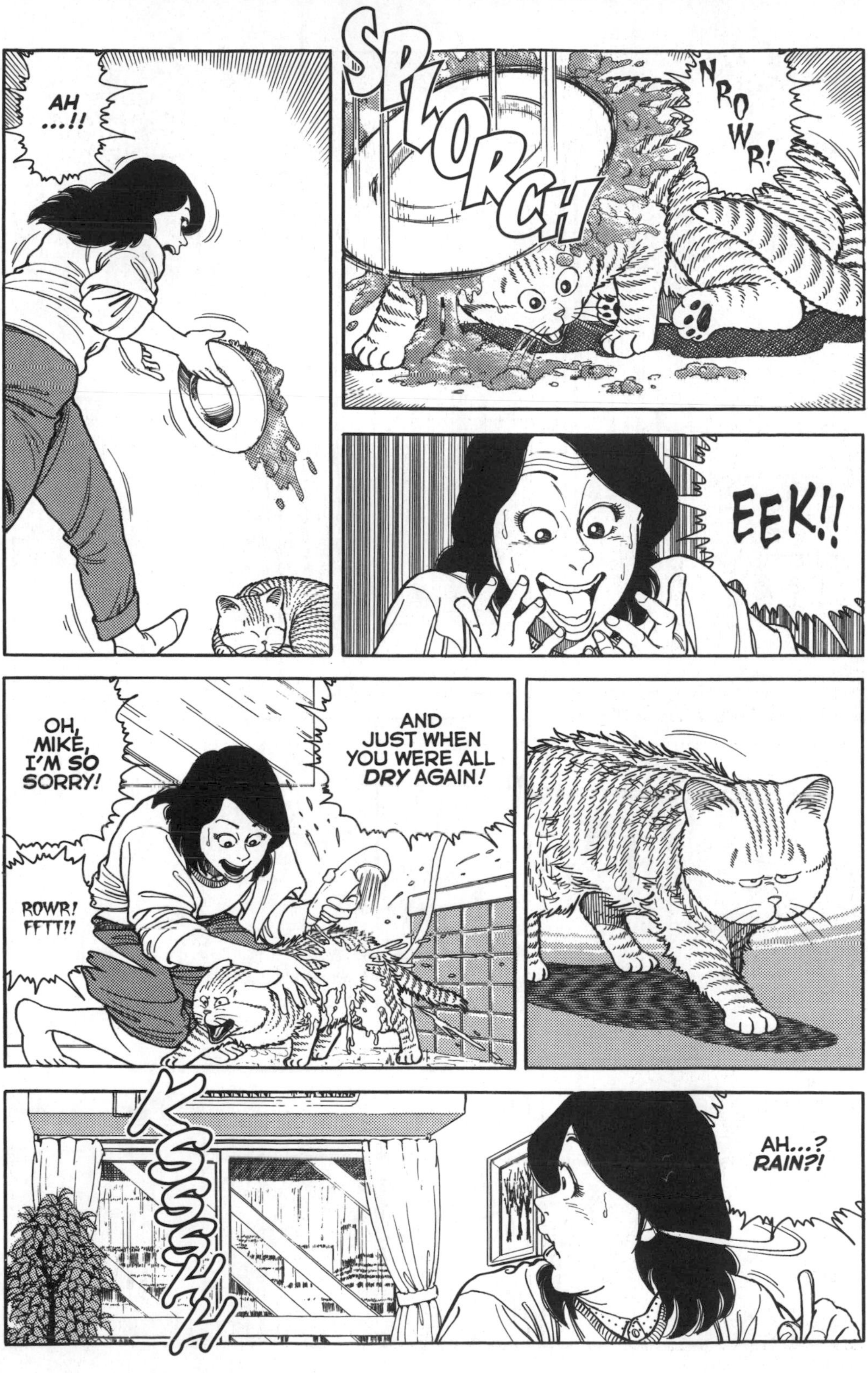
AH ...!!
SPLORCH
NROWR!
EEK!!
OH, MIKE, I'M SO SORRY!
AND JUST WHEN YOU WERE ALL DRY AGAIN!
ROWR! FFTT!!
KSSSHH
AH...? RAIN?!

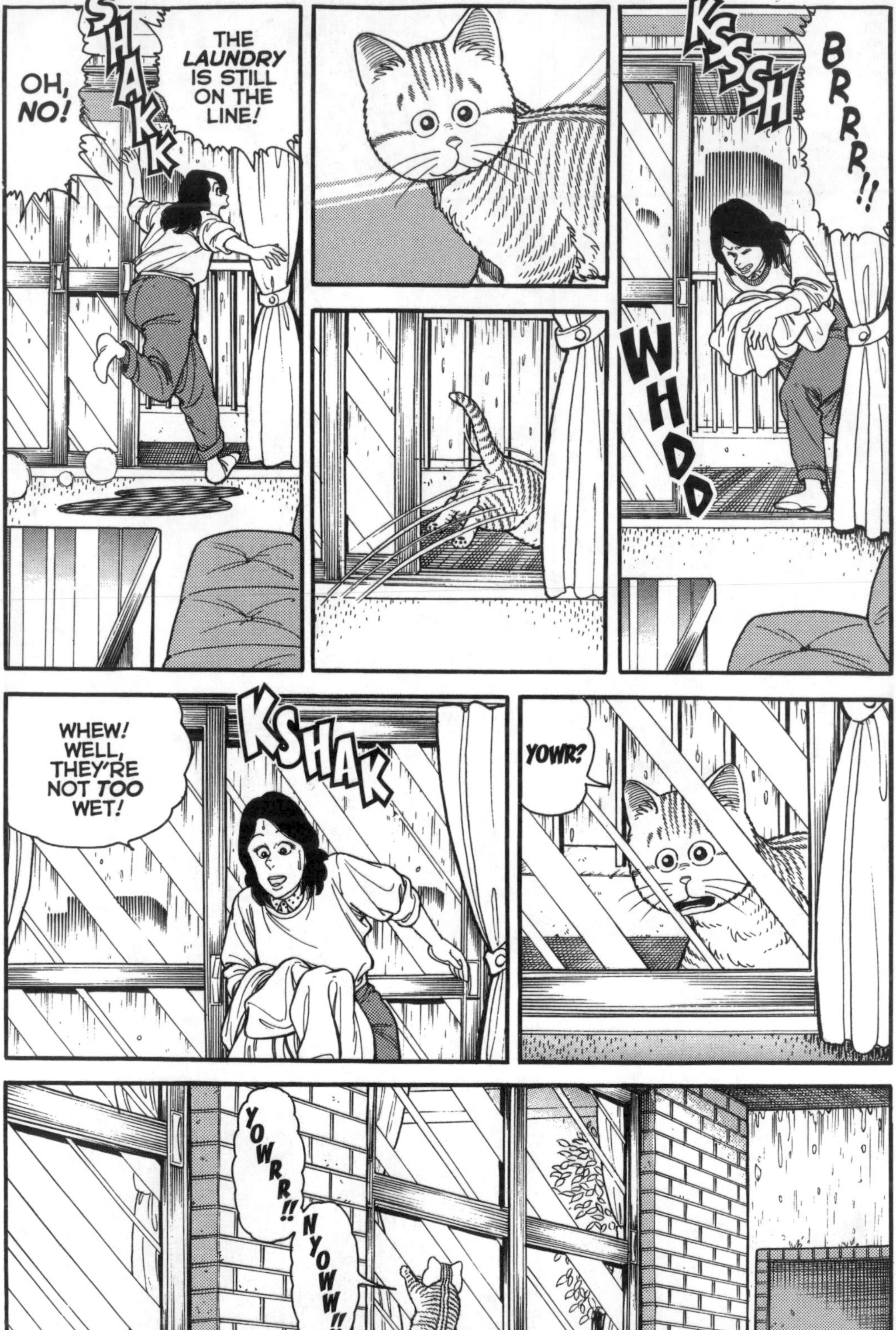
SHAKK
OH, NO!
THE LAUNDRY IS STILL ON THE LINE!
KSSSH
BRRRR!!
WHDD
WHEW! WELL, THEY'RE NOT TOO WET!
KSHAK
YOWR?
YOWRR!!
NYOWW!!

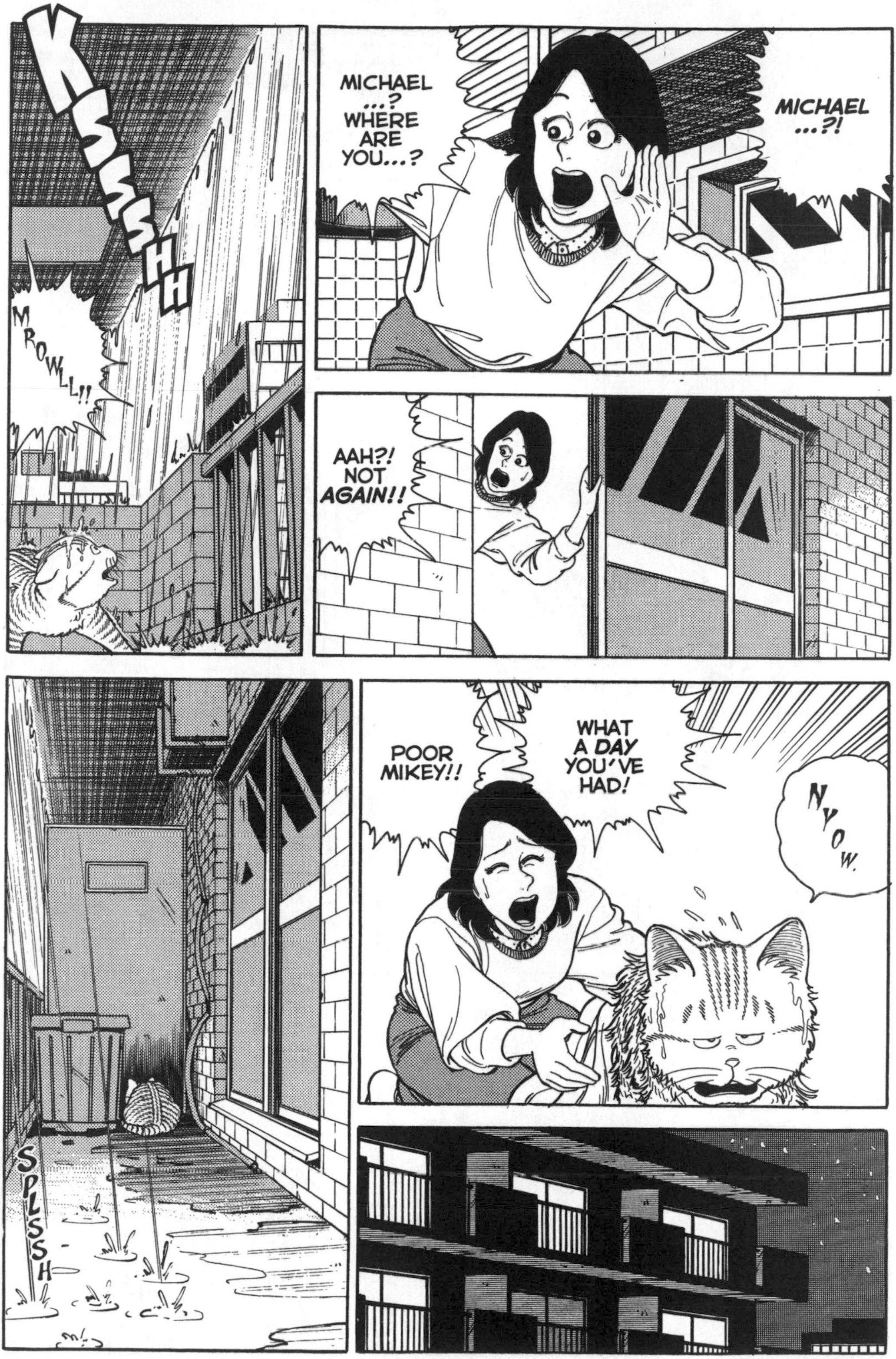
KSSSHH
MROWLL!!
MICHAEL ...? WHERE ARE YOU...?
MICHAEL ...?!
AAH?! NOT AGAIN!!
SPLSSH
POOR MIKEY!!
WHAT A DAY YOU'VE HAD!
NYOW.

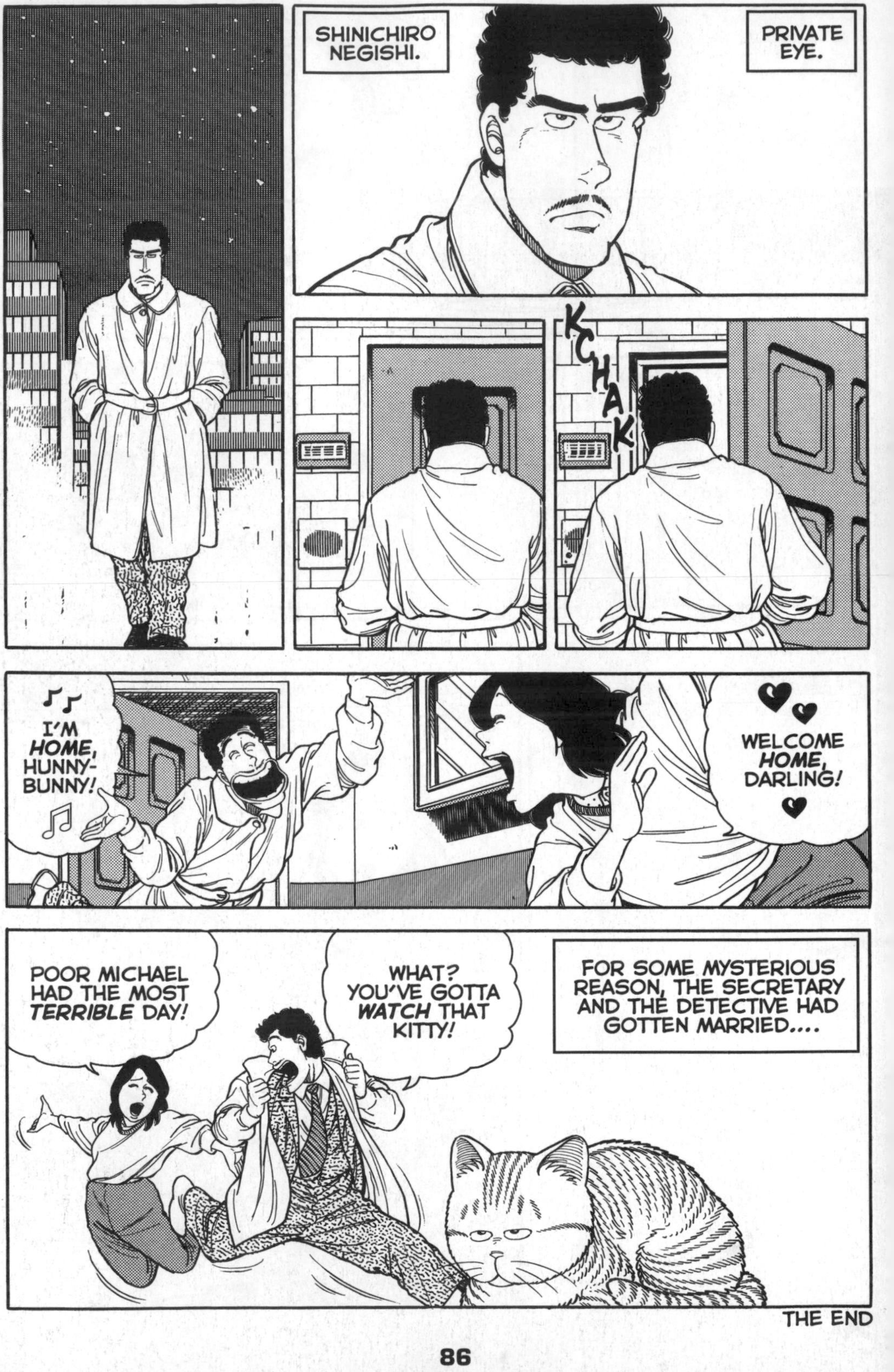
SHINICHIRO NEGISHI.
PRIVATE EYE.
KCHAK
♪♪ I'M HOME, HUNNY-BUNNY! ♪
WELCOME HOME, DARLING!
POOR MICHAEL HAD THE MOST TERRIBLE DAY!
WHAT? YOU'VE GOTTA WATCH THAT KITTY!
FOR SOME MYSTERIOUS REASON, THE SECRETARY AND THE DETECTIVE HAD GOTTEN MARRIED....

THE END

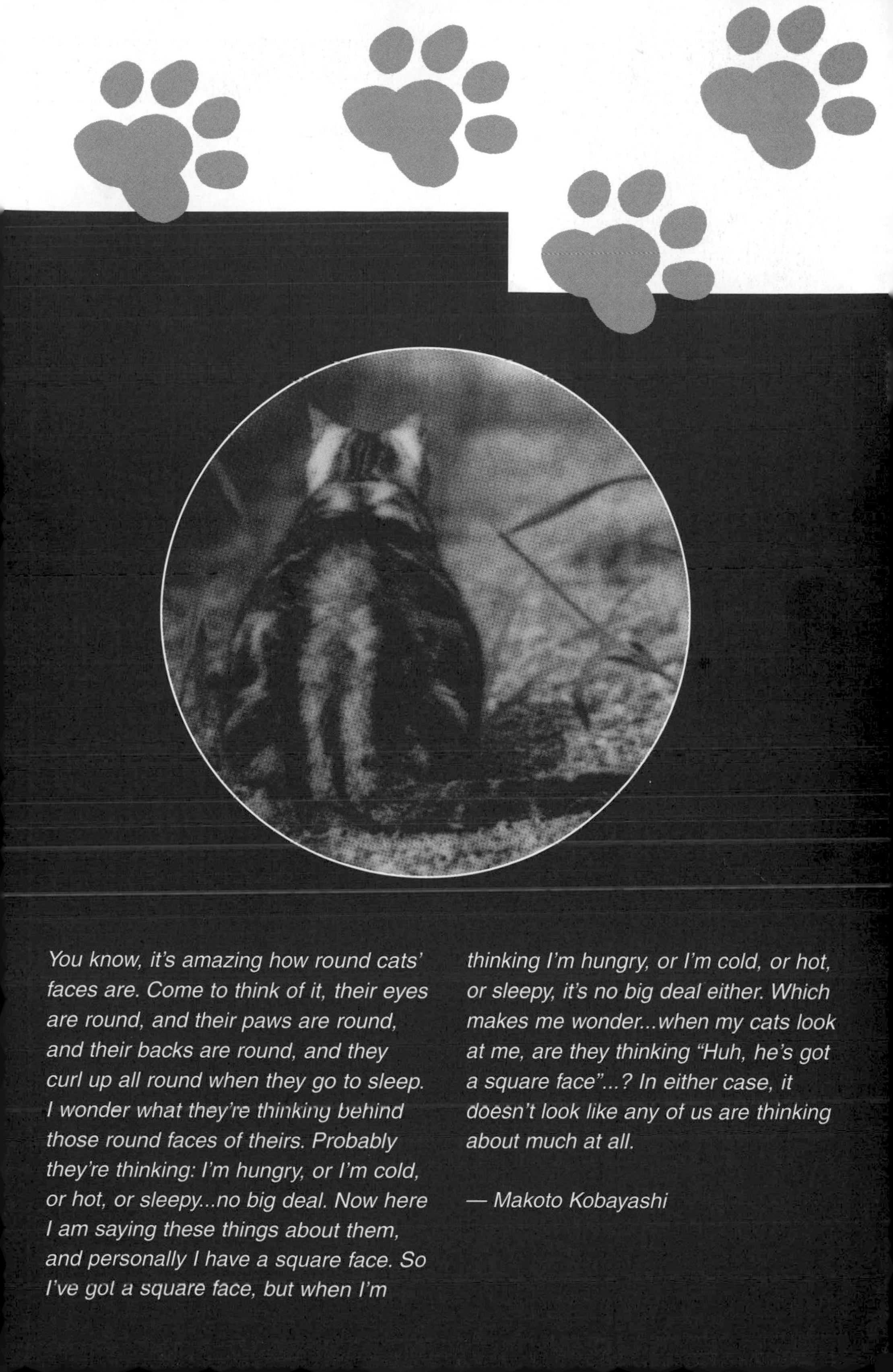

You know, it's amazing how round cats' faces are. Come to think of it, their eyes are round, and their paws are round, and their backs are round, and they curl up all round when they go to sleep. I wonder what they're thinking behind those round faces of theirs. Probably they're thinking: I'm hungry, or I'm cold, or hot, or sleepy...no big deal. Now here I am saying these things about them, and personally I have a square face. So I've got a square face, but when I'm thinking I'm hungry, or I'm cold, or hot, or sleepy, it's no big deal either. Which makes me wonder...when my cats look at me, are they thinking "Huh, he's got a square face"...? In either case, it doesn't look like any of us are thinking about much at all.

— Makoto Kobayashi

MANGA! MANGA! MANGA! DARK HORSE HAS THE BEST IN MANGA COLLECTIONS!

AVAILABLE AT YOUR LOCAL COMICS SHOP OR BOOKSTORE
To find a comics shop in your area, call 1-888-266-4226
For more information or to order direct visit darkhorse.com or call 1-800-862-0052
Mon.-Sat. 9 A.M. to 5 P.M. Pacific Time

**Prices and availability subject to change without notice*

AKIRA
Katsuhiro Otomo
BOOK 1
ISBN: 1-56971-498-3 . . . . $24.95
BOOK 2
ISBN: 1-56971-499-1 . . . . $24.95
BOOK 3
ISBN: 1-56971-525-4 . . . . $24.95
BOOK 4
ISBN: 1-56971-526-2 . . . . $27.95
BOOK 5
ISBN: 1-56971-527-0 . . . . $27.95
BOOK 6
ISBN: 1-56971-528-9 . . . . $29.95

APPLESEED
Masamune Shirow
BOOK ONE
ISBN: 1-56971-070-8 . . . . $16.95
BOOK TWO
ISBN: 1-56971-071-6 . . . . $16.95
BOOK THREE
ISBN: 1-56971-072-4 . . . . $17.95
BOOK FOUR
ISBN: 1-56971-074-0 . . . . $17.95

BLADE OF THE IMMORTAL
Hiroaki Samura
BLOOD OF A THOUSAND
ISBN: 1-56971-239-5 . . . . $14.95
CRY OF THE WORM
ISBN: 1-56971-300-6 . . . . $14.95
DREAMSONG
ISBN: 1-56971-357-X $14.95
ON SILENT WINGS
ISBN: 1-56971-412-6 . . . . $14.95
ON SILENT WINGS II
ISBN: 1-56971-444-4 . . . . $14.95
DARK SHADOWS
ISBN: 1-56971-469-X $14.95
HEART OF DARKNESS
ISBN: 1-56971-531-9 . . . . $16.95
THE GATHERING
ISBN: 1-56971-546-7 . . . . $15.95
THE GATHERING II
ISBN: 1-56971-560-2 . . . . $15.95
BEASTS
ISBN: 1-56971-741-9 . . . . $14.95

BUBBLEGUM CRISIS
Adam Warren and Toren Smith
GRAND MAL
ISBN: 1-56971-120-8 . . . . $14.95

CANNON GOD EXAXXION
Kenichi Sonoda
ISBN: 1-56971-745-1 . . . . $15.95

CARAVAN KIDD
Johji Manabe
VOLUME 1
ISBN: 1-56971-260-3 . . . . $19.95
VOLUME 2
ISBN: 1-56971-324-3 . . . . $19.95
VOLUME 3
ISBN: 1-56971-338-3 . . . . $19.95

CLUB 9
Makoto Kobayashi
VOLUME 1
ISBN: 1-56971-915-2 . . . . $15.95
VOLUME 2
ISBN: 1-56971-968-3 . . . . $15.95

THE DIRTY PAIR
Adam Warren and Toren Smith
BIOHAZARDS
ISBN: 1-56971-339-1 . . . . $12.95
DANGEROUS ACQUAINTANCES
ISBN: 1-56971-227-1 . . . . $12.95
A PLAGUE OF ANGELS
ISBN: 1-56971-029-5 . . . . $12.95
SIM HELL (REMASTERED)
ISBN: 1-56971-742-7 . . . . $12.95
FATAL BUT NOT SERIOUS
ISBN: 1-56971-172-0 . . . . $14.95

DOMINION
Masamune Shirow
ISBN: 1-56971-488-6 . . . . $16.95

DOMU: A CHILD'S DREAM
Katsuhiro Otomo
ISBN: 1-56971-611-0 . . . . $17.95

GHOST IN THE SHELL
Masamune Shirow
ISBN: 1-56971-081-3 . . . . $24.95

GUNSMITH CATS
Kenichi Sonoda
BONNIE AND CLYDE
ISBN: 1-56971-215-8 . . . . $13.95
MISFIRE
ISBN: 1-56971-253-0 . . . . $14.95
THE RETURN OF GRAY
ISBN: 1-56971-299-9 . . . . $17.95